The Adventures of

Sherlock Holmes

and the

Glamorous Ghost

Volume One

Hardcover 978-1-80424-165-3
Paperback ISBN 978-1-80424-166-0
ePub ISBN 978-1-80424-167-7
PDF ISBN 978-1-80424-168-4

Published by MX Publishing
335 Princess Park Manor, Royal Drive,
London, N11 3GX
www.mxpublishing.co.uk

Cover design Brian Belanger

Contents

Dedicated to GTP

A Most Extraordinary Bear

And to the late Ms. Woof

An Extremely Sweet and Loving
Dog

Acknowledgements

These stories have evolved over a long period of time and under a wide range of influences and circumstances. I am indebted to many people for helping to bring my versions of Holmes, Watson, Lady Juliet and Pookie to the printed and electronic page. Thanks most especially to my wife, Virginia, for her insights and clever suggestions as well as her unfailing enthusiasm for the project and patience with its author.

To Derrick and Brian Belanger for publishing and backing *The Glamorous Ghost* and many of my other Holmes and Solar Pons efforts. To Steve, Sharon and Timi Emecz, Dan Andriacco, and Gretchen Altabef for their enthusiastic encouragement for my Holmes pastiches and Octavius Bear series. And to all of my generous Kickstarter backers.

And very special additional kudos to Brian Belanger for his wonderful illustrations and covers.

To my sons, Mark and Andrew and their spouses, Cindy and Lorraine, for helping to make these stories more readable and audience friendly. To Cathy Hartnett, cheerleader-extraordinaire for her eagerness to see this alternate world take form.

If, in spite of all this support, some errors or inconsistencies have crept through, the buck stops here. Needless to say, all of the characters, situations, and narratives are fictional. Some locations, devices, historical figures, and events are real.

Thanks to Wikipedia for providing facts and figures, liberally borrowed and used throughout this book.

A Glamorous Beginning

An introduction by Derrick Belanger

The beginning of this book is actually the ending. No, I'm not giving anything away; no spoilers here. What I mean is the start of this glamorous friendship is at the end of Lady Juliet Armstrong's life. Thus, from the end of Juliet's life, the Glamorous Ghost is born, and we are all better for it.

One of the golden rules to our publications is that Holmes and Watson must be their traditional canonical selves. Whether it is in a very traditional pastiche such as in the work of David Marcum, or some of the stories in our "In the Realms of" series where Holmes might face a Martian tripod, a steampunk airship, or the red death itself, the great detective remains himself, true to Doyle's vision.

I'm happy to report that in Harry DeMaio's world of the Glamorous Ghost, you have the traditional Holmes despite his new celestial companion. And what of the ghost herself? Well, with Baroness Crestwell, you will find a rather sassy companion with a biting sense of humor who keeps the great detective on his toes.

Lady Juliet doesn't come alone; she brings with her an eclectic assortment of heavenly figures, most notably her faithful companion Pookie, a fun-loving dog quite similar to Holmes's own reliable canine friend, Toby. These characters give us a taste of Heaven, a very jazzy Heaven reminiscent of what you might see in an old black and white movie. We get the wings and halos, the fluffy clouds, the choirs, the Elysian Fields, the pearly gates.

Contrast that Heaven with the Earthly realm of London at the turn of the twentieth century where we encounter murderers, thieves, and scoundrels. Holmes and Watson are there to solve the crimes, but in these adventures, they get a little help from divine intervention.

In the six stories and one novella which make up *The Adventures of Sherlock Holmes and the Glamorous Ghost*, Mr. DeMaio does just as good a job at creating zany characters and whimsical settings as he does in his ever-growing series of Octavius Bear books. I hope you enjoy getting to know Lady Juliet as much as we did. And fear not, when you get to the end of the book and wish for more adventures with these holy ghosts, the end may not be the end after all. Mr. DeMaio has promised another collection of adventures with these characters.

This isn't the end. It is just the beginning.

Derrick Belanger

December, 2021

Rite of Passage

"Where in God's name am I, and how did I get here? And what am I doing wearing this dowdy, shapeless white robe? White is definitely not my color."

Her last memory was of stepping with her husband into the foyer of their Belgravia home, fresh (maybe not so fresh) from a rather boring house party, dressed in a fashionable red Parisian gown that caressed all the salient points of her still-spectacular figure. Now suddenly, she was here.

"Wherever 'here' is! Just that damn sun above, and this interminable grass surrounding me."

The former actress and Baroness Crestwell, Lady Juliet Armstrong prided herself on her intelligence and sharp intuition. Something traumatic had definitely happened.

"What kind of trauma? Am I caught up in a nightmare? I'll wake up any moment now and fill in the blank spots in my memory. Come on Juliet—wakey, wakey!"

Nothing!

A creeping sensation invaded her senses. Close to panic, she fought to regain control. Suddenly, the unthinkable crashed in on her:

She was _DEAD_!!

Is this what befell you when you "passed on?"

"Passed on!" she gasped. "What a polite, genteel way of saying I've croaked."

After all these years off the stage, she could still not abide the politesse that pervaded the society she was immersed in… or was once immersed in. Being married to a Baron had its compensations but being bored out of her mind by stuffy grand dames and their pea-brained spouses was not one of them.

"Concentrate, Juliet, let's review the bidding!" She paced, loudly talking to herself. "It's September 10th 1900. London. One minute, I was stepping into the house. The next minute I ended up here. Where? What, if anything, do I remember? A noise, and… a sharp pain in my chest. A heart attack? No, heart attacks don't make noises! Damn it, I was shot! How many times when I was on the stage did I fake dying? This time it was real. Did everything go black as it's supposed to? No! A blink of the eye, a lovely dress switched into this stupid robe, and here I am. My act never included quick clothes changes.

"How dare they—whoever they are! Shot entering my own luxurious home. This is intolerable. I suppose I can't do anything about being done in, but I certainly want to find the blighter who did it and bring him or her to justice before going to my heavenly reward."

She assumed there was a heavenly reward, and that she was entitled to it. All those years of putting up with Reginald and his family, going to church and giving her time and money to the widows and orphans… Juliet believed it must be worth something.

"Speaking of Reginald, where is he? We were together entering the house. Was he shot? Is he dead, too? Or… oh my

4

God, did he shoot me? No, that can't be. Where are the Pearly Gates? I want to file a complaint."

She turned and found herself facing an individual who had not been there a moment ago. A middle-aged male, tall, dressed in morning *(mourning?)* clothes, clean-shaven, not a hair out of place, dark eyes, color undetermined. He seemed to be floating inches above the grass.

"Baroness Crestwell, greetings! I am Raymond, one of Heaven's Senior Directors. Did I hear you wanted to go to the Pearly Gates to file a complaint? If it's about your current status, I'm afraid that is immutable. You are irretrievably deceased. Shall we leave for the Rainbow Bridge? It leads to the Pearly Gates."

Juliet huffed. "Rainbow Bridge? That's for cats and dogs, not the aristocracy."

"All the same. Milady, you *must* cross it. Now, please, I have a rather full schedule today."

"Where is my husband?"

"I don't know, milady. I only deal with those who have passed on." *There's that damn euphemism again*, Juliet thought. "He is not on my list of transfers. May we please depart?"

"No! I've been killed. I'll have justice done before I go."

"Forgive me for pointing out that, in your current condition, that will be quite difficult. You're incorporeal, don't you see? You're no longer extant. Quite ephemeral!"

"Well, let's get help from people who are "corporeal, alive and extant."

"The rules are rather firm in that regard. We can't have you going around haunting mortals."

"Fie on rules! All my life, I broke rules. Now fetch me up some colleagues among the living and give me back my red dress. This robe is most unbecoming."

The Director was irked. He periodically ran into resistance that he could easily overcome, but this one seemed highly determined, and he did have a large group he needed to meet shortly. A tragic train wreck. "Well, Baroness, it's highly unusual… but I suppose I could invoke Loophole M and allow you to contact one individual. Only *one*, mind you. And only for five days. That's the extent of my flexibility. Otherwise, I shall have to summon an archangel or two. Now, what's it to be, and who's it be?"

"Why, that's easy, you silly git! *Sherlock Holmes, of course!*"

*****

The Great Detective was sitting alone and pensive in a basket chair with his eyes closed. Boredom had set in with a vengeance. No new case had arrived to satisfy his need for stimuli. Suddenly, he sensed a presence. He opened his eyes and beheld an extremely attractive female standing before him in a startling red dress.

"Mr. Sherlock Holmes? I am, or was, Lady Juliet Armstrong, Baroness Crestwell. Having been murdered, I am deceased, and require your assistance."

With his usual aplomb, Holmes replied. "Madam, I can see that you have made a major journey. But your feet do not seem to be touching the floor, and the unusual September heat does not seem to have affected you. Are you a phantom? This agency stands flat-footed upon the ground, and there it must remain. The world is big enough for us. No ghosts need apply." He looked at her. "However, in your case, I might alter my opinion. I assume you are a ghost."

She put her hand on a chair and passed right through it. She laughed. "That seems to be the case. I am, shall we say, evanescent."

"I have had unusual clients in the past, but I can't recall an attractive spirit such as yourself."

"Oh, I'm not a client. I wish to be your partner. I certainly do not plan to sit idly by while you exercise your formidable powers. I want justice but as you can see, I am hampered by my present condition. I'm sure my estate will handle any fee you may choose to charge but we must work together on this."

"I have a partner. Doctor Watson has been my invaluable companion for lo, these many years."

"Unfortunately, the good doctor will not be able to see me. Heavenly rules restrict that ability to one person – you. And we only have five days to bring this affair to a conclusion. So, what's your pleasure?"

"A ghostly partner! I insist on telling Watson."

He heard the door to his rooms open and a voice said, "You insist on telling Watson what?" The doctor entered the room. After the death of his wife, Mary Morstan, Watson had eventually returned to Baker Street.

"Watson, I believe you should arm yourself with a snifter of brandy before we discuss this most unusual client."

"What client, Holmes? I daresay I won't refuse a libation, however." He headed to the decanter on the sideboard and poured a generous tot for both of them.

Holmes took the glass and said, "Watson, we have a ghost in our midst. May I present the late Lady Juliet, Baroness Crestwell."

"Your sense of humor sometimes exceeds limits, Holmes. I have just read of Lady Juliet's demise in the afternoon papers. Her husband, the Baron, is hanging on at Barts Hospital. On entering their home last evening, they were both shot by a long distance rifle. Scotland Yard believes the Baron was the target. The Lady's death was the result of poor marksmanship."

The Baroness stamped her ephemeral foot. "Ohh, this is too much! I'm just 'collateral damage,' as they say. How impertinent! I always had top billing in all of my stage performances. Holmes, that's insult added to injury!"

"Yes, Baroness. I'm sorry."

Watson reared back. "Who are you talking to?"

"I told you. Lady Juliet's ghost. I'm sorry, I cannot chide you for 'seeing but not observing'. Apparently, you can't see her, or hear her, but she is here. You'll have to take my word. "

"Has boredom overcome you? Have you taken leave of your senses? Ghostly clients, indeed!"

"No, not a client. She is a partner! And she's not imaginary."

*****

Holmes had Mrs. Hudson summon a cab and Watson reluctantly tagged along, still shaking his head in disbelief. As they headed off into the late London afternoon, he asked. "Where are we going?"

"To the Crestwell manor in Belgravia. I suspect Scotland Yard will still be there, adding major damage to the scene. The Baroness is probably already *in situ* since she has no need of earthly transport."

"Oh, come off it, Holmes."

Sure enough, the wraith in red was waiting for them at her former home. She laughed as Holmes and Watson descended from the cab. "There is something to be said for being incorporeal. It saves on cab fare. There's a large Scotland Yard Inspector interviewing the staff. He looks quite interesting! What's his name? Could you kill him so I could meet him? Sorry, that was tasteless. Poor stupid Reginald is hanging on at Barts, and here I am being the scarlet woman. Or, at least, my dress is scarlet."

"That is Inspector Tobias Gregson, one of the Yard's better practitioners. I shall not introduce you. I think you'll be most effective if no one else knows you are about. You can move around freely and watch and listen at will. You would have been extremely helpful if this was a locked room mystery."

"Oh, I shall be most valuable, regardless," said Lady Juliet. "I am quite talented."

"I have no doubt. Now, please, let me approach the good Inspector."

Gregson smiled as he saw Holmes and Watson. "Ah, Sherlock Holmes. I wondered if you would appear, and I am not to be disappointed. This is a strange case. Rifle shots from the neighboring park. We believe the Baron was the premeditated target, but the Baroness got in the way."

She bridled. "Really, Holmes! *I got in the way.* So much for me! Don't kill this policeman off. I've lost interest. Why shouldn't I have been the intended target? I'm sure there are scads of people who would like to see me dead. Well, now I am. So there!"

Holmes chuckled quietly. The lady was a true theatrical prima donna. *She will be an interesting collaborator*, he thought.

He looked at Gregson. "I assume you have transferred the Baroness's body to the mortuary at Barts. Is that also where the Baron is undergoing treatment for his wounds?"

Gregson nodded.

Juliet gasped. "Why am I wasting precious time here when I should be at the hospital?"

Holmes whispered, "No, stay for a few moments longer. There is nothing you can do for him… and are you sure you want to see your own mutilated body?"

Holmes turned to Gregson. "Inspector, you have no doubt interviewed the staff. Has any information come to the surface that might be valuable?"

"In fact there is, Mr. Holmes. At seven last evening, two men arrived at the manor asking for the Baron. The butler, Mr. Stevens, told them the couple were not at home. He offered to take their cards and pass them on, but they refused, and left."

"Did Stevens recognize them?"

Gregson consulted his notes. "No. They were not gentlemen, according to the butler. One was tall, slim, bearded and sporting a full moustache… dark hair… blue eyes. Clad in an ill-fitting suit. The other was an exact opposite. Short, portly, clean-shaven. Brown eyes. Similar clothing. In fact, the butler said they reminded him of a Music Hall Comedy Act."

Juliet thought, *"Hmm!"*

Holmes experienced an epiphany. A revelation! He suddenly realized he could now communicate with his new found partner telepathically. A great convenience. He wouldn't have to explain whom he was talking to. Holmes closed his eyes and quietly directed his thoughts towards his ghostly partner.

I just heard your thoughts in my own mind. Can you hear mine? Any reactions to the two gentlemen we're discussing, Baroness?

She looked Holmes in the eye, and responded in kind: *Yes, I can hear your thoughts! As for those gentlemen, they could be any one of the vaudeville acts that filled the music halls when I was in my glory. Or they may just be an unlikely looking pair. Reginald may know of them. I don't.*

Holmes wasn't sure she was telling the whole truth. He was certain she recognized the descriptions. Could it be she was actually the target?

Sherlock Holmes turned towards the inspector. "Let's take a few moments and examine the park opposite the home. The police believe the shots came from there, isn't that so, Gregson?"

"Right you are, Mr. Holmes. We searched but found nothing, no weapon. No spent cartridges!'

"Footprints?"

"Heavy grass!"

Holmes wandered around the perimeter of the park with his glass at the ready. Once again, the police had done an efficient job of obliterating anything that might have been of value.

Holmes concentrated. *Lady Crestwell, are you familiar with this common?*

Oh, yes! I used to walk my little dog, Pookie, around the area. Poor Pookie passed away last year. I wonder if she'll be at the Rainbow Bridge when I return. I'll have to ask Raymond.

Raymond? thought Holmes.

A 'Heavenly Director'. I mean, he's from Heaven. He's managing my episode in avoiding the Pearly Gates so I can work with you. A shame you can't meet him.

Holmes smiled. *Yes, well. Someday, perhaps, but hopefully not yet. On to the hospital and the wounded Baron.*

Once again, she arrived at Reginald's room well in advance of Holmes's plodding cab ride. She shook her amorphous head in sympathy for his injury.

"Well, old boy, I wish you could hear me. You can recover at leisure and spend your time mourning my demise, if in fact you really care. Selma Fairfax should be delighted that I am out of the picture. Now the two of you can carry on, respectably of course, in the public eye."

Juliet frowned. "You know, Reginald, if I was of a mind to shoot you, I wouldn't have missed. And of course, I wouldn't have stood in the way, to quote that oaf of a policeman."

She turned to see Holmes, Watson and Inspector Gregson walk in. "Oh hello, Holmes. I see you made it. The Baron is conscious. What does the doctor say?"

Rite of Passage

On cue, the medico entered the room with a smile on his face. "Gentlemen, our patient is on the mend. The bullet missed the vital organs and he will be on his way to a complete, but painful, recovery. Pity about the Baroness." Unaware that she was standing right next to him.

Juliet smiled at the word "painful," and agreed with the word "pity."

Gregson looked at the Baron, who stared back bleary-eyed. "Lord Crestwell, I am Inspector Tobias Gregson of Scotland Yard. These two gentlemen are Mr. Sherlock Holmes and Doctor John Watson."

A female voice rang out in the detective's mind: *And I am your former wife, Reginald dear!*

Holmes chuckled, causing a round of frowns in the group. Gregson continued: "We are here investigating the shooting that wounded you and caused the unfortunate death of Lady Crestwell. Do you feel up to answering a few questions?"

That same voice wafted through Holmes's thoughts: *Of course he is. The man is strong as an ox, and just as intelligent.*

The Baron replied (weakly), "I suppose I am. Although I'm in the dark over the whole affair."

As usual.

Holmes remarked telepathically, *I gather you and your husband were not on the best of terms.*

She replied, *That sums it up. A society hussy named Selma Fairfax has taken his attention. I don't play understudy for anyone.*

Gregson called, "Mr. Holmes, do you wish to ask the Baron anything?"

Holmes recovered from his ghostly communications and said, "Sorry, I was just musing about this situation. Lord Crestwell, do you have any idea who would want to kill you, if indeed you were the target?"

"I don't know. Of course, I was the target. Who would want to kill poor Juliet?"

The ethereal voice began to reel off a list of names, mostly female and more than a few of them being the Baron's relatives. Selma Fairfax led the parade. *I wasn't all that popular among the aristocracy*, she fumed. *The theater-going public, however, loved me.*

Watson replied, "Who indeed, m'lord? Why do you suppose you were the target?"

"Affairs of state, Doctor, which I am not privileged to share. Mr. Holmes, you might want to consult your brother."

Holmes arched an eyebrow at the mention of his brother; but before he could speak, Juliet snorted aloud, "Affairs of state? Ha! I'm sure of the affairs, but not their state. God help the Empire if my husband was involved in any diplomatic or military activities. Oh well, that's up to you to unravel, partner. Who is your brother? Never mind, I'm going to look at my body. Where's the mortuary?"

Holmes winced, focusing his thoughts on Juliet. *Please, let's speak with our thoughts for now. You'll meet my brother Mycroft shortly. The mortuary is in the basement. Are you sure you want to see your earthly remains?*

Of course! How else will I know I'm really dead? See you there.

Wait a moment, my lady, until we complete this interview.

14

Oh, all right!

Gregson asked about the two men who arrived earlier that evening. He gave Stevens's description of the two and asked if the Baron knew them. He got a blank stare in reply.

"They don't sound like anyone I would know or care to know," said the Baron. "Are they our assailants?"

"Too early to determine," replied Gregson, "and Mr. Holmes despises assumptions."

Holmes nodded. He turned to the doctor, "How soon can the Baron leave the hospital?"

"I'm afraid he will have few more days of Barts' food and care before we can release him."

The Baron shook his head. "I must speak with my lawyer; and arrange a funeral for Juliet. Inspector, will there be a coroner's inquest?"

"I'm afraid so, but I'm sure it will be straightforward. The doctor here performed a postmortem and pronounced her dead from a rifle shot to the heart. No doubt the coroner's jury will decide on 'death by misadventure' caused by a shooting by person or persons unknown."

But soon to be discovered, right, partner?

Holmes mentally shushed his ghostly companion as the Inspector continued: "There must also be a reading of the will. Juliet had substantial assets of her own from her days on stage. I'll have to contact her solicitor about her estate. I'm not the executor. I don't know what's in her last will and testament."

Nothing for you and yours, old boy, except for our niece Clarissa. Holmes, Reginald and I had no children. I was past child bearing age. Clarissa is our surrogate adolescent – a lovely young lady. All the rest of my holdings goes to charity.

Holmes pondered. *Baroness, it seems the 'cui bono' trail will lead us nowhere unless Clarissa is murderous and knew about her proposed inheritance. What is the value of her share?*

One hundred thousand pounds. The charities get the rest, but… she isn't a killer, and knew nothing about her inheritance.

I suspect your testament will be contested, Lady Armstrong.

Just let them try. Now, I'm going to the mortuary. Coming?

Holmes wished the Baron Godspeed on his recovery, and announced that he wished to view the victim down in the morgue. The doctor who had performed the autopsy joined them and they proceeded to the basement.

Watson, Gregson and Holmes were all hardened to the prospect of a dead body, especially one that had been shot. Not so the Baroness, who immediately regretted her willfulness in wanting to view her remains.

"Oh Lord, Holmes," she said aloud, "I-I think I may be sick... but of course, I can't, can I? I look awful. I… I hope the undertaker is skilled at makeup. I want to make my last exit looking beautiful."

No doubt you will, my lady, thought Holmes. *Have no fear. I shall ask Watson to attend the coroner's inquest and report any unusual events. We need to find Mr. Stevens's Music Hall comedians. But first, you and I must pay a visit to my brother Mycroft, to determine the Baron's 'affairs of state.' You will find Mycroft interesting.*

Rite of Passage

Juliet narrowed her gaze, concentrating. *My only interest is finding my killer, Mr. Holmes.*

*****

The irony of a woman, albeit a deceased woman, entering the Diogenes Club was not wasted on Sherlock Holmes. The Diogenes, of which Mycroft Holmes was co-founder, was a very well-appointed refuge for men reluctant to have any dealings with their fellow creatures. Total silence throughout the establishment was mandatory with one exception – The Stranger's Room. There, members could quietly engage in tolerably subdued conversation. As she sailed past them, Lady Juliet thumbed her nose at the footman and Majordomo who carefully guarded the entrance to the all-male enclave. They led Holmes and Watson to the Stranger's Room where they were asked to await the arrival of Mycroft. Gregson had returned to Scotland Yard. The Baroness left them and wandered through the club rooms, making faces at the incumbents, reading over their shoulders and making gestures, most of them obscene.

Just as Mycroft arrived, she returned.

Well, that was certainly fun, Holmes, thought Juliet. *Several of the members I saw might even be considered alive. Being discorporate has certain advantages. I'll have to explore it further. So this is your older brother? I can see the resemblances, but he is going to eat himself into an early grave. He's fat! Hmph—listen to me talking about early graves.*

Baroness, thought Holmes, *if you please?*

17

All right, Mr. Holmes, chat away. I'll be quiet as a little mouse in the corner. A bodyless mouse.

Holmes took a seat. "Good evening, Mycroft. I trust you are well."

"As well as possible, Sherlock. You, no doubt, are here seeking information, advice or assistance in another one of your escapades. You impose on our fraternal relationship far too often."

"It's information this time. I believe you are acquainted with Lord Reginald, Baron Crestwell."

Mycroft sighed and shrugged his shoulders, "Yes, to my regret. But wait, wasn't he and his lovely wife shot the other evening? How are they?"

"He was wounded and is in hospital. She is dead."

"A pity the roles weren't reversed."

The Baroness silently applauded and bowed to the elder Holmes brother.

"I gather you are not enthused about Lord Crestwell?"

"Hardly! The man is a pompous twit and an infernal pest. (Cheers from Juliet!) Unfortunately, he has major connections to the Government. The Royal Household, even! More specifically, he and Crown Prince Bertie are carousing playmates!"

Watson chortled, "I thought *you* were His Majesty's Government."

"Sarcasm doesn't become you, Doctor Watson. Crestwell has been responsible for more agency cockups than a regiment of chimpanzees." (More silent applause from the Baroness.)

"What agencies?"

"Take your pick. Home Office, Foreign Office, the Army, the Admiralty... and me. We pass him around like yesterday's dirty laundry. None of us will throw him out for fear of angering His Highness."

"Someone had the courage to take a shot at him," said Holmes.

"Did they? He couldn't even die efficiently. Or was his wife the real target?"

Juliet moved closer. *Come on Mycroft, open up. What's he talking about, Sherlock? Was I really the intended victim?*

Holmes looked at Mycroft. "What makes you think she was in the assassin's spotlight?"

"There are some who believe the lady is a spy. Her husband is the perfect foil... or fool. Information that was entrusted to him has ended up in the hands of foreign adversaries on more than one occasion. He swears he knows nothing about it. "

The Baroness would have come apart if she had parts. *Of all the preposterous, libelous, inane accusations! Make him take that back. Me! A spy! What utter nonsense.*

"You have proof of this, Mycroft?"

"Nothing you would honor, old boy. I didn't say I believed it. Some Foreign Office hotheads have their own suspicions, however. Anyway, it no longer matters."

"Of course it matters. We're dealing with murder here. Someone must be brought to justice."

Bravo, partner, you tell him! urged the Baroness. *I'm not just hanging around here to kill time. Oh, that's silly, isn't it? I still have to get used to my immortal status.*

"All right. I'll make inquiries but don't expect anything substantial."

Nothing is substantial, Mycroft old dear, said Lady Juliet, *especially me.*

Holmes and Watson exited the Diogenes Club. The Baroness could not resist making faces at the Majordomo as she floated out.

"Well, Watson and Lady Juliet, what do we make of that?"

"Holmes, do you still insist on acting as if you're in contact with a ghost?"

"Yes, Watson, I do… because I <u>am</u>. I ask again—what do we make of all that?"

"I know what I make of all that," said the Baroness. "Reginald is a stupid blowhard. I really wonder why I married him. Oh, I guess I do. I liked being a Baroness. Anyway, he's always ready to prove how important he is to anyone who'll listen. So, who was listening?"

"A good question, Lady Juliet."

"What did she ask, Holmes?"

"*Cui bono*, Watson. 'Who profits?'"

"I thought we discussed her will?"

"Not her will, Watson. His information. I think it's time to have another chat with his Lordship."

"Go to it, partner," said the Baroness. "Want to make a small bet? No, I guess you can't bet with a spook, can you?"

I'm beginning to think you may be a poltergeist, my lady, thought Holmes.

"You do me a grave injustice, sirrah. I am a noble lady of pure objectives… at least most of the time. I have no capabilities or intentions to throw things around or pinch people or make loud noises. Raymond would have an archangel on me in a trice if I did. I await your apology."

"You have it!" Holmes blurted out.

"I have what, Holmes?"

"A rare capability to tolerate my eccentricities, Watson. The evening is getting late and I doubt we will be able to interview the Baron until tomorrow. The medical profession can be quite stuffy about visitors. No insult intended, Watson. I suggest a little sleep would be most helpful."

Lady Juliet waved them away. "You two mortals go ahead and waste your time with Morpheus. I don't need any sleep. Another advantage to being dead. I have an objective I propose to pursue. I'll see you in your morning. Ta, Ta!"

She disappeared.

*****

Lady Juliet made her ghostly way through the corridors of Barts Hospital to the room in which the wounded Baron lay. He was not alone. Lady Selma Fairfax was at his bedside. The staff didn't seem to be too stuffy about this visitor.

"Oh, Reginald, you poor dear. When I heard of your accident, I was beside myself with concern."

"It was not an accident, Selma. Someone shot at Juliet and me. Killed her! Wounded me."

"Yes, I heard about Juliet. How tragic! But you are on the road to recovery, are you not? The Empire needs you, and so do I."

The deceased Baroness uttered a series of epithets ending with a reference to Lady Selma's illegitimate parentage: "Husband-stealing wanton! True, I didn't want him anymore; but that wasn't an invitation for you to move in. Oh, I wish you could hear me! What in heaven's name do you see in him? Oh, wait! Is this what I think it is? You don't care about him. You care about what he knows and is willing to tell you, the stupid braggart. He used to engage me in pillow talk about his connections, contacts and conquests until I told him categorically I wasn't interested. But you are, aren't you? Why? Are you the spy they're worried about? I wouldn't put it past you. They should have shot you instead of me. I need to talk with Holmes."

Lady Selma patted the Baron's hand and said her goodbyes, promising to return in the morning. Outside the hospital, she summoned a cab on her way to a late evening assignation. "The Alpenrose Club, quickly!" Little did she know that she had company.

"The Alpenrose Club! Sounds German," said Lady Juliet, swirling into the cab. "What are you up to, Selma, my dear? Oh, I do love intrigue. It reminds me of my starring role in the operetta, Lady of the Evening. The critics loved me as a mysterious courtesan. So did the audiences. We had a little trouble with the Lord Chamberlain's office. Stuffy old git, but he could be persuaded."

The Alpenrose was a discreet and nondescript bistro of modest pretensions. With its Germanic décor and overtones, it was an ideal venue for circumspect meetings, one of which was about to commence. Baron Von Meyer was hardly a circumspect individual. Brash, and something of a hell-raiser, he was nevertheless one of the Kaiser's most effective operatives. He was seated at a table for two in a dark corner of the room when Selma made her unobtrusive entrance. Juliet floated right behind her.

She mused, *I never realized how slow London cabs can be. Flitting is a much more efficient way of getting around. A shame you have to be dead to use it. Now, who is this young Teutonic specimen?*

Von Meyer rose and clicked his heels. "Lady Selma, always a pleasure!"

"Baron Von Meyer, the pleasure is mine."

Aha! She has this thing about barons. Who knows, she may also have a duke or viscount in her stable. The peerage isn't safe. I assume Holmes knows him. I'll give him a full report in the morning.

"A glass of schnapps, my lady?"

"That would be very pleasant. Danke!" She giggled.

The baron snapped his fingers at the waiter standing nearby and ordered the drinks. They engaged in small talk until the server arrived with the liqueurs and then calmly withdrew. "Now, what have you to tell me?"

"I now have a full and open channel to my source. Baron Crestwell is no longer encumbered with that harridan wife of his."

"Harridan?" Juliet huffed. "Jezebel!"

"I saw in the press that she was killed, and he is wounded. Was that your doing?"

"Of course! She was a hindrance and had to be eliminated."

"Hah! I knew it," said Lady Juliet, throwing her hands up and venting. "The woman's a murderess in addition to being a spy. Wait till I tell Holmes that I was indeed the target. That stupid Inspector Gregson! Collateral damage! Reginald's the collateral damage and a big-mouthed fool. Now, how do we bring her to justice and get him to shut up?"

"But why did you shoot the Baron? He is the goose who has been laying all those golden eggs."

"I didn't shoot either of them. I hired two professional assassins to do her in. They came highly recommended. I thought they were competent. The fools hit him as well. Naturally, I have curtailed their payment."

"Fantastisch!"

"Danke! I assume our arrangement will continue, perhaps with an increase in compensation?"

"Your demure façade is most impressive, Lady Selma. You are indeed a formidable woman."

Juliet laughed, "Oh, Sonny Boy. You don't know the meaning of the word 'formidable'. Just you wait! We're going to get the wheels of justice rolling."

*****

"Holmes! Wake up, sleepy head!"

Lady Juliet attempted to shake him but discovered it wouldn't work. Her amorphous hand fell away empty.

The great detective raised an eyebrow, yawned and frowned. "Really, Baroness, we need to reach an agreement on maintaining privacy," he mumbled aloud. "This will not do. There must be rules involving the behavior of disembodied spirits. I suggest you consult with your friend, Mr. Raymond."

"Sorry, but I have news and you have to act on it. Now come on, wake up!"

Holmes groggily acknowledged her determined presence and negotiated a truce until he could consume a cup of coffee and a scone provided by Mrs. Hudson. That good lady had an inkling that something unusual was happening, but then again, with Mr. Holmes, the unusual was always happening. She shook her head and beat a slow retreat down the stairs to her rooms.

"Now, Lady Juliet, what is your news?"

Juliet proceeded to narrate the proceedings of Lady Selma's attendance on Baron Reginald and then her meeting with Von Meyer. At the mention of the German's name, Holmes reacted violently. "So that blaggard is active again. And he's working with this traitorous harpy. She admitted to having you killed?"

"She was proud of it. She hired two known assassins to do the deed. I think they were the ones Stevens identified. Although, I'm not sure why they called at the manor."

"To determine where you were and how best to do away with you. We need to find those two. You say she reduced their payment because of Reginald's wounding? They can't be happy about that."

"She bragged about it and Von Meyer was all over himself in admiration."

"I think it's time we had another talk with Inspector Gregson. He may be able to identify those thugs once we make the connection for him. Those two can hang Lady Selma if they're properly manipulated. I must also speak with Mycroft again. We must do something about Reginald, the leaky sieve."

"Well, let's get on with it. I have an appointment at the Pearly Gates and they won't take 'no' for an answer this time. Raymond has an archangel all prepared and motivated to drag me over the Rainbow Bridge if I offer any resistance."

"I will be sorry to see you leave, Baroness. We have become a Yin-Yang."

"Why, thank you, Mr. Holmes. I actually understood that. I shall miss you, too. Even Doctor Watson, that unbeliever."

*****

"I'm pretty sure I know who you mean, Mr. Holmes," said Inspector Gregson. "If it's them, your Lady Selma was sold a serious bill of goods. Wally Sheffield and George Sykes! Murder for hire! A bigger pair of incompetents has never crawled the streets of London. They may no longer be in London but if they are, we'll find them. Lady Selma Fairfax, hmm? She's a new one on me but she sounds like someone we ought to know."

"Thank you, Inspector. We'll wait to hear from you."

We'll wait to hear from you? Gawd, Holmes. He may take forever, and I don't have forever.

Fear not, my lady. We have other resources. Holmes and Lady Juliet had reverted to their telepathic means of communication while in the presence of Inspector Gregson.

26

Watson looked askance at Holmes, muttering quietly to himself as they all exited the police station.

Not that overweight brother of yours!

I need to see Mycroft about dealing with Reginald; but no, my lady, for these situations I have one of the finest search teams in England at my disposal.

"Watson," said Holmes, in his regular speaking voice, "can you contact Timpkins, Wiggins's successor? We need the Irregulars. Please have Timpkins assemble as many of them as possible at our apartment; and have them wait for me there if I have not already returned."

'Irregulars?' They sound like people I would like. Who are they?

Holmes concentrated. *You'll meet them as soon as we return from the Diogenes Club.*

Ah, the Diogenes Club! My favorite home away from home. I simply adore their Majordomo. He's the Soul of Gracious Welcome. I'll flit over and meet you there. I've developed a severe dislike for London cabs, even though I adore horses. Those smoke-belching automajigs are going to ruin this city. See you in the Stranger's Room. I'm probably the strangest stranger they've ever seen... or never seen.

The Soul of Gracious Welcome sourly perused Holmes as he entered the club. He bowed and directed Holmes to the Stranger's Room where the Baroness sat waiting, her chair partially visible through her ghostly appearance. She was fussing with her dress.

I've lost a lot of weight. In fact, <u>all</u> of my weight, and this gown doesn't do anything for me anymore; but I'll be damned *(oops, sorry) if I'm going to go around in one of those dowdy white robes. Absolutely non-negotiable. Archangel or no archangel. So there!*

She looked up as the Majordomo returned, standing at the door with Mycroft.

Oh, look who's here. Mr. Joyful himself, fresh from his meal of lemons and sour prunes. Smile, sweetheart! Oh, never mind. Holmes, read your brother the Riot Act about Reginald.

Mycroft made a feeble attempt at humor. "We have to stop meeting like this, Sherlock. People are beginning to talk, and as you know, that's against the club rules."

Holmes gave him a wan smile in return. "I have news," he said, and proceeded to present chapter and verse of the Lady Selma Fairfax saga, with a healthy supply of digs against Baron Crestwell. "Prince's friend or no Prince's friend, Mycroft—the Baron needs to be silenced and exiled, and Lady Fairfax needs to be hung for the willful murder of Lady Juliet Armstrong, Baroness Crestwell."

The red-begowned spirit jumped to her feet, almost losing her dress in the process, and cheered. *Lay it on him, Holmes. Tell your brother to ship that stupid blighter out; and string up Lady Fairfax!*

Mycroft, ever the spoilsport, remained nonplussed. "These are serious charges. Do you have sufficient evidence, dear brother?"

"Shortly, Mycroft, shortly. Be ready to visit His Highness. You may wish to gather some allies before you venture forth. I'm sure you'll find plenty of proof of Lord Reginald's braggadocio and stupidity. He's not a deliberate traitor. He's just a pillow-talking fool with an eye for an attractive ankle."

Her ankles are not attractive. They're shaped like trees. Von Meyer is another idiot. Demure, my Aunt Louise. She's a nasty piece of work. I hope those murderous clowns she employed turn on her. Let's go meet your Irregulars.

Holmes left Mycroft in a very unhappy state of mind.

*****

Back at Baker Street, Lady Juliet was occupied once again in adjusting her gown when the door to the rooms burst open. Mrs. Hudson let out a scream of frustration from below. "Mr. Holmes, I thought we'd seen the last of these delinquents!"

A half-dozen street urchins cascaded through the door. "We found 'em, Mr. 'olmes. Doctor Watson gave us the 'looks-like,' and the names, and we found 'em." They looked expectantly for their rewards. When none were forthcoming, reality creeped in. "Oh, they're holed up in Seven Dials at a flophouse. Mrs. Washburn's."

"Excellent! Here." Several half-crowns landed in their dirty hands. "Share with each other. Play fair!"

They tumbled down the stairs and the amazed deceased aristocrat gaped. "Holmes! Those were *children*."

"Very astute of you, Baroness," said Holmes. "The Irregulars are my most potent investigative force, along with a wonderful dog named Toby. No one notices children or canines. They can pursue, identify, and even capture wrongdoers without creating a ripple in the atmosphere. Somewhat like an ethereal

29

personage with whom I have recently become acquainted. Although I suspect your abilities at capture are severely limited."

"Sad but true. You continue to amaze. Now what?"

"We gather up Inspector Gregson and a few bobbies and proceed to Seven Dials, where hopefully our two inept assassins have gone to ground. And then we bluff. We need a confession and a tie-in with Lady Selma."

*****

A Black Mariah pulled up in front of Mrs. Washburn's. Several constables rushed in front of the amazed onlookers and took the stairs in several leaps. The bobbies ran into a large common room and, brandishing batons and handcuffs, grabbed two individuals—one tall, slim, bearded and sporting a full moustache. Dark hair, Blue eyes. Clad in an ill-fitting suit. The other was an exact opposite. Short, portly, clean-shaven, brown-eyed. Similar clothing. A Music Hall Comedy Act.

Inspector Gregson, accompanied by Holmes, Watson and the unseen Baroness, advanced on the pair.

"'ere, you rozzers. What's the meaning of this? Assaulting peaceful citizens who happen to be down on their luck."

"You have our sympathy. Wally Sheffield and George Sykes, you are under arrest for the willful murder of Lady Juliet Armstrong, Baroness Crestwell."

"Wot? You're off your chump, you are. We don't know any Baroness. Wot would she want with a pair like us?"

"Nothing! You just killed her off on hire from Lady Selma Fairfax."

"Wot? George, the bint has done us in. She's squealed. I told you she would be trouble."

"Shut up, Wally. You just got us a one way ticket to the gallows."

"I won't shut up! She's the one who should swing, not us."

Gregson hauled the two of them to their feet and turned them over to the constables. "We'll talk again, lads. Meanwhile we have a murderous she-cat to bring in. Thanks for the information."

"Wally, you're a damned, big-mouthed fool!"

Juliet laughed. *He's not the only one, George,* she thought, loud enough for Holmes to hear. *I married one.*

Back at 221B Baker Street, Holmes and Watson sat with snifters of brandy in hand. "Well, Holmes, it seems the law has caught up with our murderers, all three of them. Selma Fairfax is a very dangerous woman. The two riflemen have been spilling their guts and implicating her in the hopes of getting off with a lesser sentence. No such luck. Not if Lady Selma has anything to say about it. She seems to have plenty to say."

"Indeed, Watson. Mycroft has sent me a wire announcing the appointment of Baron Reginald Crestwell as His Highness's personal representative to the court of the Maharajah of Sailendra."

"Where is that?"

"I don't know, and I am not motivated to find out."

Juliet, who had been listening to this attentively, chuckled. "You'll find out soon enough, Holmes. That idiot will probably set off a revolution."

"Alas, too true, my lady," said Holmes, raising his snifter in her direction.

"Well, gentlemen. I must leave now. You have been an excellent partner, Holmes. Perhaps it may not be goodbye but simply 'Au revoir.' A pity I cannot hug or kiss you."

"Au revoir, my lady. Consider yourself kissed."

*****

Standing in a sun-drenched open field, the former actress and Baroness Crestwell, Lady Juliet Armstrong *(recently, violently and definitely deceased),* looked around her. She was still attired in scarlet.

She turned and found herself facing an individual who had not been there a moment ago. A middle-aged male, tall, dressed in morning *(mourning?)* clothes, clean shaven, not a hair out of place, dark eyes, color undetermined. He seemed to be floating inches above the grass.

"Hello Raymond. As you can see, I have returned."

"Yes, Baroness. Welcome back. Was your journey successful?"

"Yes, Raymond. Justice has been done, and I am ready to accept my fate."

"Nothing so dire, My dear Baroness. The Pearly Gates await you… as does someone else."

"I really don't need an archangel to enforce my entry."

"Not an archangel, but a little angel covered in white fur with a very active tail."

She looked down and saw a lovely vision running towards her.

"Pookie! My little Pookie, my one true love! Come, sweetheart, come! There's my good little dog. Let's cross the Rainbow Bridge together and go to the Pearly Gates. Thank you, Raymond. Thank you!"

Swing Low, Sweet Juliet

A very attractive female figure in a scarlet gown (none of those dowdy white robes for her) soared down from the celestial choir loft in the Cosmic Cathedral. Her dark brown coiffure was undisturbed by the descent. Her face held a radiant smile. She adjusted the song book in her hands and looked back at the gold and white edifice that stretched into infinite space.

Across the enormous square, a Mosque projected its slender minarets high into a cerulean sky. Further along, Solomon's gold-encrusted temple gleamed in the sun. Tabernacles, oriental shrines, chapels and assorted other places of worship dotted the heavenly landscape. She sighed. Contented! She was followed by a little white dog whose tail beat a calypso rhythm.

"Well, Pookie, choir practice was glorious, as usual. Herr Handel was once again his marvelous self. He asked me to perform a solo, citing my splendid lyric contralto. I was delighted. The heavenly host was at its otherworldly best, although I sometimes think the angels are a bit jealous of us ex-mortals who performed while alive in the opera and music halls. Ah, well, another blessed day. It's good to be alive… sorry, dead."

The dog responded with a robust bark and dropped a sparkling ball at the dainty red shoes of Lady Juliet Armstrong, one time Baroness Crestwell and former sensation of the London musical stage.

"Oh. are we to play, Pookie? All right, but you cheat, you know. You can't possibly catch all of those throws on the fly without divine intervention. I think the Almighty has a sweet spot for dogs. I know I do. Anyway, let's go over to the Elysian Fields and have at it. Do you know the French have Elysian Fields in the middle of Paris, of all places? The Champs-Élysées. Not sure you can play ball there."

Lady Juliet was a recent arrival in Heaven and was still settling in after her violent death at the hands (guns, actually) of two hired assassins. She created a bit of a stir by refusing to cross the Rainbow Bridge and enter the Pearly Gates until her killers were found and brought to justice. When it was pointed out to her by Mr. Raymond, a Senior Heavenly Director, that in her discorporate state, she would be unable to interact with living, breathing humans, she insisted on partnering with the one individual who could compensate for that lack and respond to her requirements.

That someone was Sherlock Holmes. Long story short, the Director somewhat grudgingly acquiesced to her taking a short sabbatical back on Earth where she could join the Great Detective, find her killers and bring them before the British Bar of Justice. Unexpectedly, Holmes agreed to the arrangement. He was the only one who could see and telepathically converse with the lady. That left a befuddled Doctor Watson in a state of disbelief that he only overcame when the culprits were brought to book.

Now, Holmes's erstwhile partner Lady Juliet and her dog, Pookie, were enthusiastically exploring Heaven and its delights until a funny thing happened on the way to the playgrounds. She met an old friend, Eric Crescendo, world-renowned acrobat and aerialist. That wasn't his real name, but she didn't know his real name.

He enthused, "Juliet, sorry, *Milady Crestwell*. Wie wundervoll! How hervorragend you still look after all these years!"

As you've probably concluded, Eric was German.

Juliet's reaction was mixed. She appreciated having her beauty admired but she wasn't all that pleased about being reminded of her age before she expired. "You too, Eric. So nice to see you again."

"The last time we were together we shared the bill at the Orpheum. We both flew after a fashion. Then of course, you retired and married a Duke. Sorry to hear of your death. It made Celestial news. But here you are. Your same lovely self."

Juliet smiled. "He's a Baron, Eric. And as you can see, I'm not exactly my same lovely self. But tell me, why are you here? An accident? Did you finally fall off your high wire?"

"Yes. but it was no accident. Someone tampered with the rig. Like you, I was murdered."

"How awful! You say 'someone.' You don't know who?"

"No, and my wife, Clotilde, had a similar episode on a broken trapeze. Fortunately, she survived. Someone has it in for the Flying Crescendos. Our whole family is at risk. Clotilde, Walter, Eric Junior, Katrin and Friedrich."

"Have the police been involved?"

"Yes, but they just think it's the dangers of our profession. Aerialists are vulnerable. We Crescendos don't use nets. They don't believe there was any meddling. We're just excitable artistes. Besides, we're German. Who cares about us? My poor wife and children are helpless. We've, I mean, *they've* had to suspend their performances."

"That's terrible!" She paused. "I think I know someone who can help. How can I reach Clotilde?"

"They're in London staying at a hotel. But how can you help? You're like me, a ghost."

"I may be a ghost but I'm not like you. I have a mortal partner. You may have heard of him. Sherlock Holmes."

*****

"No! Absolutely not! I had a terrible time explaining why I invoked Loophole M on your behalf the last time. It's only supposed to be used in emergencies. You used it to track down your killers."

"Well, Raymond, this is an emergency. Someone is trying to wipe out an entire family of aerialists and I can get them help."

"Sorry! There's a lot of evil in that world you just left, Baroness."

"I can't believe you're going to let that evil succeed."

"I can't interfere!"

"Sure you can. Heaven has been interfering since Adam and Eve. And if you can't, I can. Come on! Where's the old Raymond I've come to love? You're such a sweetie."

"Your flattery won't work."

"Of course, it will. Now, same arrangement. Five days, one mortal; namely, Sherlock Holmes."

"Oh, all right—but this is absolutely the *last time.*"

*****

The snuffling and panting sounds of a dog echoed in Sherlock Holmes's head. He grunted and said, "Good dog, Toby. Is somebody down a well? Go search!" The sound continued. "Toby?" As he awoke, squinting, he realized that his hound assistant was probably at his usual home at Pinchin Lane, Lambeth. Who was this? He opened his eyes further and saw a small white Bichon Frisé standing on his chest. He saw and heard it but didn't feel it. He looked over the top of the black nose and curly tail and spotted a more familiar figure. Baroness Juliet. The glamorous ghost had returned, this time with an ethereal canine in tow. Clad in a new dress of dazzling red, she smiled and said telepathically, *Hello, Mr. Sherlock Holmes! Remember me?*

My lady, he mentally replied, *how could I forget? I thought we had reached an agreement on not invading my bed chamber. And who is this charming puppy?*

Say hello to Pookie. She is hardly a puppy. She died of old age over a year ago but we're back together again beyond the Rainbow Bridge. Now, she is my constant other worldly companion. As for me, I am here to reinvigorate our partnership.

Holmes reached out to pet the dog but his hand went through the fur-covered body. A spectral canine, indeed. But certainly not the Hound of the Baskervilles. Holmes stretched, and said aloud, "Let me see. You can't have been murdered again. Lady Selma and her associates are facing the noose. Baron

Reginald is in exile, so this must be something new. Give me a moment to don my dressing gown, and we can discuss it after I ask Mrs. Hudson for some coffee."

Holmes sat up, while Pookie jumped off his chest and rolled around and through the bedsheets. "So, Lady Armstrong, have you been released by celestial management to engage in another pursuit of wrongdoers? Poor Mr. Raymond. Browbeaten again!"

"Yes," Juliet said, "only this time it's to protect a family of German aerialists. The father is a former theatrical associate of mine. His act preceded me when we were on tour years ago. Like me, he is now deceased. Someone tampered with his rig and sent him falling to his death. His wife also came close to the same fate. He is sure it was sabotage—and before you ask, the police were involved. They believe it was a pair of accidents. Sloppy maintenance or some such thing. Eric knows otherwise."

"Who is Eric?"

"The now deceased patriarch of the Flying Crescendos. Clotilde is the wife and Walter, Eric Junior, Katrin and Friedrich are the children. They are world famous, but as a result of these events, they have cancelled their performances and are hidden away here in London."

"Ah, they are not in Germany. Good! That will save us a continental journey."

"So, you'll work with me on this?"

"I'm sure you knew the answer to that before you and your dog arrived. Now, where are they staying in London and which policemen have investigated this so far?" He looked up and shouted: "Mrs. Hudson, coffee and a few scones, please!"

"Yes, Mr. Holmes," came the reply from the floorboards, followed by a sniffing sound. "Is there a dog in there? You know how I feel about animals in the house."

"No dog, Mrs. Hudson. Is your imagination running away with you?"

He turned to the Baroness and thought, *She smelled Pookie. You may want to give her a bath in holy water.*

Very funny, thought Lady Juliet, *I have the address of the hotel where the Crescendos are staying, the London Grantham. And it was our old friend Gregson who managed or mismanaged the investigation. First, we need a story to tell Clotilde and the Inspector. We can't mention my contact with Eric. That would well and truly kill our credibility.*

We can't even mention you, Baroness.

Oh, yes, of course. I'm the 'silent partner.' Silent, but effective.

How true! Unlike you, I need some nourishment, if only occasionally. Let me finish these scones and get dressed. I'll send a few wires, then we can head for the Grantham and after that, Scotland Yard. I'll take a cab and you can fly though the air with the greatest of ease. You and your little dog, too. No broomstick required.

*****

At the London Grantham, Holmes inquired at the desk for Madame Clotilde Crescendo. He forwarded his card with a note asking to see her about a matter affecting the family's professional activities. She recognized the name of the famous detective and, somewhat puzzled, told the desk clerk to send him up.

Needless to say, Lady Juliet was there ahead of Holmes and was standing inside the door looking at Clotilde and her oldest son, Walter. She remembered them from her theatrical ventures and felt frustrated that she could not renew acquaintances. *Ah well, C'est la vie!* she thought. *No, C'est la morte! Drat!*

Clotilde responded to the detective's knock, walking through Pookie to open the door. The dog was insulted and came out with a ghostly growl. Juliet laughed, thinking *"Steady on, Pookie, my dear. You'll have to get used to being invisible to all but us immortals; and of course, Mr. Holmes. He's a different kind of immortal."*

"Mr. Sherlock Holmes," said Clotilde, "please come in. I must confess I don't know why you're here. This is my son, Walter. My other three children are down in the hotel dining room demolishing breakfast. Eric Junior, Katrin and Friedrich all have strong appetites. Walter and I are more restrained as was my husband, Eric, rest his soul."

The Baroness nodded. Using her telepathic connection, she broadcast to Holmes, *Eric's soul is not resting, Clotilde. Not yet. We'll fix that, won't we, Holmes?*

Clotilde Crescendo was a small, slim, but muscularly defined woman, as you might expect of an experienced aerialist. Her specialty was the trapeze rather than the high wire. She was in her late thirties with short black hair and an attractive theatrical face. Walter was by comparison, a tall, strong and burly individual, obviously skilled at catching and grasping flying entities like his brothers and sister. He was also a high wire walker like Eric Senior.

Holmes said, "Madame Crescendo and Herr Crescendo. My sincere condolences on your loss. It is the reason I have come."

Walter frowned. "My father's death was tragic, and so was the near miss that my mother endured when her trapeze collapsed. Are you here to take advantage of those events by poking your nose around and charging us an enormous fee for your services? Lord knows, the police were useless."

"I understand and sympathize with your cynicism, Herr Crescendo. I am here at the request of a friend of your father who wishes to remain nameless. That friend will bear my fees and expenses, if any."

Oh, dear! The deceased Baroness wondered how to set up payments through her estate. *I'll have to talk to Raymond, won't I, Pookie? Lawyers won't help; they don't believe in ghosts.* The dog wagged her tail.

Holmes continued, "I have been asked to investigate the circumstances of Eric Senior's death and the subsequent accident that almost resulted in your demise, Madame Crescendo."

Walter snorted, "No accidents, Mr. Holmes. Someone has been tampering with our gear. We need to find them out and stop them so we can safely return to our act."

The lady joined in. "I will not have my children put in danger, Mr. Holmes. We are not penniless and can continue to live on our savings until this villain is found."

Walter added, "Mama is worried and cautious. I want revenge."

"That is a subject for future discussion. Right now, let's concentrate on putting an end to these acts of violence. You say your gear was tampered with. May I see the evidence?"

"The Scotland Yard inspector has taken the high wire and the broken trapeze shackles into police custody. Why, I don't know, since he believes it was a case of shoddy maintenance. It was not. We need those props and equipment. Is there anything you can do to get it all back?"

"I plan to visit Inspector Gregson immediately after we end our conversation here. I'll be back to you in short order. Meanwhile, a few questions. I assume you wish me to work on your behalf?"

Clotilde responded. "Oh, yes, your reputation is outstanding, and if some unidentified friend is paying your fees, we would be fools not to take advantage. Wouldn't we, Walter?"

Walter nodded affirmatively but rather cautiously. Lady Juliet picked up on it. *He's hesitant, Holmes. I wonder why? Something's strange here. I mean, stranger than usual.*

Holmes replied telepathically: *I share your opinion. Walter needs some further study and observation. That's your specialty.*

Yes, I am rather good at it. So is Pookie, aren't you, girl? Another spiritual bark! Inspector Pookie was on the job!

"Now, Madame, the usual question: who would want to sabotage your equipment and cause death and injury? Who has means, motive and opportunity?"

Walter responded, "As to motive, we have rivals like all theatrical acts. But I'm having a hard time imagining who would have such a reservoir of hatred to do us in. Any high wire performer would have the means. It's the opportunity I find hard to deal with. We keep very careful guard on our equipment."

"You say 'we.' Who is that specifically?"

"Well, obviously Eric Senior when he was still with us, but now Mutter Clotilde and I share the responsibility. The kids are too scatterbrained to trust with the apparatus and tackle. We have a company of riggers who gets us set up when we first take on a show commitment. Merriwether Brothers. They're from Liverpool. Of course, on the continent, we use other companies."

"Both incidents took place here in London?"

Clotilde replied, "Yes, we came off tour and took on a long engagement at the Palladium. That's down the drain now."

"You don't think you can salvage any of the dates?"

"Well, we've been replaced for the time being"

"By whom?"

"A troupe of trained horses and dogs. It's humiliating."

At the mention of dogs, Pookie growled again. The Baroness calmed her. *Quiet, girl! Although, no one can hear you besides me and Sherlock Holmes.*

Holmes smiled at this. The Crescendos looked at him in puzzlement.

"Sorry, a stray thought just crossed my mind. One last question. Have you received any threatening notes or messages?"

"Yes! As you know, we are German and in 1901 Germany is not too popular with England. The Queen is dead and this country is still in mourning. Kaiser Wilhelm may have been a pallbearer at Victoria's funeral, but he is stirring things up again and we get abusive remarks and materials from time to time. Our kids go to a theatre school here and their classmates are not kind. "Go back to Germany, you dirty Huns."

The Baroness shuddered and Holmes frowned. "I am on my way to see Inspector Gregson. I will see what I can do about getting your materials restored to you. We'll get to the bottom of this."

"My turn to ask, Mr. Holmes. Who is 'we?'"

Lady Julia chuckled. *Oops!* Pookie looked at her expectantly. Could Lady Julia have dropped a heavenly doggie treat? No such luck!

Holmes didn't even blink. "I plan to ask my colleague, Doctor Watson, to join me in this investigation. And of course, there is your nameless benefactor."

Nice recovery, Sherlock. Let's go see that oafish Inspector again. He actually referred to me as 'collateral damage' when he was investigating my assassination. Dumbbell! Anyway, we got that slattern Lady Selma, and those two yobs who shot me. I wonder how my former husband Reginald is doing with the Maharajah of Sailendra. Maybe they stranded him in the desert or is it an island? Reginald can't swim. She giggled and floated out of the hotel room with the dog running lazy circles around her red satin slippers.

*****

The Baroness rode along with Holmes as they went across town to the Victoria Embankment and the newish home of New Scotland Yard. They conversed telepathically.

I am foregoing my celestial transportation mode so we can have a strategy session, Mr. Holmes. Though I've really come to

45

hate cabs. Flitting is so much more fun. Pookie likes it too, don't you, girl? The bichon had decided it was nap time and was quietly snoring at Juliet's feet.

Well, my lady, strategize away. What thoughts are wandering about in your aristocratic and theatrical head?

The first idea that occurred to me is that I can fly. If we can get those aerialists ready to go back in the air, I can examine their rig, observe what is going on and report to you. Fortunately, I do not suffer from fear of heights. It might be jolly to skitter along a tightrope or flip from a trapeze, especially knowing I'm not going to fall.

A splendid suggestion, but first we have to get that tightrope and trapeze back from the police.

Ah, yes, there is that. Tell me, Holmes, what is your opinion of Walter Crescendo?

Holmes frowned. *There is more there than meets the eye. I need more data.*

Lady Juliet shrugged. *I'm suspicious too, but I can't imagine him trying to kill his parents.*

Why not? History is full of stories of parricides. I, myself, have brought several to justice.

What would be his motive, Mr. Holmes?

I don't know but, dear partner, that is the sort of question we detectives have to answer. Holmes looked out of the window. *Here we are. I sent a message to Gregson that I was coming. By the way, Watson will be joining us. I told him you were back, but he's still dubious about you. Doesn't trust what he can't see. I'm afraid part of that is my fault. I also filled him in about the Crescendo tragedies.*

Holmes looked down at Juliet's scarlet-encased feet. Pookie stirred when the rhythm of the cab's movement came to a halt. *I guess I had better tell Watson about the dog. Of course, Mrs. Hudson knows nothing about you or Pookie. She'd be frightened to death. Not literally, of course.*

Holmes paid the cabbie and strode into the building, waving at the desk sergeant. The Baroness floated along with him, taking in the bustling activity with a raised eyebrow. *It looks like London's criminal element is busy.*

He chuckled, *Welcome to Scotland Yard, Milady!*

"Welcome to New Scotland Yard, Mr. Holmes." The voice belonged to Inspector Tobias Gregson. "Good to see you again. Doctor Watson is here already. Come join him in my office."

The Baroness looked askance at the Inspector. *Hello, stupid. It's me! Good old collateral damage. Here to save your reputation once again. You got all the credit for putting away my killers while Holmes and I did all the work. Ooh, I wish you could see and hear me. I'd really fry your senses. I'd have Pookie bite you if she could. Holmes, sometimes being incorporeal is so frustrating!*

The detective smiled and telepathed, *...but it has advantages.*

Watson noticed the smile and whispered, "Is she here with you?"

Holmes whispered back. "Yes, with her little dog, Pookie."

The doctor grinned and sniffed, "The dog needs a bath."

"Well, gentlemen, what can the Metropolitan Police do for you? I assume you're here on some sort of criminal case."

"Yes, Inspector. We're here representing the Flying Crescendo family."

"No criminal activity there. Just a tragic case of shoddy apparatus maintenance."

"They think otherwise, and I am investigating the possibilities of sabotage. If you believe there was nothing in this for your department, why are you holding on to their equipment?"

"We submitted it to the Building Safety chaps for evaluation. They found nothing out of the ordinary besides loose shackles. Just unattended wear and tear. If you want their gear, take it. It's in storage here. I'll be glad to get rid of it."

"Good! I'll be happy to tell Madame Clotilde and Herr Walter. They can have the Merriwether Brothers make a pick up. Maybe they can re-install it unobtrusively in the theatre. Trained dogs and horses don't use high wires or the trapeze. I plan to meet with the manager of the Palladium and see what the situation is with the Flying Crescendos' contract. I'm not sure what they plan to do. Madame Crescendo is unwilling to expose her children to hazards, although their profession is one long hazard."

The Baroness laughed, *Unless, like me, you really can fly! Did you know Pookie can fly too? She could work on a high wire. We're right out of Peter Pan. I guess I'll never completely leave the stage. Heaven has several theatre guilds. Although there are not too many actors or playwrights who make it beyond the Pearly Gates. Glad I did! All right, Holmes. No further satisfaction to be gotten here. On to the Palladium. Did you know I once played there? The critics loved me.*

Swing Low, Sweet Juliet

*****

Over to Soho and Argyll Road to the Palladium Theatre. Less of a theatre and more of an arena, rebuilt and modified by Fredrick Hengler, the son of a tightrope walker, the Palladium specializes in circus-like performances. The Flying Crescendos had been regulars on the bill as were the dogs and horses who were currently replacing them, Major Merwyn's Menagerie. They were just finishing a matinee performance when Holmes, Watson, Lady Juliet and Pookie arrived.

Holmes approached the stage door, identified himself and asked for the manager. The doorkeeper recognized the famous name, stood aside and called out for one of the stage hands. "Charlie, see if you can fetch Miss Jenny Louise."

After a few moments wait, during which Pookie managed to pursue several of the Menagerie dogs and caused two of the horses to shy, Miss Hengler appeared. The animals sensed the two ghosts and Major Merwyn was puzzled and upset by their reaction. The lady, herself a famous equestrienne, calmed the horses, shrugged at the Major and turned to Sherlock Holmes.

"Mr. Holmes and, I assume, Doctor Watson, what brings you to the Palladium, honored though we are by your presence?"

"Miss Hengler, I am here representing Madame and Herr Walter Crescendo. We are trying to unravel the mysterious events leading up to Herr Eric's recent demise and the near tragic trapeze mishap with Madame Crescendo. Hopefully, we can help them resume their act here."

"Oh, yes, come up to my office. This is hardly the place to have a conversation especially since something has spooked

49

the horses and dogs. Very peculiar. They are usually so well disciplined."

The 'something' floated back over to the Baroness and settled in her arms. *Bad girl, Pookie. You're giving us away!*

The bichon yawned and proceeded to lick her chops.

They walked and floated around the stage platform area and entered a fair sized office. "Please be seated. Shall I order tea?"

"None for us, thank you!"

I would have liked a spot of sherry. That's something I really miss in the celestial realm. No food, no drinks, no champagne. Not necessary, they tell me. I think the Almighty is a teetotaler. I may organize a campaign in protest. Pookie gets her treats and water, though. Animals are a special case, especially horses, cows, camels, dogs, lambs, goats, sheep and donkeys. Cats are still on trial.

Miss Hengler heard none of this grousing, of course. "Now, how can I assist you?"

"I understand you are descended from a family of tight rope walkers. Can you shed any light on the accidents that befell the Crescendos?"

"Actually, Mr. Holmes, I am a bit of a black sheep. I'm a championship equestrienne, not an aerialist. I manage the Palladium out of respect for my father and our family. I'm afraid of heights and I always shuddered when I saw Eric, Clotilde and their brood flipping through the air or balancing on high."

"What is the contract situation for the Crescendos?"

"Oh, they can resume their place on the bill any time they want. Major Merwyn expanded his act to fill in their slot as well as his own. They're not really replaced."

"Excellent! We are recovering their equipment from Scotland Yard. They found no examples of tampering. Actually, it was the Building Safety unit that made the analysis."

"We see them all the time. With a large audience and dangerous acts, to say nothing of fire hazards, they're a theatre manager's constant burden. If they've signed off, we can reinstall the Crescendos' apparatus."

"Then, I suppose, we could have the Merriwether Brothers set up the high wires and trapeze again. Now comes the difficult part. Finding who tampered with the gear in the first place, arresting them and convincing Madam Crescendo to resume their performances. Do you have any useful insights?"

"I do know they have received threats here at the theatre from anti-German fanatics. But they have always been very easy to work with. Not like some of the prima donnas we get here."

The Baroness raised an ethereal eyebrow but said nothing.

Watson, who had remained relatively quiet up till now, asked. "Are there any rival companies who would like to replace them on the bill?"

"Yes, several! There are the Winged Fitzgeralds, Max and Elise and the Sky Dwellers. None of them compare to the Crescendos for daring or skill. Although I wonder about that now that Eric is no longer with them. Walter is very talented but for the last few seasons, it's been Clotilde who is the highlighter with the trapeze act. She is no wire walker, though. That's Walter's domain and the kids are a sort of special added attraction, especially for our younger audience members. I can't believe any of those acts would stoop to sabotage."

Lady Juliet snorted, *Oh deary, little do you know about show business rivalries. Stick with your horses.*

"How can we contact these acts?"

"I'll give you their agent's name and location. George Forsythe on the Strand. He manages them all, but not the Crescendos. Their agent is in Germany. I do know that the Fitzgeralds are on the road in Scotland. I don't know about Max and Elise or the Sky Dwellers."

"You've been most helpful. We'll contact Walter Crescendo and tell him his equipment has been released. He can make the arrangements with Merriwether Brothers. Thank you for your assistance."

As we crossed the stage toward the exit, Watson said, "Holmes, don't you think we ought to interrogate the representative from Merriwether Brothers?"

"Exactly what I intend to do, Watson. Two great minds in agreement."

The Baroness laughed. *Make that three and add a half for Pookie.* The dog did a series of leaps.

*****

A handsome and exceedingly well-built man in his late thirties rose from his desk to greet Holmes and Dr. Watson.

Goodness, Holmes, what a splendid specimen. Why do I keep meeting all these interesting men after I'm dead? I guess it was the price of being a Baroness. Reginald was a lot of things. Interesting wasn't one of them.

"Yes sir, Mr. Holmes! Simon Hargreaves, at your service. London representative for Merriwether Brothers, Riggers Extraordinaire to the Crown and Common Folk! What can I do for you?"

"Several things, Mr. Hargreaves. Doctor Watson and I are here on behalf of Madame Clotilde and Herr Walter Crescendo."

"Oh, yeah. Very sad thing. I liked Eric. Can't understand it. Never saw him fall or even lose his balance. And then the lady had a near miss. The Yard said it was equipment failure. Don't you believe it! When Merriwether Brothers rig an aerial extravaganza, it's done right and it's done completely. That setup was right as rain when we left it. Somebody got at it. The police have it all wrong. Faulty maintenance! Fah! I never knew an artiste who was more careful and attentive to detail than Eric Crescendo. 'Check! Check and check again!' That was his motto. No, no! Something smells."

Juliet giggled, *He's not talking about you, Pookie, but you are a bit ripe. One bath coming up when we get back. Interesting that all my senses are sharp and complete. Sight, smell, hearing. I don't know about taste. I haven't eaten or drunk anything since I crossed over. But not touch. That's limited to contact with the deceased and of course, the angelic groups. I've watched them driving their chariots. Carrying people home, they say. Speed demons, all of them.* The dog barked. *Shh, you little noise box.*

Holmes smiled at the ghostly byplay. "Do you have any ideas you can share with us, Mr. Hargreaves?"

"I'd take a look at that Sky Dwellers crowd. Bunch of roustabouts who decided they wanted to break into show business. Spend most of their time at circuses. Unprofessional toughs, if you ask me."

"We plan to meet with their agent,"

"Hah, there's a piece of work. George Forsythe. Up to his ears in debt. We won't work with his clients any longer. At least not till he pays up what he owes us for services rendered."

"What about Max and Elise?"

"They're actually quick change artists. They just shimmy up poles or run behind curtains as part of their distraction act. We fix them up in half an hour. They're prompt payers. They're good at what they do."

I bet they're not as good at changing clothes as I am. I can get rid of a white robe and into a gorgeous red dress in nothing flat. Change shoes too, although shoes aren't a necessity in Heaven. You know, Pookie, we'll have to get you a fancy red bow so we match. The dog didn't seem enthused.

"Do you happen to know if the Crescendos have received threats?"

"Of course! They're German. Not a good country to be from nowadays. I'm not sure. We only saw them when we first set them up. That Walter is a strange one. Still waters run deep. Are they going back in the air? Are we going to have to set them up again?

"I believe so but I'm not certain when. You'll hear from them, no doubt."

*****

Outside, once again!

Watson coughed, "Holmes, we seem to be going around in circles, chasing our tails."

Pookie took it upon herself to do exactly that. *Stop, you silly twit. Not you, Holmes, the dog.*

"Patience, Watson. There's a pattern emerging here but it's not complete."

"And as usual, Holmes, you are not going to share any of your thoughts or impressions."

"Correct! At least, not yet."

Mr. Holmes, is this the way you treat your partners? I expected to be inundated by your mental gymnastics. I feel totally left out.

Lady Juliet, I abhor half-baked assumptions based on impartial information or rumor.

You would never have survived as a diplomat or member of the aristocracy. That's how we lived.

I am all too well aware of that, Baroness. Once again, patience. I do not theorize. I analyze, synthesize, experiment and confront the truth when it arrives.

Well. Tell it to hurry up! Who's next on our visitation list? The agent?

Not yet. I want to return to the Crescendos.

Aha, Walter!

No, Clotilde. Back to the Grantham.

*****

Lady Juliet, I have an assignment for you, thought Holmes.

Oh good. I was beginning to feel quite useless. Do I get to sit on a trapeze?

Only if you want to. I'd like you to shadow Madam Clotilde.

Aha! 'Cherchez la femme' and all that. Is there more to the lady than concerned mother and aerial artiste?

That's what I want you to find out.

Definitely up my street! I loved skulking about when I was on the stage. Leave it to me. Come, Pookie, we're on the prowl. Where are you and Watson going, Mr. Holmes?

First, we need to tell Madame and Walter that their equipment has been released by Scotland Yard. Then a visit to George Forsythe, the agent, while you follow the lady.

They once more approached the apartment at the Grantham where the Crescendos held temporary residence. This time the youngsters were in attendance. Pookie wagged her tail furiously and ran through the door (literally) and flopped, disappointed. So many young hands and eyes but none of them could see to pet or tickle her. Watson knocked on the door and was greeted by Walter.

"Herr Doctor, Herr Holmes. Back so soon. Did you forget something?"

"No, Herr Walter. We have news. Scotland Yard has released your apparatus. You may pick it up at your convenience or perhaps have Simon Hargreaves, of Merriwether Brothers, reinstall it at the Palladium. Miss Hengler is eager for you to return."

"Just a moment! Mama, Herr Holmes and Doctor Watson are here. We have our equipment back from the police."

Clotilde plowed through the sea of eager teen-agers and approached the detective. "Thank you, Mr. Holmes. Have you any word on who meddled with our apparatus?"

"Nothing definite but we suspect one of your rivals may be to blame. We are looking further into it. I hope to have results, shortly."

Mr. Holmes, I thought you didn't theorize.

Holmes closed his eyes. *I don't, Baroness!*

Ah, a little deception at play?

A modest ploy!

One of the children called out, "Mama, Miss Hengler wants us back at the Palladium."

Clotilde turned to them. "Well, I guess we can't hide forever. I'll go and see Mr. Hargreaves and ask him to get us set up again, but we must be very cautious."

Smiles from Walter (unusual), Eric Junior, Katrin and Friedrich. "Hurray, up in the air again!"

Juliet shook her head. *These children are fearless. I hope they don't end up like their father. Anyway, Pookie and I are on stalker duty. I wish I could borrow your hat, Mr. Holmes.*

Farewell for the moment, Milady. Come to 221B Baker Street when you have anything to report. Holmes and Watson said goodbye to the aerialists and headed for the lobby, and then to the office of George Forsythe, theatre agent.

*****

"Sherlock Holmes and Doctor Watson, eh? Yes, I've heard of you. Thinking of packing in the detecting and going on stage? Well, I'm your man."

Watson smirked. He had often told Holmes the theatre lost an amazing talent when he decided to devote his life to the pursuit of wrongdoers and the prevention of criminal activity.

"Not at the moment, Mr. Forsythe. but thanks for the offer. We are just here for a little information if you can spare the time."

Watson looked around. Time seemed to be in ample supply in the sparsely furnished office. Forsythe was a portly and sleazy individual only partially clean-shaven, with sparse dark hair combed over his otherwise balding head. He had prominent blood vessels on his nose and face. Probably alcohol induced. His clothes, long past current fashion, fit him poorly. He was, in street parlance, a slob.

The office was in careless disarray with theatrical posters, playbills and old newspapers scattered on a table and chairs. There was no assistant or secretary in attendance.

"Well, I am quite busy but I guess I can spare you a few moments. Clear off those chairs and have a seat. I'd offer you something but my assistant is out running an important errand. Now, what is this all about?"

"We have been commissioned to investigate the untimely death of Mr. Eric Crescendo, the aerialist."

"Yeah, a real shame… but his troupe were not clients of mine."

"We are aware of that, but several rival groups are your clients, however. The Winged Fitzgeralds, Max and Elise, and the Sky Dwellers."

"Hold on! If you think any of them could be involved in Eric's death, you're barking up the wrong tent pole. The Fitzgeralds have been on the road in Scotland for the last six months. Max and Elise never get off the ground more than eight feet, if that, with their quick change routine. She has acrophobia. And as for the Sky Dwellers, those swine broke up last month and skipped off owing me a packet. They were a lousy act anyway. Their so-called lead damn near got killed several times. I guess he got smart and decided to switch to something on the ground. Aerial acts are the bane of my existence. Too few of them, too. Only a couple of venues where they can appear. I suppose you got my name from the Palladium."

"In fact, we did."

"Well, give my regards to Jenny Louise. Tell her I could use some business from her."

Holmes smiled. "Thank you for your time, Mr. Forsythe."

As they exited out onto the Strand, surrounded by theatres on both sides, Watson turned to Holmes and said, "Has it occurred to you that we have been increasingly caught up in the world of show business ever since you have taken up with your glamorous ghost?"

"She is not my glamorous ghost. I thought you didn't believe in her or her dog?"

"I don't have much choice. You really believe she is tracking Madam Crescendo!"

"Yes!"

*****

Back at the Grantham, Clotilde Crescendo, went into her bedroom, changed into a fashionable street dress, adjusted her jaunty hat, checked her medium-heeled shoes and advanced to the door of the suite. "I am going to see Mr. Hargreaves and arrange for the restoration of our apparatus."

Walter asked. "Do you want me to come with you? I know a bit more about the equipment than you do."

"That won't be necessary this time, Walter. You can supervise when they actually set up the rigs. I'm just going to negotiate the contract."

The Baroness looked down at Pookie. "Well, my dear canine companion, to quote the Master, 'The game is afoot,' or in your case, 'apaw.' Let us proceed to Mr. Simon Hargreaves' office once again. He certainly is a fine-looking example of male humanity."

The dog growled. "Don't like him, huh? Let's give you credit for your feminine intuition. I'll trust your judgement. Pity, though! He's very pretty. Ah, here we are. Let's wait here for Madame. No, better yet, let's do some spying…"

She and the dog glided into the office and set about peeking and peering, and in Pookie's case, sniffing.

Hargreaves was sitting at his desk, looking at diagrams and making notes in pencil. The Baroness wished once again that she could reach out and open cabinets and drawers. Frustrating! Nothing much of consequence and certainly nothing evidential on the surface.

Clotilde had taken a cab and arrived at Hargreaves' office about ten minutes after Juliet. She entered, strode over to his desk and promptly embraced him with a passionate kiss. "I've missed you."

He returned the kiss and said, "Me, too! But now, he's out of the way."

"Simon, I didn't expect you to kill him."

"What did you want? He was going to take all of you back to Germany and keep you there. I couldn't allow that. Besides, he was a martinet. The Teutonic bully! And Walter is just like him. We may have to deal with him, too."

"Nein!"

The Baroness laughed, "Well, Pookie, seems you were right. He's a rotter and she's no better."

"You have nothing to be concerned about, Clo! The Police are convinced it was an unfortunate accident and I have that fool, Sherlock Holmes, chasing after imaginary rivals."

Clotilde frowned, "Holmes is not a fool. He worries me. He has a reputation for uncovering crimes when nobody else can."

Juliet snorted, "You should be worried, my high-flying friend. The clock is running out for both of you. You're right. Holmes is no fool and you and your handsome lover are going to find that out. Pookie, why am I always attracted to good-looking swine or stupid cops?"

Clotilde looked at Hargreaves. "Simon, I did come here on business. Scotland Yard has released our equipment and the Palladium wants us back on the bill. I can stop pretending I'm fearful for our lives. That fake collapse of the trapeze should stop any suspicions about me. Walter is a bit dubious about that whole event. He doesn't like me. I'm not really his mother. The kids are mine, but not him."

"As I said, we may have to deal with him."

"Ach, Gott, No more killing, please."

"No, just a crippling accident. All right. I'll contact Jenny Louise Hengler and arrange to set your rig up again. You can start rehearsing. Those horses and dogs will have to move over."

Pookie growled. "You're right, Miss Dog! I think we have to get back to Holmes right away. We can't let this go on. Walter's in danger. Come. We have to leave these deadly lovebirds for the moment."

Back at Baker Street, Lady Juliet excitedly shared her newfound knowledge with the Great Detective. He, in turn, relayed it to Doctor Watson who reacted. "Holmes, Hargreaves is a scoundrel. We must warn Walter."

"I believe Walter knows already, Watson. I'm sure he's aware that his 'mother' is having an affair with the rigger. He may not know that, like his father, he is a target."

The Baroness intervened. "You can't rely on his knowledge, Holmes. Tell him! At least tell him that Hargreaves was responsible for Eric's death and you suspect Walter may be next."

*****

They arrived at the Grantham only to be told that the Crescendos had all checked out.

The manager, Mr. Frobisher, raised his eyebrows and said, "Believe me, Mr. Holmes, I was quite surprised. I thought they were quite content with their accommodations. Mr. Walter said they were leaving the country. They had a great offer on the continent and needed to rush to accept it."

"How long ago did they leave, Mr. Frobisher?"

"Early this morning, sir. They took a cab for the station. Something about catching the first channel ferry from Dover. Madame Crescendo didn't look too happy and neither did the kids but that Mr. Walter is a very forceful man."

Lady Crestwell said, *Leave this to me, Holmes; or would you rather use your Irregulars to find them? The police won't do. Leaving the country is not an offense unless a crime is involved. Pookie and I can get to Dover in a twinkling.*

"Yes, Baroness, please do!"

"Do what, Holmes?

"She's going to trace the Crescendos, Watson."

****

An ephemeral little white dog and a scarlet-clad wraith floated across the Eastern ferry dock in Dover just as the boat was preparing to leave. On the second deck stood Clotilde, Eric Junior, Katrin and Friedrich… but no Walter. Where was he? Had he gone for refreshments? No, he'd have the kids with him. "Where is he, Pookie? Find Walter!"

The dog ran off and speedily circled the decks. She ran back to the Baroness, tail lowered with a look of annoyance on her canine face. She barked.

"He's not on board, is he? He never left London. Back we go, swiftly. Holmes is probably at Baker Street."

The two of them shot through the door of the detective's sitting room. If she could breathe at all, she would have exhaled violently. Pookie panted for a moment but recovered her lady-like composure. A true aristocrat among dogs. The Baroness all but shouted in Holmes's head: *He's not with them! I think I know where he is! The Palladium!!*

Holmes replied, "Yes, of course. Very perceptive… partner! Watson, quickly!"

"Yes, yes, I know: 'The game is afoot.' Where are we going?"

"The Palladium. We have a murder to forestall. Contact Gregson and then join Lady Juliet and me… *(A momentary growl)* …and of course, Pookie."

*****

Simon Hargreaves had arrived at the theatre early with two assistants and a cart full of aerial equipment. He checked in with Jenny Louise Hengler and then proceeded to lay out the high wires and trapeze rigs according to a set of plans he held in his hands. One of the assistants was up on the traverse bars that ran across the ceiling over the stage attaching a swinging trapeze and lowering a flying trapeze platform. There were no nets. The Crescendos never used them.

A high wire had been already installed to run from a platform attached to the balcony, over the theater and onto another on-stage platform and ladder. Eric (and now Walter) would proceed on the wire from the stage platform to the balcony, turn and repeat the walk back to the platform, performing a series of short dance steps and keeping his equilibrium with an extended balance pole. All this, thirty feet in the air, exceeding the international specifications for "high wire" performances. Without a net!!

Swing Low, Sweet Juliet

The Baroness had arrived, as usual, ahead of Holmes and Watson and was perched on the flying trapeze stand while the technician lowered it into place. The dog remained on the auditorium floor looking up at Juliet. *"Pookie, I wish I could make this thing swing," fretted Lady Juliet. "I sat on a trapeze, sang and swung when I still did my act in this very theatre. That's how I knew Eric. He showed me how to keep a trapeze moving smoothly. When I return, I shall have to ask Raymond to have a rig like this installed in Heaven. Of course, the thrill will be artificial. We all can fly, and we're already dead so the risk is zero, but it's another diversion. Oh, look. Herr Walter is making an appearance."*

The aerialist strode down the aisle to where Hargreaves was standing. "Good morning, Simon. I see you are here bright and early. Clotilde and the kids will be down later."

The Baroness burst out, *"Liar, liar, pants on fire! Why is he here if the family is on its way to the continent? Oh no, does he plan to kill Hargreaves? Murder and more murder!"* Of course, only the dog heard her.

Hargreaves nodded. "We're working on the trapeze set-up. The high wire is already installed. Do you want to try it?"

"Of course! Let me just shed my jacket and change my shoes. Do you have my balance pole?"

"It's right there by the ladder. Go over and check out the balcony attachments first and then we can both go up and examine the stage-side platform when you return."

Walter went up to the balcony and went through a set of procedures, checking the attachments, testing the tautness of the wire, looking for any signs of wear or fraying, examining the

65

platform for stability and steadiness. Satisfied, he returned to the auditorium floor and then climbed up on the stage where the ladder and his balance pole awaited.

Hargreaves said, "I'll go up with you. You can show me any changes or fixes you want made." He climbed up, reached the top and stood against the steel fence that surrounded the platform on three sides. "Come ahead, Walter. The ladder, fence and platform are secure. You'll have to check the wire and attachments on this end."

The aerialist made his way up carrying the balance pole in one hand. He turned at the top and slid past Hargreaves, bending over to examine the connection points. Out of the corner of his eye he caught the rigger moving over to get behind him and push.

Walter shouted, "You bastard! You killed my father and now you're trying to kill me. You and that so-called mother of mine. Well, I'll get you first." He struck Hargreaves with the balance pole and the two of them locked in a tight embrace, pulling back and forth. Suddenly, one side of the fence gave way as Hargreaves had intended it to. What he had not intended was to be caught in Walter's arms as the two of them fell over onto the stage thirty feet below. Two necks simultaneously broke.

Holmes, Watson and Gregson arrived together. "My God" said the Inspector, "The both of them. They couldn't have survived a fall like that."

They didn't.

The Baroness frowned. "Very perceptive, Inspector. I suppose you're going to write it up as a tragic accident. Too much trouble to figure out who killed whom. I guess I should get down from this trapeze and talk with Holmes. Oh, dear! Poor vengeful

Walter. He wanted to kill Hargreaves. Do you think he wanted to die as well? I doubt if I'll be seeing him or Hargreaves again. They're headed for the nether regions."

Holmes walked over to Lady Juliet, pretending to survey the crime scene so he could telepathically speak with her in private. *Well, Milady, I don't know about Walter. I'm sure he felt betrayed by Clotilde and mourned the loss of his father. As far as Eric is concerned, we know who the true killer was, even if Gregson doesn't. If he persists in regarding Eric's death and now these two as mishaps, I think we'll let him go on in his ignorance. Here comes Miss Hengler.*

"Good Lord, Mr. Holmes, Inspector, Doctor. Are the two of them dead?"

Inspector Gregson removed his hat. "Yes, Miss Hengler. We've summoned an ambulance and the Medical Examiner but it's clear they both fell while testing the equipment."

"How does this happen? Twice with the same troupe in only a few weeks. That settles it. No more aerial acts at the Palladium without nets. Horses and dogs are less sensational but they're a lot safer. Audiences come to see the wire and trapeze artists fall but not get killed. Where are the rest of the Crescendos?"

"Somewhere on the continent, by now. I'm afraid," said Holmes. "You may have to search out another act. George Forsythe would love to hear from you."

"Not on your life. George Forsythe will never book another act in this theatre as long as I'm Director. Good day, gentlemen. Please have the medical people stop by my office when they arrive."

*****

Once more at 221B Baker Street, goodbyes and farewells were being exchanged.

Well, thought the Baroness, *it's time for Pookie and me to exit stage left and head back to the Elysian Fields. I will break the news to Eric that we discovered his killer. I guess I'll have to tell him about poor Walter. A shame Walter won't be able to tell him, himself. I'll pass over Clotilde's dalliance, but I will tell him that what's left of the troupe is back on the continent, probably Germany.*

Say goodbye to Doctor Watson for me. Maybe, if we meet again, he will be able to see and converse with me as well. Au revoir, Sherlock Holmes. I hope we can be partners again but meantime, if I can't persuade Raymond to let me come back, I may at least be able to wheedle a trapeze out of him. Or maybe just a swing.

A Major Issue

The Heavenly Theatre Guild had just completed another perfect rehearsal of Saintly Spectaculars, the longest running revue in unrecorded history. Over 2 million consecutive performances, and now featuring the lovely Lady Juliet Armstrong, Baroness Crestwell. A former sensational London actress/singer and British aristocrat, she arrived on the spiritual scene as a result of an assassination plotted by a rival. She has become, to put it mildly, something of a phenomenon in celestial circles.

She had just finished off a songfest and dramatic performance that left the angelic choir and virtuous virtuosi in awe. Lady Juliet had captured the divine audiences and was well on her way to celestial stardom. She picked up her scripts and flitted away from the extravagant stage.

On her way back to her fabulous mansion with her dog, Pookie, Juliet found herself once again face to face with Mr. Raymond, one of Heaven's Senior Directors. A middle-aged male, tall, dressed in morning (mourning?) clothes, clean shaven, not a hair out of place, dark eyes, color undetermined, floating inches above the grass. He held his halo in his hand.

"Ah, Milady Juliet. Just the woman I was coming to see."

"Hello, Raymond. Am I guilty of another cosmic infraction?" Ever since her relatively recent transfer to Elysium,

Lady Julia had been building a bit of a reputation for herself as a rebel. She refused to wear the white robes favored by most of Heaven's denizens. Instead, she went about in a daring scarlet dress. Her dog giddily chased the other ghostly animals for fun. But perhaps most perturbing were her sojourns back to Earth to partner with Sherlock Holmes and Doctor Watson in their crime-solving activities. It's just not done, don'cha know!

"No, Baroness. Paradise seems to be adjusting to you pretty well. So much so, in fact, that I have a request from On High to enlist your services."

"From the Very Top? All Three of Them?"

"Indeed! You have caught their attention, a somewhat normal phenomenon in your case."

"Sorry! I have never been a shrinking violet, or lily, or even a daffodil. Maybe a rose. They have barbs. Whatever could They want with me?"

"Not just you - your earthly associates - Holmes and Watson."

"Aha! I should have known. Another trip to my former home! What's this about? Who's involved?"

"A Major Monahan!"

"The military has plenty of investigators and police. Why do they need us? Who is this soldier? What did he do to attract the attention of the Almighty?"

"Major Philomena Monahan is an important member of the Greater London Salvation Army. Very devout, hard-working, charitable and sincere. We are answering her prayers for assistance. She is accused of murder."

"Oh dear! Who's the victim?"

"A colleague. A Lieutenant Abercrombie. He was the leader of their brass band. You have just exhausted my knowledge of the situation. Now, I find myself in the awkward position of asking you to do something I tried to refuse to let you do in the past."

"But, softie that you are, you gave in on both occasions. I'll do it, but I have two conditions."

"Why am I not surprised?"

"One - Pookie comes with me."

"Granted!"

"Two - Holmes and Watson are a team. If I am to collaborate with them, they must both be able to see me and converse with me telepathically. Right now, Watson isn't even sure I exist."

"Not so easy, but it can be arranged."

"Oh, one more thing!"

"That will make three conditions."

"Sorry, I was never very good at maths. I need an understudy for my act in Saintly Spectaculars. Perhaps an angel?"

"A devil would be more appropriate, but we don't have any of them. I'll take care of it. Are you ready to go?"

"No time like the present, especially in eternity. Pookie dear, come to Mommy."

*****

Doctor Watson, good morning!

Watson, who believed he was sitting alone in his medical consulting room, looked up in shock at a beautiful woman in a startling red dress who was staring at him. *I'm sorry, Madam. I didn't see you come in the door.*

I didn't.

Watson frowned. *I beg your pardon?*

She laughed. *Doctor John H. Watson, boon companion and associate of Sherlock Holmes, we've not actually met, but in fact, we have. I'm Lady Juliet Armstrong, one-time Baroness Crestwell.*

Good God!

Yes, He is. Isn't He? Actually, it's They. A Trinity. They've sent me back to you and Holmes to investigate another murder. I thought I'd stop here first before flitting over to Baker Street to renew acquaintances. This is a sort of 'test run,' so to speak. I got tired of you not being able to perceive me and so I stipulated that on my next trip back to Earth, you, Holmes and I would all be able to see each other and communicate directly. You may have noticed that we're talking telepathically.

Watson's jaw dropped when he realized he wasn't actually speaking.

She chuckled, *Well, I see the test is successful.*

So, you actually exist!

She smiled. *In a limited sense, yes. Not exactly like the good old days. But it has its advantages.* She switched to her regular speaking voice. "As I said, I can speak directly with you now."

I'll be damned!

Watson caught himself and spoke aloud. "I… I mean, I'll be…"

"Oh, I sincerely hope not. That would be most inconvenient... and inopportune. Look, I'm here to enlist the aid of the two of you in helping clear a Salvation Army Major of the charge of murder. If you're free, let's go see Holmes and discuss it. Oh, and watch out for my little white dog over there. Pookie is very sweet, but she still hasn't got this ghost thing down completely. I don't like cabs and I usually just flit to where I'm going, but I'll ride along with you and we can get further acquainted."

*****

"Oh, Doctor Watson. Come in, come in. It's good to see you again. How are you?"

"Very well, indeed, Mrs. Hudson. Thank you for asking. I assume Holmes is in? I hear movement up there in the rooms."

"Yes, he is. He's into another one of his experiments. I shall have to air out the place again. Funny, I smell a dog right now, but surely that can't be right. You don't need me to announce you." She went off to her rooms.

The Baroness laughed, "I'm sorry, Pookie. Time for another bath." The dog whined.

Watson stomped up the seventeen steps while Juliet and the dog popped up to the top. Watson opened the door and saw Holmes crouched over a series of glass tubes, foul-smelling materials and open flames. "Holmes, it's me. We have guests."

"Tell them to go away. I'm in the middle of a sensitive experiment."

"I'll be quiet as a ghost, Mr. Holmes."

73

He looked up. A brief smile. "I was wondering if you'd return, Baroness. Can you see and hear her, Watson?"

"Yes, we had a long conversation on the way over here. I am still somewhat amazed."

Lady Juliet smiled. "I've always been amazing, Doctor. Don't let it bother you."

Holmes poured an evil looking concoction into a beaker and set it over a flame. "This should not take long."

It didn't. The beaker promptly overflowed, burning what little paint was left on the work bench.

She giggled, "Exactly the result you were expecting, right?"

"Progress comes in slow bursts. That was not one of them. I assume you are here to re-establish our partnership."

"Yes, this time it's an important member of the Salvation Army. She's accused of murder. The mandate comes directly from the Heavenly Throne."

"So, refusing to participate is not an option."

"I don't have the option. You can take your own risks."

"Well, if I can serve the King and the House of Saxe-Coburg and Gotha, I guess I can serve an even higher regime. What do you think, Watson?"

"I'm intrigued. What do we know about this Salvation Army Officer?"

"She's a Major. Major Philomena Monahan. Very important in the London organization. Highest ranking woman below the co-founder. Obviously, very important to the Almighty. We're answering her prayers for help. She is accused of killing another Church officer. A Lieutenant Abercrombie. He was in charge of the British Salvation Army Brass Band. A significant position for a young Lieutenant. I believe that, in spite of the murder charges, she is out on bail. The Army has vouched for her. Her life, until now, has been totally above reproach. Shall we contact Scotland Yard? Please God, not Gregson."

Watson grimaced. "With our luck, it will be Athelney Jones."

Holmes said, "Before we do that, let's contact the head of the SA here in London. General Booth and his wife are the founders and overall commanders of the entire organization. Who is the local London commander or commissioner? I'd like to hear his perspective. Do we have a name?"

Watson went to one of the many haphazard indices maintained by Holmes seemingly at random and said, "Yes. Commissioner George Scott Ralton. Headquartered in East London."

"What say you, Lady Juliet? Shall we call on the Commissioner?

"Of course, Mr. Holmes. The Major needs our help."

*****

"Sherlock Holmes and the famous Doctor Watson. I must say I am honored, but also surprised, by your presence. What may I do for you gentlemen?"

"First, thank you for seeing us, Commissioner. I am immodest enough to think it is we who can do something for you. It is about Major Monahan."

"Ah, yes! Poor lady. One of our very finest officers. How are you aware of her predicament?"

"Let us just say that we detectives have our sources."

Juliet unleashed an unheard chuckle. Her ethereal dog wagged its voluminous tail and settled down beneath the Commissioner's spartan desk. Besides the usual chairs, table and desk, there were few signs of any authority or personal style in his office. Two wall-hangings with the SA shield and crest were the sole ornaments.

The Commissioner himself was a spare individual with an ascetic face, sparse hair and full beard. His eyes were piercing and alert. He wore a unique uniform of blue, adorned only with the letter S and the Army's crest on the collar of his jacket. A shirt bearing an embroidered golden cross and the words "Salvation Army" peeked out from beneath his formal coat. A formidable individual. One of God's true warriors.

Holmes continued, "We are here to assist in finding Lieutenant Abercrombie's killer and restore the Major's good name."

"Excellent! You are convinced of Major Monahan's innocence?"

"We have it on the very highest authority."

The Commissioner raised an eyebrow but said nothing.

Watson interjected, "We need to meet the Major as soon as possible. May we assume we have your permission and assistance?"

"Yes, of course. She is on administrative leave at the moment. We convinced the police that the evidence against her is insufficient to warrant imprisonment. We firmly believe she is innocent. In spite of Inspector Jones's objections, she is free on bail supplied by the Church. Needless to say, she cannot continue in her duties until this is cleared up."

Watson groaned telepathically, *Athelney Jones, that bumptious fool. He'd arrest God if he could.*

The Baroness laughed, *That would be worth watching! We could include it in the Saintly Spectaculars as a comedy skit. Oh, you didn't know. That's a celestial theatrical production in which I have a major lead. At least, I did until this task came along. There's an angel substituting for me until I return. Righto! Where do we find the Major?*

Holmes looked at the commissioner. "Where do we find the Major?"

"At our Officers' Quarters." He presented an engraved card. "Here is the address."

*****

The rooms at the Salvation Army's Officers' Quarters were modest affairs. Major Monahan's apartment was on the top floor.

When they arrived, her door was open. The Major's bedsit was outfitted cheerfully with plants and small religious paintings. She too, had wall hangings with the Army's Shield and Crest. On a chair rested her uniform jacket with red epaulettes and silver crests, and a red collar patch with the letter "S."

She looked up at the two men and rose to greet them. Dressed in a modest white blouse and long dark blue skirt, she was tall and slender, with light brown hair showing traces of grey. Her blue eyes showed signs of distress as did her facial expressions. The Baroness guessed her age to be late forties or early fifties.

"God bless you, gentlemen. How may I assist?"

Holmes smiled. "You are Major Philomena Monahan?"

"I am, although perhaps not for much longer."

"I am Sherlock Holmes and this is my associate, Doctor John Watson."

"Oh, I have read stories of your exploits, Mr. Holmes. Hardly spiritual tracts, Doctor Watson, but most entertaining."

"We are here to assist you in your hour of need, so to speak."

Her eyes widened and a smile broke across her mature face. "Can it be, my prayers have been answered?"

The Baroness, who had plopped on the major's bed with Pookie in hand, shouted telepathically: *Yes, they have. And I should know! Sing Halleluiah!"*

Holmes ignored Lady Juliet. "We have come from the Commissioner's office. He has the fullest confidence in your innocence and has given us permission to search out the true nature of the Lieutenant's death."

She hesitated. "I'm afraid I won't be able to afford your fee, Mr. Holmes. We members of the SA live frugally. Did the Commissioner say the Church would provide recompense?"

Holmes looked at the Baroness. "Our recompense has been assured, Major. Cast that concern out of your mind."

Lady Juliet nodded vigorously.

"Will you please share your knowledge of the incident with us? We have not yet been to Scotland Yard. It is next on our agenda."

"Oh, then you have not yet met Inspector Athelney Jones. He is my accuser."

Watson scowled. "We are quite familiar with the Inspector. Our experiences have been neither pleasant nor fruitful."

"I am encouraged to hear that. I found him to be quite unreasonable... but then who am I to judge?"

"The only way to deal with Inspector Jones is to hand him a culprit other than yourself and let him take all the credit for solving the case. We hope to be able to do that."

"Oh, God is being so good to me. I really cannot deserve this rescue."

Juliet laughed, and quietly thought: *You don't know the half of it, Major, and you probably never will. As of now, you're on the Almighty's highly preferred list. I wish I were!*

Holmes and Watson both smiled. "Now, please tell us your story."

"There really isn't very much to it. I have supervisory responsibility for our London Thrift and Charity Shoppes (the so-called Sally Stores); Unwed Mother Support and, oddly enough, our Music Programs. I say 'oddly enough' because I am partially deaf. I suspect no one else wanted the Bands or the Singers, and they ended up with me.

"Anyway, we have been formulating plans for our annual Hyde Park Concert and Lieutenant Abercrombie headed up the Brass Band. He was a very talented musician, as far as I can tell. I went down to George's, that is, Lieutenant Abercrombie's rooms to discuss several unsettled issues and discovered him, stretched out on the floor, dead. The police said he was struck repeatedly with a heavy brass musical instrument. One of the other SA officers on the floor claimed they heard us shouting at each other earlier in the day. Of, course, we were shouting. As I said, I am partially deaf. Forgive me if I'm shouting at you."

Holmes smiled and nodded.

"That seemed to be enough for Inspector Jones. He promptly arrested me on strong suspicion of murder. The Church's solicitor was quick to get me set free on bail, but I remain the prime suspect for the Lieutenant's death."

Watson snorted, "Another triumph for Athelney Jones, the classic incompetent."

The Baroness cast her eyes to heaven and thought, *Are there any intelligent beings in Scotland Yard?*

A few, Milady, a few, thought Watson. *You have not had the good fortune to meet them yet.*

"Major Monahan, do not despair," said Holmes.

"Oh, Mr. Holmes, despair is a serious sin. I am a sinner but not in that way."

Lady Juliet winced. *If you're a sinner, what am I? Don't answer that, Watson! Holmes, I have a suggestion.*

Holmes inclined his head slightly in the Baroness's direction. *By all means.*

I assume Abercrombie was a devout member of the Church and has gone to his eternal reward. Why don't I flit back to the angelic realm, track him down and just ask him who did him in? Then you can do your 'game is afoot' act and pursue the villain. Dump him or her at Athelney Jones's feet, exonerate the Major, and we can all go out and celebrate.

Holmes nodded. *A splendid idea, partner.*

*****

"Baroness Juliet! Back so soon? Is there something amiss with your assignment?"

"No indeed, Raymond. I think we are about to stage what they call a 'breakthrough,' but I need to be back here to bring it off. You can help. I must find Lieutenant George Abercrombie and interrogate him. I assume he is a recent arrival. Can you locate him for me?"

The Heavenly Manager closed his deep, dark eyes and hummed a brief tune. Pookie looked at him enquiringly.

"I regret to inform you that Lieutenant Abercrombie is nowhere to be found on the celestial plane, infinite though it may be."

"That's impossible—or highly improbable, as Holmes would say. Please check again!"

"Our admissions system is perfect, Milady. He is not here."

"Perhaps under another name?"

"We can see through aliases, noms de plume and any number of adopted identities. He is not here."

"Oh, Hell!!"

"That alternative is quite likely, but we do not have access to Satan's rolls. A mutual concession."

"How does a member of the Salvation Army end up in the nether world?"

"Are you aware of how many popes, cardinals, bishops, imams, ayatollahs, rabbis, ministers, priests, vicars and monks have gone down the road to perdition? So-called pious women as well. Religious affiliation does not guarantee salvation."

"I suppose not. Well, so much for my easy solution. I'll have to return to Holmes and Watson with my disappointing news. Goodbye, Raymond."

"Hurry back, Baroness. We'll keep a candle lit for you"

*****

"He's not there! No George Abercrombie in Heaven."

Holmes nodded. "I might have known. Our victim had feet of clay. That means we have some more in-depth investigating to do. Watson, let's return to the Commissioner."

"Wait for me! Or better yet, I'll wait for you. Come, Pookie. The game is apaw." They flitted and vanished.

*****

"It is good of you to see us again, Commissioner."

"Of course, Mr. Holmes, Doctor. Have you news about Major Monahan?"

"Not specifically, but we have strong suspicions that Lieutenant George Abercrombie was leading a double life and engaging in clandestine criminal acts that led to his murder."

Perched on the commissioner's desk, Lady Juliet chuckled. *We have more than strong suspicions. He's gone to Hell with himself, hasn't he Pookie?* High-speed tail wags!

"That is a very serious accusation, Mr. Holmes. Do you have proof?"

"Nothing that will stand up in court or with Inspector Jones. That is why we are here. What more can you tell us about the Lieutenant?"

"Very little. I hardly knew him. I suggest you speak with Captain Ernest Ferguson. He was Abercrombie's immediate superior and of course, you can interview members of the brass band. We need to clear this up rapidly and restore Major Monahan to her rightful position."

Watson replied, "That is our immediate objective, Commissioner. How do we reach Captain Ferguson?"

"His office is in this building. Tell him you are making these inquiries with my full blessing. Please keep me posted and, if you can, keep that Scotland Yard inspector out of my sight."

The Baroness reached down and patted her dog. *Pookie, this Athelney Jones sounds like a real classic. It's a shame you can't bite him and make it count. Where are you, Captain Ferguson?* She swooped through the Headquarters Building and landed in an empty office exactly the same as the Major's, minus the plants and pictures. Group photos of SA members hung on the walls, but no sign of the Captain. *Holmes, I'm in his office, but he's not here.*

Thank you, Milady. We'll be there in a moment. He and Watson entered the office. He looked around and said, "I shall leave a note asking him to call at Baker Street. What is that sound?"

Out in the courtyard, a blare of trumpets, a "barump" of tubas and a swoop of trombones announced that the Salvation Army Brass Band was practicing. The Baroness braced herself, took on the pose of a majorette and strutted out of the room, down to the enclosure and over to the music where she swayed, keeping time with the drums and bass horns. Pookie pranced around her. She sang out,

> "I love a parade, the tramping of
> feet,
> I love every beat I hear of a drum.
> I love a parade, when I hear a
> Band
> I just want to stand and cheer as
> they come."

"Hello Holmes, Doctor. That's my grand finale song in Saintly Spectaculars at The Heavenly Theatre Guild. It hasn't been written yet but it will be. Shame you can't come and see it. This band is wonderful. I'd love to use them but I guess killing them all off would never do. Anyhow, that's the new leader over there. Let them finish their number and then we can interview him."

Holmes stood by until they finished and then approached the leader, a sergeant.

"Excuse me, Sergeant, my name is Sherlock Holmes and this is my associate, Doctor Watson."

And I'm their friendly theatrical ghost. A top performer, I might add.

"Oh yes, Mr. Holmes, Doctor. I've heard of you. Read one of your books, Doctor. Enjoyed it. Name's Pepper. Sergeant First Class. What can I do for you?" He turned. "Alright, you lot, take ten!"

The band rose, casting quizzical looks at the detectives as they wandered away from the courtyard.

"Your organization sounds splendid, Sergeant. My congratulations. I understand Lieutenant Abercrombie was the leader until his untimely death. We're investigating that event."

"Scotland Yard was here about it. Some blighter called Jones. Unlikely name. Didn't take to him at all. Understand Major Monahan is in a spot of trouble over it. A dirty shame. She's top notch. Not like old Georgie. We're practicing to play at his funeral. Why, I don't know. Nobody liked him. Full of himself, irritable and mean as they come."

"Did the Lieutenant have enemies who might have wanted to kill him?"

"Only anybody who knew him."

"Were you aware of any activities that the Lieutenant might have been engaged in that would have gotten him murdered?"

"We were hardly best pals and he didn't confide in me. Just, 'Pepper, do this! Pepper, do that. That sound is awful. Get rid of that trombonist.'"

"Did he have a lot of money?"

"Now that you mention it, he did. If you're a member of the SA, you're not wallowing in cash but Georgie seemed to have a good supply of the ready whenever he needed it."

"Any idea where it came from?"

"Nope. You might want to ask Captain Ferguson. Oddly enough, those two got along. Don't know why. "

"We plan to. He wasn't in his office."

"Not surprising. He seldom is."

That last remark caused a buzz among the three partners.

The band members were wandering back and the sergeant excused himself.

Holmes said, "Let's go back to the major once more and then on to Baker Street. I asked the Captain to visit at his convenience."

The Baroness flitted off. They found her sitting next to the major in her office. Eyes closed, the officer seemed to be caught up in meditation.

She opened her eyes and said, "Oh, Mr. Holmes, Doctor Watson. I didn't see you. I was just saying prayers of thanksgiving for my hoped-for deliverance. You two are a Godsend."

Lady Julia smiled. "For the record, Major, even though you can't hear me, I was the one sent by God—not these two reprobates."

Watson laughed telepathically. *Touché, Milady. Credit where credit is due.*

"Major, what can you tell us about Captain Ferguson?"

"Not a great deal, Mr. Holmes. Theoretically, he works for me, but he is very much an independent spirit. I suspect he resents reporting to a woman. Truth be told, since I am partially deaf, he has overall responsibility for the band. Lieutenant Abercrombie got most of his orders from him. He also supervises some of the stores although they are my responsibility. It's a two-person job. He leaves unwed mothers to me."

"Are the stores audited?"

"Yes indeed, the Church uses a professional firm. In fact, the annual audit is just about to begin. I personally supervise that activity on the commissioner's behalf."

"Do you have any reason to suspect the audit will turn up discrepancies?"

"I do. That's why I've accelerated the process, The books at several of the stores simply will not balance. I have had the managing officers in for discussions. They believe the records have been tampered with and that major sums have been removed. But, as of the moment we have no conclusive proof."

"Have you any suspicions as to the identity of the culprits, if there are any?"

"Yes, but I hesitate to besmirch someone's good name on simple suspicion."

"Do you consider yourself to be in danger?"

"My goodness, I am in danger of being hanged for a murder I did not commit!"

"We discovered Lieutenant Abercrombie was not very popular."

"Speak no ill of the dead, but... I'm afraid your information is correct."

"Out of curiosity, who was it that reported to the police that you and the Lieutenant had a shouting match that morning?"

"I'm not certain, but I suspect it may have been Captain Ferguson. As I told you, I shout because of my hearing disability."

"We need to have a conversation with Captain Ferguson. Hopefully, he will call on us this evening. Meanwhile keep your courage up. You have the Commissioner's fullest confidence."

Juliet smiled. "And God's."

*****

Mrs. Hudson welcomed them back and, after another splendid meal, Holmes and Watson settled down with a snifter of brandy to await the arrival of the captain, if indeed he was coming. Having no need for sustenance, Lady Juliet and Pookie had flitted off to the West End theatres to spy on the latest productions. Watson promised to summon her back when their guest arrived. At eight, a cab pulled up in front of 221B Baker Street but instead of Captain Ferguson getting out, Holmes spied the rotund shape of Inspector Athelney Jones, the 'pride' of Scotland Yard.

He turned to Watson. "You had better bring the Baroness back. She wouldn't want to miss this."

Mrs. Hudson climbed the time-honored seventeen steps followed by the thudding strides of the policeman.

A knock, and his clumsy rush through the door almost threw the poor lady to the floor.

Juliet arrived just in time to witness his arrival and Pookie broke out her loudest, spectral barks.

"Well, Sherlock Holmes, we meet again. You, too Watson."

"So it would seem, Inspector. What brings you out on this rainy night?"

"I am informed that you are poking your nose into the Salvation Army murder. I insist that you cease immediately."

"I am afraid that is impossible, Inspector. Our client is no less than the Army's Commissioner Ralton."

A slight but forgivable bending of the truth, thought Lady Juliet.

Holmes continued: "He has requested our assistance in exonerating Major Monahan, whom you have so rashly accused."

"That woman is as guilty as sin. I shall see her in the dock and hung upon the gallows."

Juliet choked, *The man's an idiot! To say nothing of being a boor and a blowhard!*

Holmes responded telepathically, *Right on all counts, Baroness.*

"Inspector," asked Holmes, "what evidence do you have to support your claim?"

"She found the body and was heard to have a shouting match with the victim."

"She shouts because she is partially deaf and you yourself have found bodies in the past. Are you a murderer?"

Juliet laughed. *He's certainly a fool. By comparison, Gregson is a genius. Thank you, Holmes. I thought that between my husband, high society and the government I had exhausted all the imbeciles in the world. I see I am wrong.*

Jones snarled, "Oh, you're so very clever, Holmes. I am going to Commissioner Ralton in the morning and insist that he relieve you of all rights and responsibilities in this case. I will not be interfered with."

"By all means, Inspector. You are free to do as you please, wrongheaded though you may be. Now, will you please leave? We are expecting a guest."

"Who?"

"Forgive me, but it is none of your business. Goodbye!"

He huffed and tromped down the stairs past the irate Mrs. Hudson who loudly slammed the front door at his exit.

The Baroness frowned. "Major Monahan wasn't exactly forthcoming with her suspicions, was she? Do you think she may be guilty of something?"

"No, she knows what it means to have her reputation destroyed and is unwilling to do that to another. I think the woman is guiltless. Should I remind you? The Deity seems to agree with me. Otherwise, why are you here?"

"I bow to your superior logic, Mr. Holmes. When is this Captain Ferguson supposed to make an appearance? I'm getting suspicious of him."

Watson chimed in. "As am I, Holmes. If it was he who told Jones that the Major and Lieutenant had a shouting match, it sounds to me like he was trying to frame her."

"The two of you may well be right, but let us see what the Captain has to say for himself. I hear a cab approaching."

Mrs. Hudson, who seemed to have recovered from Athelney Jones's loutish behavior, once again trotted up the stairs, knocked and introduced Captain Ernest Ferguson of the Salvation Army. She beamed at him. He nodded in return.

Dressed in his formal blue uniform with two stars on red epaulettes, he made an impressive sight.

"Mr. Sherlock Holmes? I am responding to the note you left in my office. I assume this has something to do with poor Lieutenant Abercrombie's death?"

"It does, Captain. Let me introduce my associate, Doctor John Watson." The captain seemed unfamiliar with him. "We are seeking the truth about the Lieutenant's murder."

"I hope you find it, but I'm not sure how I can help."

"You knew the Lieutenant, of course."

"In a non-personal way. He was my subordinate."

"We have learned he was not very popular."

"Lieutenants seldom are."

"You, in turn, report to Major Philomena Monahan."

"On paper. But we have our separate functions and tasks that keep us apart for most of the time."

Juliet snorted. *He's not going to admit to working for a female boss. A chauvinist.*

"You know, of course, that she has been accused by Scotland Yard of killing the lieutenant."

"Yes, I am aware."

"Do you have an opinion?"

"No, I do not. Look, what is this all about?"

"Information gathering, Captain. Data is the detective's lifeblood."

"Well, I want to see justice done, but I'm afraid I can't provide you with much information."

"Was it you who told Inspector Jones that the Major and Lieutenant had a shouting match the morning of his killing?"

"Yes, it was. I felt it my duty to supply meaningful evidence."

"You are aware that the Major's hearing is impaired and that she shouts as a general rule?"

"No, I was not aware of that."

"Even though you report to her?"

"I seldom see the Major. We operate in separate spheres."

"Do those spheres include the stores?"

"Yes, but different stores."

"I suppose you know that an impending audit of all the London shoppes is about to begin."

"That's earlier than usual, but... so what?"

"Will you be involved?"

"I suppose I will. Look here, I don't like the tone this discussion is taking. If you wish to accuse me of something, come out and say it."

"I make no accusations, Captain. As I said I am simply data gathering. Do you have any opinion on who may have killed Abercrombie?'

"None. I thought the police believe it is Major Monahan."

"The police have been known to be wrong. Well, thank you for stopping by, Captain. I appreciate your coming out on such a rainy evening. May we call on you again, if necessary?"

He nodded, made a military turn and headed for the door.

The Baroness grinned. *I believe there is a saying about a cat among the pigeons.* At the word 'cat,' Pookie growled.

"Abercrombie's funeral is tomorrow," said Holmes, speaking aloud. "I propose to attend. Are you up for it, Watson? I assume you are, Baroness."

The Doctor replied, "I may have to rearrange a few appointments, but I will try."

Lady Juliet also spoke aloud. "Oh yes, if nothing else, I want to hear that brass band again and listen in on conversations. Meanwhile, I shall do some late-night shopping at several of the Thrift and Family Stores. Sleep well, gentlemen."

She left and flitted with Pookie in hand to the East End where a large Salvation Army Thrift Store stood, closed for the night. This, of course, was no problem for the evanescent Baroness and she passed through the doors into the darkened interior. "Now, let us see. Where would the records and unbanked cash be? Of course, the safe. I can't open it, but I can make myself small and steal inside it. Stay here, Pookie. Mommy's going to do some research."

A list with the day's receipts lay on top of a register, waiting to be copied into the book. A small stack of bills and a bag of coins rested next to it. The total on the list was over a hundred pounds. Yet the stack of currency was far too slim to match that number. Her suspicions were aroused. "Where is the missing cash? Let's explore further!"

On to another shop. This time a smaller family store. It, too, was closed. She was about to repeat her performance with the safe, when she heard the front door open, and saw a tall figure stealthily advance to the shop desk. He (she was sure it was a he) looked familiar. He held a lit candle to the safe's lock and taking out keys, opened it, reached in and retrieved a stack of bills. He peeled off a small number, pocketed them and returned the rest to the safe's shelf, not bothering to alter the list of the day's receipts. Either sloppy or uncaring! No wonder an audit was called for. She stared at the culprit. Was it? Yes, it was. Captain Ferguson! The scoundrel! Holmes and Watson needed to know and then tell the Commissioner. She could hardly wait until morning.

*****

A small, uniformed group gathered inside the chapel. A company of choristers intoned a mournful hymn as the brass band positioned itself along a side aisle. They were resplendent with their military garb and glistening instruments. Holmes made his way into an empty pew and sat next to the invisible Lady Juliet, walking through the snoozing Bichon Frisé in the process. Pookie didn't move an inch.

She silently blurted, *I have news for you! Ferguson is a thief. You have to catch him and report him. Where is Watson?*

Detained. A broken leg. Not him; a patient. As for Ferguson, let us discuss it after the service.

Juliet noticed Major Monahan seated off to the side by herself. Captain Ferguson was in a pew next to the band. In the back sat Inspector Athelney Jones, staring about and alternately giving Holmes and the major the evil eye.

Suddenly a drum roll and a blare of trumpets echoed through the sanctuary, and a coffin, carried by six cadets, was moved down the center aisle to the chapel altar. The funeral service began. The commissioner, looking none too healthy himself, presided. Songs, prayers, martial music; a lengthy eulogy by an unidentified officer disingenuously extolling the virtues of the deceased; more music, and then the coffin began its journey to the Salvation Army's cemetery.

At the conclusion, Jones rushed up, trying to get the attention of the commissioner, but failed miserably. The Baroness heard something about making an appointment. Obviously, he had not struck up a pleasant relationship with Ralton. He turned to Holmes, pointed at the major and loudly and petulantly proclaimed, "Her days of freedom are numbered. I'll have her back in gaol, bail or no bail."

"Good morning, Inspector. Moving service, was it not?"

Lady Juliet directed a not very lady-like raspberry in his direction and Pookie growled.

Athelney turned away in frustration and Holmes asked telepathically, *What is this about Ferguson?*

The Baroness proceeded to tell him about her late night shopping expedition and her discovery of the captain's thievery.

Holmes thought for a moment. *Let us speak to the major. The audit cannot come too soon. The thought had occurred to me that one way of forestalling the examination would be to see the major re-incarcerated. The captain's evidence of the so-called shouting match was extremely convenient, but misguided. But none of this sheds any more light on Lieutenant Abercrombie's murder, unless you believe Ferguson is responsible for that as well.*

I do, Mr. Holmes. He's a nasty piece of work.

As was the lieutenant. I thought several members of the band would choke during the eulogy. I wouldn't write the sergeant off as a suspect. His nemesis is gone, and now he has control of the band. There's motive enough, and certainly sufficient means and opportunity. Abercrombie was struck on the head several times with his own heavy cornet. His blood was on the instrument, but all fingerprints were wiped off. No, I believe Sergeant Pepper bears careful watching.

Mr. Holmes, I have a terrible thought! Do you think the major may have actually killed him? She looks tall enough and strong enough. Maybe that shouting match was real.

Highly unlikely, but not out of the question. What would be her motive?

I don't know. I hate to admit it, but maybe Athelney Jones is not all that wrong.

Holmes's eyes widened. *It would be a first. The man is impossible. Let us concentrate for the moment on Ferguson's thefts. Are the only stores affected the ones to which he has access and authority?*

Let's ask the major. We also need to warn the auditor that defalcation and thievery are at play. Defalcation! I love that word. Don't hear that one in Heaven.

I should hope not.

She sang aloud, "I have the Defalcation Blues, oh yeah!"

Holmes winced. *Baroness, for goodness' sake.*

Oh, of course, always for goodness' sake. Oh. look, here comes Watson. Hail, hail, the gang's all here. Welcome Doctor! Don't mind me. I'm just being winsome.

Dr. Watson tipped his hat to their spectral companion and sat down. Holmes quietly said, "Lady Juliet observed Captain Ferguson stealing money from one of the Salvation Army stores. We must devise a way to communicate this to the major and commissioner. Telling them a ghost saw Ferguson at it will not be very credible. We also need to encourage them to get started on the financial audit. The captain is pretty brazen with his thefts, but not all that clever."

"He's obviously a swine trying to implicate the Major, and that fool Jones fell for it."

"Probably, Watson, but we're withholding judgment for the moment."

"You don't believe the Major is guilty, do you Holmes? You especially, Baroness. Could the Almighty be wrong?"

Their track record is spotless, Doctor. Mr. Holmes is being something of a doubting Thomas.

You brought the issue up, Milady. All right Watson. Let's go see the Major.

*****

"I must admit I've had my suspicions, gentlemen. Ernest Ferguson is not very bright. It wouldn't occur to him that thefts from the stores that he oversaw would point to him."

"Are you saying, Major, that only his stores were showing cash shortages?"

"Yes, doctor, that's what I'm saying."

"How much has disappeared?"

"Several hundred pounds over time. This has only been going on for quite a few months."

"I suppose he thought the store managers would be blamed. There were no signs of a conspiracy, were there?"

"None at all. If only one store was victimized, I would have suspected the manager, but when several were involved, that would have been too much of a coincidence. Besides, those managers are specifically chosen for their honesty. I know several of them personally. They are true Christians. No, I believe it's Ernest."

Juliet shook her head. *What a dope! Why didn't he just hang a sign around this neck? 'See the stupid thief'.*

"Mr. Holmes, how did you get your information?"

"It's best if we don't reveal our source, Major. Suffice it to say it's quite reliable."

Reliably dead. Oh well! I'm not in this for the credit. No top billing for this act.

Holmes ignored Lady Juliet and continued, "I originally was going to suggest that you start the audit posthaste, but that might put an end to his thefts. Why don't we wait a few days and hide guards at the stores at night. He might get overconfident and we could catch him in the act."

"It's worth a try. I shall take care of that immediately. Now, forgive me for being concerned but what about Lieutenant Abercrombie's killer? That Scotland Yard inspector is still convinced it's me."

"He's in a quandary. We'll give him information of the captain's thefts to sooth his ego and then we'll pounce on the murderer. We're closing in."

Juliet looked surprised. *We are? Nobody told me.*

Watson looked similarly nonplussed but said nothing.

"A little more patience, Major. By the way, I have heard rumors that the commissioner is making another journey to America."

"The General's son, Bramwell, insists that Commissioner Ralton once again take personal charge in the United States. I hope it doesn't ruin his health. Can we please clear this killing up before he leaves in the next few weeks? I have come to rely heavily on his good will."

"We shall make every effort. Be of good heart and stay faithful."

The Baroness shook her head. *That's quite an exit line, partner! Who's next? Pookie's getting bored.*

Out in the corridor, Holmes said telepathically, *I think it's time we made another visit to the brass band and the sergeant.*

Watson, showing a bit of irritation, said, "Holmes, you know how I feel when you become enigmatic and mysterious. I'm sure Lady Juliet is equally annoyed."

Right you are, Doctor. Come on, Holmes, time for the Big Reveal.

Holmes turned to Lady Juliet: *I believe our friend, the Lieutenant, was engaged in a bit of extortion and it caught up with him.*

"Blackmail?" asked Watson.

Or something similar. I also believe the sergeant knows more about it than he is saying.

Well then, let's go listen to the band and the sergeant.

Precisely what I had in mind, Milady. They are in the courtyard again. Although I think they are working on more upbeat sounds than the funeral dirges we heard the other day.

Indeed they were. Rhythm!! Drums, cymbals and trombones dominated. Cornets, tenor horns and trumpets flared against an "oom-pah" background supplied by the tubas. A lone flugelhorn inserted itself and a euphonium played counterpoint. Clearly the band was enjoying itself as was Sergeant Pepper. The Baroness swung her shapely hips and Pookie twitched her tail in perfect time. With one final cymbal crash, they came to a climax. One waggish cornet player blatted a final flatted note.

Lady Juliet applauded wildly but silently, while Holmes and Watson clapped enthusiastically aloud. The sergeant turned and bowed to his small audience. Recognizing the two detectives, he called for the band to take a break and walked over to them, carrying his cornet.

"Greetings, gentlemen. Here for entertainment, or are you still searching for who did old Georgie in?"

Watson laughed, "A bit of both, Sergeant. Most enjoyable!"

Holmes agreed, and decided to bluff. "We have reason to believe, Sergeant, that Lieutenant Abercrombie was supplementing his income."

"If you mean Old George was running a 'pay to play' scheme, you're right. All the lads and lassies had to shell out in order to belong to the band. Called it an 'instrument usage fee.' Most of them couldn't afford it."

Watson was appalled. "Didn't you report it?"

"To Ferguson? A hell of a lot of good that would do. He was in on it. I suppose we should have told the major. She would have helped."

"Captain Ferguson seems to be quite skilled at bringing in money from a variety of sources."

"Too true. A little thievery here, a little extortion there. Subtle and not so subtle threats. If you want my opinion, it was him who bashed in Georgie's skull. A falling out among thieves."

"Do you have any proof of that?"

"Not that I'm willing to swear to. I have a strong desire to keep my head intact."

"Let me ask you a very blunt question, Sergeant."

"Wait, let me guess. Did I kill George Abercrombie? Answer: Hell, no! Although I salute the bloke or lass who did it. The bastard deserved everything he got. I hope he rots. No, Mr.

Holmes. I'm afraid I don't have the courage of my convictions. By the way, whoever is trying to frame the major is barking up the wrong tree. She's a peach."

Pookie let out a rapid fire salvo of growls.

Back to Baker Street.

*****

The Baroness had returned after another evening of prowling the West End playhouses. While Holmes and Watson had their breakfasts, she regaled them with her opinions of the offerings being presented to the theater-going public.

"The London stage is at an ebb, gentlemen. A major dearth of talent combined with a total lack of imagination by playwrights, producers and directors. I'm sorry to say the music is atrocious and the musicians even worse. Simpering ladies of the chorus demonstrating their bovine proclivities. Poorly designed and executed scenery. Pookie was bored stiff. Say, if I ever have a chance at reincarnation, I think I shall return as a drama critic."

Watson chuckled. "Don't hold back, Milady. What did you really think?"

She blew another ethereal raspberry!

Mrs. Hudson knocked at the door. "Excuse me, gentlemen, but there is a message for the two of you. From Salvation Army Headquarters."

Holmes took up the envelope. A few brief sentences on SA stationery. "We've caught him. Ten AM in the commissioner's office. I have notified that awful Scotland Yard

Inspector." It was signed Philomena Monahan, Major, Salvation Army.

"Ha! My worthy companions, the game is in play. Our villain has been flushed out."

"What? The game's not afoot? Honestly, Holmes! Sometimes I despair of understanding you. Oh, despair is a sin, isn't it? Well, let's off to the office of the noble commissioner. I am all atwitter. Come Pookie. Flit, we must!"

*****

Every seat in the Commissioner's sparsely furnished office was occupied. He sat behind his desk with Major Monahan on one side and Athelney Jones on the other. Holmes and Watson took up hard back chairs and the Baroness perched unseen on a desktop in a ladylike pose. The dog was at her feet. Two SA guards and a police constable stood by the door. The object of this meeting, Captain Ferguson, sat disheveled in front of the commissioner's desk, head bowed and hands cuffed in front of him.

The commissioner cast his ascetic eyes on the officer and with a deep accusing voice, asked, "Well Ferguson, caught pilfering from our charitable stores. What have you to say about this disgrace? This violation of your sacred trust! And for what? Filthy lucre! Are you not ashamed?"

The officer kept his head bowed but slowly nodded affirmatively.

The commissioner rumbled on. "The sums you have stolen may not be that significant, although our forthcoming audit will attest to the true amounts." He looked at Major Monahan who nodded. "It is the arrant abuse of your position, giving scandal to your fellow Army members and demonstration of the sin of greed that calls for extreme punishment. I am expelling you from the ranks of the Salvation Army with a total loss of all privileges and rights and turning you over to the inspector here for prosecution. I do this with a saddened heart, but justice must be done."

Athelney Jones rose from his seat, signaled the constable and said, "All right, my lad, it's off to the cells with you."

Holmes raised his hand. "One moment, Inspector. Commissioner, we are neglecting something here. The death of Lieutenant George Abercrombie still remains unsolved... or would you like to confess, Captain?"

An electric shock permeated the room. The commissioner jerked his head at the inspector and ordered Ferguson back to his seat.

Holmes continued. "The captain and lieutenant were partners in an array of unworthy schemes. A bit of theft, a touch of extortion, defalcation, misuse of resources, threats and abuse of subordinates. Attempts to frame a fellow officer. A veritable treasure chest of misdeeds. But somewhere along the line, the arrangement went sour, didn't it, captain? Abercrombie wasn't satisfied with his share of the pie and threatened to anonymously implicate you unless you paid up. That amounted to insubordination and was not to be tolerated, was it? Military discipline and all that. Discussion became argument and argument became assault. Impulse overcame you. Ironic that you chose his heavy cornet as your weapon. He was quite a good musician, I am told. Have I left anything out?"

The captain shouted, "No! It's not true. It was all Abercrombie. He was the guilty one."

"How come it is you who was captured stealing from the Thrift Store safe?"

"A one-time mistake. I needed cash."

"To pay gambling debts or worse? Come, captain, the truth."

Looking for all the world like the purveyor of doom, the commissioner calmly intoned, "Ernest Ferguson. I adjure you, before these witnesses and your God, to confess your murderous sins or suffer the eternal torment of Hellfire unforgiven."

The captain trembled, sobbed and murmured, "All right! I did it. God help me. I did it!"

The Inspector rose once more from his seat, apparently shaken, as were they all. He once again signaled the constable but before he could leave with his captive, Holmes halted him in his tracks. "Inspector Jones, I believe you owe Major Monahan a sincere apology."

"No, Holmes. Apologies are never required in the pursuit of justice. Good day!"

The commissioner shook his head. Watson murmured, "Arrogant swine." The major breathed a sigh of relief. Juliet stood on the desk and telepathically shouted, *That insolent fool! Wait till I get back to the Pearly Gates. He's going on report.*

Back in the major's office, her face wreathed in smiles, she looked at Holmes and Watson and said, "I don't know how to show my gratitude."

Watson said, "There is no need. All in a day's work, as we say."

Holmes agreed, smiling enigmatically.

"Well, thank you anyway. As I said, you were Godsends."

The Baroness laughed, *Yes we were, literally.*

"Oh. and a special thank you to Lady Juliet."

A telepathic chorus of three startled voices: *She's aware of you! How?*

Holmes had the last word. *God only knows!*

Speak of the Devil

L ady Juliet Armstrong, the onetime Baroness Crestwell, now deceased, came away from the Cosmic Cathedral and her Art Appreciation class in a state of euphoria. She had just watched Michelangelo as he was painting a new and far more spectacular version of the Creation of the World on the limitless ceiling of the glorious church. Wonderful! He didn't need to lie on his back on a scaffold as he did in the Sistine Chapel. He just floated, a palette and brushes at his elbow and created his magic. In this version, Adam and God actually touch hands!

But the highlight of the session was her chat with Leonardo da Vinci. What a charmer! She had smiled and he asked her to pose for him. Mona Juliet? Who knows?

"It's a shame you don't have an artistic eye, Pookie," she said to her faithful canine companion who trotted along at her side. "We could have such wonderful conversations on technique and perspective. But you have so many other marvelous qualities."

They had reached their mansion and she was just setting aside her halo, books and portfolios when a vision appeared. Mr. Raymond, one of Heaven's Senior Directors. A middle-aged male, tall, dressed in morning (mourning?) clothes, clean shaven, not a hair out of place, dark eyes, color undetermined, floating inches above the floor. He carried his modest halo in his hand.

"Forgive me for violating your space, Baroness."

"Oh. forget it, Raymond. What's the point of doors when we all can walk right through them? Everybody here in Heaven seems well-behaved when it comes to respecting privacy. No problem. But what brings you here? I would have thought you'd be busy with the new arrivals."

"I'm concerned because of a new departure."

"Departure? Who departs from Heaven? I guess I do from time to time, but those trips are only temporary, and authorized."

"This is different. Angus MacDougal, a soldier and major philanthropist during his lifetime. There are hospitals, medical schools, orphanages, colleges, houses of refuge and hospices that owe their existence to him. A modest soul, he never allowed his name to be used at any of those institutions. He was simply 'The Donor.' He led a quiet life during his short stay here in Heaven."

"Short stay? You keep using the past tense. Is he gone? Where?"

"We don't know. His mansion is empty. He took whatever possessions he had with him when he left. His halo is on a table in the foyer. Heaven is not a prison, but we do keep careful watch over our residents. How he left without being observed is beyond us. It's a first. Even his Guardian Angel is puzzled... and currently unemployed."

"You're obviously here with a purpose. I can almost guess what it is."

"Perceptive as always, Milady. We believe he has returned to Earth as a disembodied spirit. We'd like you and your colleagues, Holmes and Watson, to find him and convince him to return to his celestial reward."

The Bichon Frisé barked. "Oh, and you too, Ms. Pookie."

"Very unusual! I assume I have approval to flit around Earth with my boon companions in search of the elusive Mr. MacDougal's spirit. It doesn't sound like a difficult assignment finding him. It may be more of a task getting him to come home."

"He must! You know the rules about spirits wandering around Earth. We allow it in your case because you are engaged in laudable activities on behalf of the Almighty. In fact, we support it. But MacDougal is a different situation. We don't know why he returned to Earth, if he did."

"If he did? What else... oh. No!"

"Yes, we're afraid he may be stuck in Hades."

"Oh dear! That puts quite a different spin on it. Very well! I'll get to Holmes and Watson, and we'll see what can be done. But first, I want to talk with MacDougal's Guardian Angel. Who is it?"

"Filadel. I'll send him to you. Thank you and Godspeed, Milady."

(Note to readers: The more inquisitive among you are probably wondering about Lady Juliet's and Pookie's Guardian Angels. There were several. The fact is, she simply exhausted them and finally received a special exemption from requiring Angelic monitoring services. Needless to say, the Angels are relieved.)

A handsome Angel descended into the mansion, folded his voluminous wings, bowed to the Baroness and reached down and petted Pookie. "Lady Juliet, how can I be of assistance? I'm afraid

I'm unemployed at the moment. The Angelic Council is not happy with me. Nor am I. Letting my charge disappear undetected is a major dereliction."

"I'm hardly one to criticize, Filadel. Too many mistakes in my lifetime and my immortality. But I and my earthly companions are going to try to get Mr. MacDougal back." *(Her earthly companions were as yet unaware of that assignment, but Lady Armstrong was nothing, if not confident, of her persuasive powers.)* Now, what can you tell me about him?"

"He's strange, Baroness. One of the few individuals I've known who didn't seem happy to be in Heaven. He kept saying he didn't belong. Amazing! With all the good work he's done, I can't think of too many who are more deserving."

"I'm certainly not. If I made the cut for Paradise, he certainly should have."

"He did but he wouldn't acknowledge it."

"Describe him!"

"Well, obviously he's incorporeal; but if he were still alive, he'd be over six feet tall, brown hair, blue eyes, full moustache, no beard or heavy sideburns… slight limp. He was in the military. A colonel. A Scottish Laird, too. Never used his title, though. Spoke with a slight Scottish burr. They say he died of a heart attack. His wife is still alive. One grown son, Robbie."

It's always Robbie, thought the Baroness.

"His last mortal address," continued Filadel, "was Kilmarnock. Look up Robert Burns and Johnnie Walker whiskey. I think part of his wealth came from the distillery, but he had financial interests worldwide. Of course, his charities spread widely. He never contributed in his own name. Always just 'The Donor.'"

"Filadel, I don't know if you're familiar with Sherlock Holmes and Doctor Watson. They are my earthbound compatriots. Pookie and I combine our ethereal talents to their tangible gifts for detection to form a formidable investigative team. We'll find the Donor. Whether we can bring him back is another question."

"All Guardian Angels are familiar with Holmes and Watson; and you and Pookie are building quite a reputation as well, Milady."

"I hope it's a good one. May I call on your help if we need it, Filadel?"

"Absolutely, Baroness. It would be my pleasure. I want Angus MacDougal back."

"Pookie, time for another flit. Back to London. Maybe while we're there I can get a look at the latest fashions. These gowns of mine are all 'last season.' I'll bring the new designs back to Heaven with me. The folks at Miraculous Modes can do their enchantments. Everything in scarlet of course. We'll find you a sweater, although you'll hardly need one. You could use a new bow. You keep chewing through your regular ones. I give up on trying to keep you in haloes. You just keep shaking them off."

*****

Late October 1901. The nation still mourned their late Queen and Empress.

221B Baker Street. It was at that address that Lady Juliet found the Great Detective immersed in yet another foul-smelling experiment.

"Oh, Holmes, what a stink! I'm sorry I still have my sense of smell. Whatever are you concocting?"

"Ah, Baroness, back again. I'm making rubber. What is it this time? A revolution in Zanzibar? Jewels stolen from a Tibetan temple?"

"Nothing so tedious, and those probably wouldn't have involved me, anyway. No, this time it's a missing person."

"Forgive me, but missing persons are as common as tuppence. Call the police."

"Not when the lost sheep is a ghost, Mr. Holmes."

"Heaven has misplaced one of its residents?"

"In a sense, yes. The resident has misplaced himself. There is a strong belief that, somehow, he has returned to Earth in his spirit form and wishes to stay here. Or worse yet, he might have gotten himself trapped in Hades! Bit of a rum go. Not being done and all that."

"My first reaction is Heaven is better equipped to deal with inchoate renegades than I am. Where are the angels?"

"Stumped. The reason I'm involving you is that you're so damned (sorry!) good at finding missing persons, and once again the Almighty has specifically asked for you and Watson."

A bit of a stretch of the truth, but still acceptable, she thought to herself.

"Is Watson available?" she asked.

"I don't know."

"I'll flit along to Queen Anne Street and see if I can stoke his interest. Be back shortly,"

Watson's medical practice had grown, and he was taken up with the ills and complaints of his many patients. Lady Juliet arrived at his surgery in time to see his last sufferer emerge from his office on her way to a local pharmacologist.

Good afternoon, Doctor Watson. I see you are still curing the ills of the world, she said telepathically, not wanting Watson to have to look like he was talking aloud with no one.

The doctor paused, still slow to react to the presence of the Glamorous Ghost. *Ah, Lady Juliet, how delightful to see you even if no one else can*, he thought. *I assume you are here for a purpose. Mere Heavenly social calls seem to be beyond our relationship.*

Right you are, Doctor. I have a case I want to pursue with you and Sherlock Holmes. I've met with him already at Baker Street. Care to join us?

Give me a few moments to clear the day's activities and I'll grab a cab to Baker Street. I'll see you and Holmes there.

Pookie and I will flit back. Don't be long!

*****

True to his word, Watson emerged from a cab and strode up to the entrance on Baker Street. As he fumbled for the key that he kept for just such events, Mrs. Hudson, who had seen him from her window, threw open the door. "Doctor Watson, how glad I am to see you. Mr. Holmes is up to his old tricks. Smelly experiments! He did bring me a lovely gift so I can't be angry with him. At least, not for long. Come in! Come in! Mind those steps. It's getting more and more difficult to navigate them."

Difficult if you were a mortal of sixty odd years but extremely easy for a ghostly wraith and her canine companion. They flew up, floated through the closed door and she settled on the one clear table top in the room. "Watson is here, Holmes. Making his way up the stairs. It occurred to me that we might invite our fugitive's Guardian Angel to join us. Name's Filadel and he's frustrated and embarrassed with the whole situation. I'm sure he'd like to redeem himself."

"You are making the brash assumption that we are going to take up your cause, Milady."

"Well, of course! You always do!" she said, with tinkling laughter.

Watson opened the door and walked in. "I knew I recognized that laugh. Got here ahead of me as usual. Hello again, girl." This last greeting was directed to Pookie, who knew her way around the rooms and had settled on a well-worn chesterfield.

"I was just telling Holmes how you two are going to help Pookie and me track down a saint who has gone missing from Paradise. Your colleague seems a bit resistant. You're not going to let me down, are you, Doctor?"

Watson laughed, "I usually don't have a choice, Milady."

"Fine, I'm going to reach out to Filadel and invite him to join us. He's Angus MacDougal's Guardian Angel." She looked heavenward, murmured and paused. "He's coming."

Watson frowned. "Angus MacDougal? Colonel Angus MacDougal? 647th Scots Grenadiers? (She nodded.) Angry

Angus, they called him. Lost almost his entire unit in a Boer ambush in the Western Transvaal. He was medically discharged and that's the last I heard of him. So he died and went to heaven, eh? Interesting. Man was a millionaire several times over. Rich as Croesus. I think he was a Laird. You know, less than a baron but more than a gentleman. I was surprised he was in the Army, but these Scots are a tough breed, and frugal. Probably still had his first shilling."

"Not so, Doctor. He became quite a philanthropist during his lifetime. There are hospitals, medical schools, orphanages, soup kitchens, colleges, houses of refuge and hospices all over the world founded and funded by him. But he never allowed his name to be used. He was simply 'The Donor.'"

"Hmm! War can do that to people. Horror at the bloodshed. Loss of life. Loss of comrades. Sense of guilt and responsibility. Bothers *me* sometimes. Can make permanent changes in a chap's personality."

He was interrupted by a loud flutter of incandescent wings. Filadel had arrived. "Greetings! May I assume you can all see and hear me? Hello, Pookie!" He smiled at a friendly bark from the dog.

Holmes replied, "Yes, we have access to the spiritual side, courtesy of Mr. Raymond. Welcome. Lady Juliet has been trying to convince us to join in a search for Colonel MacDougal, your protégé."

She laughed again, "Successfully convincing, you may be sure. These gentlemen are pussy cats." This provoked a low growl from Pookie.

"It's highly unusual, but I would be delighted to have your assistance, especially if he is here on Earth. However, I fear that may not be the case."

Watson looked up in surprise. He was still recovering from the image of the angel. Spectacular wings. Not something you see every day. "What do you mean? If he's not in Heaven and he's not here, where is he…? Oh!" The penny dropped.

Holmes frowned, "Yes, 'oh!' I fear our assignment may require a trip to the nether world. A journey I don't anticipate with any joy. It's outside any of our experiences. Filadel, I'm afraid it's you who must supply the assistance. Are you familiar with Hell and its denizens?"

"I've never been inside, but we are permitted to approach the gates. I can lead you there. And as for its denizens, we are in constant conflict with them. I am at your disposal."

"All right. I have a few things to tidy up and Watson, I imagine you'll have to arrange for a locum to handle your practice. Tomorrow afternoon, Baroness. Back here at Baker Street. We'll see you then, Filadel."

*****

The angel spoke: "You two mortals will have to negotiate with Charon, the ferryman, to cross the River Styx. The fee is usually a Greek obol or Persian danake, but a British penny will do. He seldom has to deal with people who are still alive, so he may be a bit resistant. I'll help, if necessary. The Baroness, her dog, and I can simply float across through the air and take up our position at the gates. No doubt, we'll attract attention." He stretched his wings to envelop Holmes and Watson. "Come, I'll take you to the riverside. Follow along, Lady Juliet. You may want to leave Pookie behind or put her on a leash. There are dangerous hounds in Hell." The dog was having none of that, and flew up next to the Angel and Juliet. They proceeded in formation.

The Styx and its tributaries form the boundaries between Earth and the Underworld. Like all cabbies and boatmen throughout the universe, the ferryman responded favorably to the Victorian half- crown the two proffered as their fare for the ride. Little did Charon know, it was intended to be a round trip. He seldom had passengers on the return.

The Gates of Hell are, in a word, ominous. Tall, pitch black, with twisting posts and rails devoid of any decoration, they are hardly welcoming. To emphasize the effect, a large inscription in Italian (*who knows why it's in Italian?*) looms over the structure. "Lasciate ogni speranza voi ch'entrate," which translates to, "Abandon all hope, you who enter." The Chamber of Commerce was obviously not involved.

As the adventurers gathered before the portal, a demon dressed in black (naturally) landed in front of them. Tall, of significant girth, ugly visage and rattling voice, he fluttered his short metallic wings as he scanned them with his fiery red eyes. He wore a cloak decorated with flashing dragon images. Oddly, he did not have a pitchfork in hand. Probably required only by the infernal guard.

"Who are you, and what do you want? I doubt you are seeking entrance. You, there! Are you an angel? Is this some sort of tour group? Another heavenly innovation designed to annoy us? Get you gone!"

116

Suddenly a larger and more fearsome being appeared in their midst. It was difficult to discern his true dimensions, physiognomy or characteristics. They kept changing moment to moment.

Juliet turned to Filadel, "Is this who I think it is?"

The fiend intervened. "Yes, Baroness Crestwell, it is I - Satan, Lucifer, Prince of Darkness, Father of Lies, the Tempter, etc. etc. etc." Flickering, he turned to the first demon and shouted, "Beelzebub, what is this all about, you bumbler? Look who we have. A celestial ghost and her dog; a disgraced guardian angel and two mortals who are very well known to me: Sherlock Holmes and Doctor John Watson. We have them to thank for many of our inmates. I doubt if this is a tour group."

Holmes replied. "No, your Lordship, it is a rescue mission."

"You wish to recover one of our prisoners? Sorry, it can't be done. It was tried in the past. I remember that poor fool Orpheus trying to bring back his wife. It almost worked. Almost. We've had incursions by mortals from time to time. Beelzebub, what was the name of that Italian poet – Danny? Daniel?"

"Dante, my lord. He and that Roman, Virgil. They claimed they were cataloguing the nine circles of Hell for a guidebook. I threw them out, but… I think before they left, they got enough for a publication. And then there was the recent one."

Satan recoiled. "Wait, Beelzebub, what recent one? Why wasn't I informed, you incompetent? Who was it?"

"Some ghost, already dead. Said he escaped from heaven and wanted to enter here. Said this is where he belonged. Of

117

course, I refused. I think he was a spy. I shooed him onto Charon's boat. The guards made sure he left."

Juliet pounced. "Was he a Scot, ex-military, a Laird? Name of Angus MacDougal?"

"I never got his name. Didn't care, but I recall he did talk with a brogue, or a burr, and he limped."

"Well," said Satan, "Rescue mission. Sounds like your fugitive doesn't want to be saved. A pity he's gone."

Filadel was frustrated. "Can we trust what you're telling us?"

Lucifer laughed. "No, of course not. I'm not known as the Father of Lies for nothing. Beelzebub wouldn't know the truth if he fell over it. Enough of this persiflage. I have other important things to do. Go away!" He cupped his hands and yelled, "Charon! Bring your boat!"

They left. After a short nautical journey and brief flight back to London, the fivesome reassembled in the Baker Street rooms.

Watson and Holmes sat with snifters of brandy in hand. The ethereal three abstained, although Pookie did demolish a Heavenly Chewy treat. "Well," said the doctor, "that was quite a unique episode. We've eliminated one possibility if the Father of Lies is to be believed."

Juliet frowned. "Can we believe him?"

Holmes responded, "It was difficult to gauge from his demeanor. He kept changing instantaneously. A wonderful ploy of deception, by the way! I wish I could do it. But I would be willing to wager that, much as it may have bothered him, he and

Beelzebub were telling the truth. What do you think, my angelic friend?"

Filadel replied, "I'm sure they don't have Laird Angus. They would have paraded him out if they did. A saint who prefers Hell to Heaven? What a coup! Satan would be bragging all over the universe."

Watson shrugged, "That leaves us with Earth to deal with. My instinct says, 'Go to Scotland.' What say you all?"

The angel said, "I must return to Heaven. The Angelic Council wants to explore how Angus left without anyone knowing about it."

Watson commented, "As a member of the military, based in South Africa, I'm sure he developed very subtle stealth and deception skills against the Boers. Movement behind enemy lines, so to speak."

"Heaven was not his enemy!"

Watson arched an eyebrow at the angel. "You and I know that, but we don't know how his mind is working."

"It's working strangely, that's for sure. Well, I'm leaving! Goodbye for the moment." Filadel flew off through the walls and ceiling, vanishing as he ascended.

Watson turned to their phantom friend. "What about you, Baroness?"

"I'm up for a trip beyond Hadrian's Wall, but I have a modeling appointment tomorrow with Signore da Vinci that I'm eager to keep. He says I have an enigmatic smile. What do you suppose that means?"

Holmes chuckled, "He thinks you're a woman of mystery."

"Well, I am. Inscrutable, unknowable and unfathomable. That's me."

"If you say so."

"Yes. I do, Holmes. If you can be a man of mystery, I can also be incomprehensible."

Holmes and Watson both stifled a laugh. "Sorry," said Holmes, "I didn't understand you."

"Oooh!" Lady Juliet fumed. An enigmatic pout came on, followed by an emphatic raspberry. "Right now," she said, "I'm going to the London fashion boutiques and gather up some ideas for some new frocks. I'll pass them on to Miraculous Modes. They love me for breaking away from the dowdy white robes and displaying some style. I can model for them, too."

Watson asked, "To paraphrase Shakespeare, 'When shall we four meet again?'"

Holmes replied, "When Birnam Wood does come to Dunsinane, or when we get together at Laird Angus MacDougal's estate in Kilmarnock, whichever comes first. There is a 7:30 AM train from Euston Station that travels to Kilmarnock with one change. It arrives in the late afternoon. Join me if you can on Friday, Watson. We can stay overnight at one of Kilmarnock's excellent inns. I assume you'll flit there directly, Baroness. I'll contact Lady MacDougal and tell her I'm following up on a Foreign Office inquiry about the Boer attacks in Western Transvaal and ask for an interview this coming Saturday.

"Meanwhile, I want to contact Mycroft, and the Ministry of Defense, and learn more about the Boer ambush of the 647th Scots Grenadiers. I feel sure much of what's motivating Colonel Angus MacDougal's angst lies therein."

Juliet smiled. "You'll forgive me if I leave the pleasure of conversing with your brother to you alone. He is not one of my favorite people. Come, Pookie. Let's go look at gowns and dresses." Pookie circled Lady Juliet impatiently. "All right, one more Heavenly Chewy coming up." She grimaced. "You still need a bath."

*****

Once more to the offices of Mycroft Holmes, nominally Principal Auditor of His Majesty's Government but in actuality, Influencer in Chief. This time, he was joined by General Cartwright of the Ministry of Defense.

"What prompts your interest in Angus MacDougal, Sherlock?"

"A private query having to do with the ambush of his 647th Scots Grenadiers in the Western Transvaal early in 1900. Am I correct that it was a total rout marked by the death of nearly the entire unit?"

Cartwright shook his head. "Yes, it was a disaster. Major carnage. Only a few survived, including MacDougal, who was severely wounded. We kept the true dimensions out of the press but many a Scots family mourned the death of a loved one. MacDougal received a medical discharge after the event and returned to his estate in Kilmarnock."

"What brought about the ferocity of the attack? I understand most of the Transvaal activity consisted of minor skirmishes and guerilla raids."

Mycroft answered, "True, but this one seems to have been prompted by revenge. It has been alleged that, in 1900, members of the 647th had previously attacked a Boer settlement, burned it to the ground and bayonetted women and children in the process. The Boers took out fierce vengeance. An inquiry was initiated after the fact, but nothing was conclusively proven. There were complaints on both sides of a cover up. MacDougal was retired and no disciplinary action was taken against him. Interesting that he had since devoted his short life to major philanthropies up until the time of his death. Some believe it was to relieve a guilty conscience. Why the interest?"

"An inquiry by an historian. He felt, given my connections, I might be able to uncover the true story of the event."

The historian, thought Holmes, *being myself.*

"Thank you, gentlemen. I am much indebted. I suspect I will find little in the newspapers of the time."

Mycroft smiled inscrutably. "Not if we did our job effectively."

*****

Back beyond the Pearly Gates, Lady Juliet had just returned from a conference with the ethereal modistes of Miraculous Modes. "Oh, Pookie, fashion can be so exhausting. Madame Clarice is a genius, however. She can take heavenly cloth and mold it into such delicious confections. The London and Paris houses are well behind her in taste matched with boldness. A pity she can no longer participate in the season. She would rattle a few cages. Anyway, London's loss is my gain.

"Now I must dress in a more restrained form. I have my appointment to pose for Leonardo da Vinci. I have been practicing my smile. Perhaps he will include you in the portrait. I'll ask him. Little dogs were always favorites of famous artists. I'm glad you have had your bath."

The dog barked. Not at the suggestion, but at the Angel who had just alit in the Baroness's forecourt.

Lady Juliet looked out. Filadel was adjusting his wings for indoor movement. "God love you, Lady Juliet, have you a moment for a chastened guardian angel?"

She gave him her enigmatic smile. "God love you, too, Filadel. Of course. How did the inquiry go?"

"It was determined that we have a systemic issue we must deal with. I was just the unfortunate victim in this instance. The Angelic Council is wrestling with the problem of maximum freedom coupled with effective security. We cannot restrain our residents, but we cannot allow random clandestine excursions off the heavenly campus. You and Pookie, of course, are exceptions. But you did come up for some discussion. Mr. Raymond was called as a witness and promptly justified your travels and adventures."

"As well he should. He instigated several of them."

"Anyway, I have been charged with bringing Colonel MacDougal back to Paradise. If you have no objections, I shall rejoin your foursome on Friday evening in Kilmarnock. I believe that's where the trail leads. Thank God, we did not find him in Satan's claws. There would have been Hell to pay, literally."

"Yes, Lucifer is a nasty piece of work. No, by all means, feel free to join us at the Wheatsheaf Inn. Holmes is tracing the Colonel's military record and has set up a visit with Lady MacDougal. Her son, Robbie, will probably be there as well. It should be interesting, but more important, let's hope it leads to finding our wandering phantom. Now, if you'll excuse me, I must change for a sitting. Leonardo awaits."

*****

A nine-hour journey over 350 miles from London Euston to Kilmarnock left Holmes and Watson tired, irritable and hungry. They envied the Baroness's ability to simply flit to her destinations. Of course, one had to be dead to do so. She was accompanied by the Guardian Angel Filadel and her fur-covered companion, Pookie. They met in Holmes's chamber after he and Watson had devoured a fine Scottish dinner of salmon, neeps and tatties. No haggis, thank you! The dog looked on longingly and was rewarded by Juliet with a Heavenly Chewy treat.

Holmes related his conversation with General Cartwright and Mycroft. Watson asked. "Was the Colonel responsible for the atrocities that spurred the vengeful attacks on his troops?"

"We don't know that. The Board of Inquiry was of several minds on the subject. Of course, the commander is responsible for the actions of his troops, but whether he specifically ordered the burning of the settlement, and the murder of innocent women and children, was never satisfactorily determined. One version says a particularly brutal sergeant-major who hated the Boers gave the orders. Another accused the colonel. It resulted in a stalemate. By that time, MacDougal had been given a medical discharge because of the wounds he had sustained and was sent home. You'll know something about that, Watson."

"Yes, but my wound was the result of a Jezail bullet fired by an Afghan attacker. Quite straightforward and continually

124

painful, by the by. The only way we'll get any truth about this story is to confront the Laird's ghost. That is beginning to sound less and less likely."

The Angel groaned. "I hope you are wrong, Doctor. I must find him and bring him back. An Angelic Decree. Failure is not an option."

The Baroness sighed, "Oh dear! I didn't realize it was that serious."

Filadel nodded his head and drooped his wings. "I'm afraid it is, Milady. I must keep searching even if it takes eternity."

Pookie tilted her head and whined.

Holmes said, "I have hired a pony trap and driver for tomorrow's journey. The MacDougal estate is just outside town by the river. We will be seen by Lady MacDougal at 10 o'clock. I was quite vague when it came to the purpose of our visit."

Juliet asked, "Do you intend to tell her the truth? I doubt she'll believe you."

"That depends on the reception we get. Initially, Watson and I will merely be historians commissioned by the Ministry of Defense to develop a tome on the Boer Wars. Our names are Shaw and Walton. We shall see you at 9 tomorrow after Watson and I have breakfast."

The angel was uncomfortable with the deception but said nothing. Juliet had no desire to watch them eat in the morning. Pookie had to be content with her Chewies.

A fog had rolled up from the River Irvine and shrouded the morning sun. The pony trap arrived on schedule driven by a man who belied the image of the dour Scot. A broad smile wreathed his ruddy face. Unfortunately, he was also unintelligible to all except the Angel who had the gift of universal language.

Juliet giggled telepathically, *I assume he's speaking English but I don't understand a word.* She smiled enigmatically at the driver, who of course, didn't see her.

Filadel deciphered: "Good morning, gentlemen. 'Twill be a fine day once this fog lifts. It's to the Laird's estate we're goin.' He was a grand gentleman indeed. As is the Lady. I can't say that about the son. He's a first class rotter."

Watson replied, hoping the Scot would understand him: "And why would you say that, my man?"

The angel picked up the simultaneous translation. "He's a gambler, cheater, drinker and wencher. No Kilmarnock lass is safe from Master Robbie. My own Fiona had to fight him off. He's the Devil Incarnate." Filadel winced at that, and continued: "Someday, he'll be found strung up or face down in the river. But I'm talkin' out of turn. My apologies. It's chust that he raises my hackles. But here we are at the manor. I'll come back for ye as we agreed."

In the Scottish tradition, only an owner of a substantial estate can be called a Laird. Angus MacDougal's spread and mansion were indeed substantial. A flock of sheep grazed on a hillside. Several horses watched the approaching trap as it passed the stables. Pookie was enthralled. So much to chase and so little time.

The house itself was obviously from an earlier century. Three stories in height, grey in stone, outlined by two towers, it dominated the landscape with unquestioned authority. The trap pulled up to the sheltered portico which had been added sometime later. The three "celestials" floated by a liveried butler and entered a large foyer surrounded by ancestral portraits, suits of armor and weapons, weapons, weapons. The butler opened the large portico doors to admit the two mortals – "Mr. Shaw" (Holmes) and "Mr. Walton" (Watson).

"Gentlemen, welcome. Lady MacDougal and Mister Robert are in the Grand Salon. Please follow me."

The mixed mode entourage encountered a small, but dynamic, mature woman, who quickly rose from a sofa to greet Holmes and Watson. "Good morning, Mr. Shaw, Mr. Walton. You're quite prompt; I thought the fog would delay you, but I see Willie got you here on time. I am Agnes MacDougal, Lady of the manor. The locals used to joke about Agnes and Angus when my late husband was still alive."

Holmes looked closely at the energetic figure, dressed in a cardigan twinset and long grey skirt. Her hair was pulled back in a chignon and her blue eyes quite literally twinkled. Her gestures were active and frequent. A gracious smile filled out the picture. Juliet was impressed. As were 'Shaw and Walton.'

She gestured toward an unimpressive figure, slouching on another sofa. "This is my son, Robert MacDougal, 'Robbie' to all of us." They made a true study in contrasts. Tall, lanky, sallow of skin, bearded in the Scottish tradition, a torpid expression dominating an unattractive face. Probably a caricature of his late father. He moved not at all but grunted in their general direction. Watson was inclined to agree with the trap driver. This could be an unsavory character.

Holmes spoke, "Forgive me, Milady, but accents are a study of mine. Clearly, you are not from the Scottish mainland,

Shetlands or the Hebrides. In fact, I believe you may be from South Africa."

"How astute, Mr. Shaw, and quite correct. I am an Afrikaaner from Cape Town. Much to the dismay of his associates, Angus and I met and wed when he was stationed in the Transvaal and I was a young secretary with the new Boer government. Upon his discharge after the terrible incident, we came here to Kilmarnock to take up the Laird's residence."

Watson said, "It is that terrible incident into which we are enquiring. We have been commissioned by the Ministry of Defense to write yet another history of the second Boer War. The official record of the ambush is very short and very vague. We were hoping you could help us. Some thoughts and insights your late husband may have shared with you and of course, your son."

Another grunt from the far sofa.

"I'm afraid it was a subject Angus never spoke of. In the time since his discharge he would never bring up the subject. Neither did I."

The slouching figure, inanimate until now, spoke. "But I did. He was a stinking coward. Killed off all those dirty Boer women and kids as they deserved but didn't have the courage to stick with his men when the Boers counterattacked. He should have died with them, the bastard. Instead he comes back here, lords it over us and gives away his money to a bunch of pasty faced do-gooders. Leaves Ma'am and me with this ugly pile of stone and nothing much else."

Lady Agnes was horrified, as was Juliet, the Angel, and the dog. Holmes and Watson were not surprised. "Robbie, that's enough. In fact, it's too much. Your father was a noble gentleman."

"The Hell he was. He should have died in Africa and left us his fortune. Then we'd have the life we deserve instead of hanging about in this god-forsaken Scottish burgh. He gave it away to atone for his sins. At our expense!"

He rose, wonder of wonders, and stalked from the room, slamming the door as he left.

Lady Agnes turned to her guests with a painfully dignified expression. "Please forgive him, gentlemen. Robbie longs for the high life of Glasgow or Edinburgh, even London. We are not impoverished as he may have led you to believe, but… his desired standard of living requires far more than we can afford. I suppose when I am gone, he will sell up and leave Kilmarnock for good."

Holmes decided it was time to be open with the lady. He signaled to Watson and cast a slight wave in the direction of the ethereals. "Please forgive us, Lady Agnes, but we have a confession to make ourselves. We are not who we claim to be. I am Sherlock Holmes, a consulting detective, and this is my associate, Doctor John Watson. We are here on a mission which you will no doubt regard as impossible, or at best, highly improbable. We are searching for your husband. Please sit down."

The Lady sat, her mouth open in shock and confusion. "Searching for my husband? He's dead. Didn't you know that?"

"We do indeed, but he is missing from his heavenly reward and we are trying to locate him and restore his celestial life."

Lady Agnes regarded Holmes with contempt. "This has to be the sickest prank I have ever been subjected to. Please leave immediately, or I shall have to summon the authorities."

Watson intervened, "Please, Milady, give us a moment more of your time. We have brought along our personal credentials to prove who we are and we can tell you about the situation, incredible as you may think it is. We are commissioned by a much higher authority than the British Ministry of Defense."

Juliet whispered telepathically, *Appeal to her love for Angus!*

"We mean nothing but good for you and your beloved husband. We want to right a cruel mistake."

"I've heard of you. I've even read one of your books, Doctor Watson, if that's who you are. I don't understand what this is all about."

Holmes replied, "We didn't expect you to. Please suspend your suspicions for the moment. First, do you believe in the hereafter?"

"I suppose I do. I never gave it much thought until Angus passed away."

"It exists. In both forms. I can attest to that. What do you suppose happened to Angus when he passed on?"

"I hope he went to Heaven. He was a good man in spite of what Robbie thinks."

"He did go to Heaven, but then a remarkable thing happened. He left."

"He what?"

"He left Heaven. Voluntarily, we believe. We have reason to think he feels that he does not deserve to share eternity with the saints. Lest you be concerned, we have checked. He is not in the underworld."

"That sounds like Angus. Flooded with guilt. Here, you almost have me believing you. Well, all right. Where is he?"

"That's what we are trying to establish. Have you had any contact with him?"

"No. No, Wait! No, that's impossible."

"This whole affair is impossible. What were you about to say?"

"I have found flowers in my bedroom. Several times. African Violets. My favorites. They bloom continuously. None of the servants can account for them. And Robbie certainly wouldn't... You don't suppose...?"

Juliet blurted, *He's here! Filadel! Pookie! Help me search. Holmes, Watson, he's here! We'll see him when you can't. He's somewhere in this pile. Where is he likely to stay?*

Holmes asked, "Did he have a favorite room he would retreat into?"

"Yes, his study. I don't go in there, and I have forbidden Robbie and the servants to go there as well. It must be covered with dust by now."

"Would you take us there?"

Lady Agnes hesitated. "I'm reluctant, but... I guess I'll go along with this bizarre charade. Come! Wait. I'll need the keys."

The angel silently spoke: *But we won't. I can sense him. You're right, Baroness, he's here! Follow me!*

They floated to the second floor, down a back corridor and into a dusty but comfortable room. Pookie barked. A ghostly figure stirred. He smiled gently. "So, you found me. I didn't think I was worth looking for."

Juliet chuckled, "Au contraire, you silly man. Heaven has been on alert. The Angelic Council has this poor guardian angel of yours on tenterhooks. We have the world's greatest detective on your trail. Your heavenly mansion is standing empty, waiting for your return. You have nothing to feel guilty about. Your history was carefully vetted before you were admitted beyond the Pearly Gates. That vindictive sergeant-major was responsible for the slaughter. You weren't even there. He perished in the Boers' ambush. You, of course, were wounded."

By this time, the lady of the manor arrived with Holmes and Watson. She took the keys and slowly opened the door. "You see, gentlemen, nothing and nobody."

Two pots of African violets bloomed on a desktop. Three spectral figures and a dog sat around it.

"On the contrary," said Holmes, "he is here."

She spied the flowers and sucked in her breath. "Angus, oh, Angus. You're really here. Oh Angus, what are you doing? I love you, but you cannot stay. Go to your reward, my dear. I hope I'll join you shortly. Go and for the first time, be happy. Let the angel take you back."

They all looked puzzled. How did she know about the angel?

The colonel rose. "I'll wait for her, of course. Ah, weel. This is no place for a dead man, I suppose. By the way, it wasn't a heart attack that took me, ya ken. It was Robbie. Poison. Let's go, Filadel."

Epilogue

Six months later to the day, Lady MacDougal passed to her eternal reward and joined her husband in their celestial mansion. Juliet stops by from time to time with Pookie on her way to another sitting with Leonardo da Vinci. Filadel hovers nearby. Holmes is retiring to Sussex, and Watson's practice grows.

Robbie MacDougal acceded to the status of Laird but before he could reap any advantage, his body was found in a Kilmarnock back street. Strangled. The police had no clues.

On a fiery throne overlooking the nine circles of Hell, an ominous figure laughed diabolically. "Well Beelzebub, at last we have a MacDougal. The right one."

What's What, Watson?

Paradise time: Perpetuity **Earth Time:** January 1902

Lady Juliet Armstrong, the onetime Baroness Crestwell, came floating out of her celestial villa accompanied by her dog, Pookie, on their way to the Elysian Fields for a game of "fetch." Speaking of fetching, her new custom-made halo from Millenial Millinery was exactly that. She had replaced her standard issue corona with a jaunty little number that sat precariously on her brunette coiffure. "What do you think, Pookie?" she asked. "I believe it goes well with my scarlet gown. The stars add a certain sophisticated historical touch. My theatrical background and all that.

"You, on the other hand, my silly twit, *insist* on trying to shake yours off. I keep trying to tell you it's not a rash recovery cone, but you won't listen. By the way, I will not tell you again. Stop chasing the sheep! You do realize you look like a lamb, yourself." The Bichon Frisé barked, stood on her hind legs and rotated. "Yes, I know a lamb can't do that, Pookie, but you still look like one."

They had gotten part of the way to the park when she was intercepted by Mr. Raymond, one of Heaven's Senior Directors. A middle-aged male, tall, dressed in morning (mourning?) clothes, clean shaven, not a hair out of place, dark eyes, color undetermined, floating inches above the grass. He carried his modest halo in his hand.

134

"Ah, Baroness, I have come to see you. I have news. Your former associate, Doctor John Watson has been shot. Real Estate is preparing a mansion for him as we speak."

Juliet was shocked. "Watson is dead?"

"Well, not yet. I am being a bit premature, but his chances of survival are slim, and we do like to plan ahead for our new arrivals."

"Where is he?"

"St. Mary's Hospital in Paddington, on Praed Street. They specialize in trauma. Also, Mr. Sexton Blake has his domicile nearby. Are you familiar with him?"

"No! Strange name, but then so is 'Sherlock Holmes.' Are you going to allow me to attend the victim while he's still alive?"

"Under the circumstances, yes. But the same rules apply—"

"Yes, yes. I know! I can stay no longer than five days. I'm only visible and available to Holmes and Watson, although that Salvation Army Major sensed I was abroad. Holmes and Watson can hear my thoughts, as well."

She mused. "Pookie comes, too. No hijinks or mischief. Oh, I'll need an angelic understudy at Saintly Spectaculars."

"Noted. I hope Dr. Watson survives. We're running a bit short of mansions at the moment and could use the respite. A temporary situation, of course. We are infinite, after all."

"You are such a sentimentalist, Raymond. Tell the Real Estate Office not to go too far in their preparations. Sorry, Pookie. No fetch today. Mommy has to make a trip. Down we go!"

*****

St. Mary's Hospital is a stately pile noted for its excellent care and skilled physicians. If Watson is to stage a dramatic recovery, this is the place to do it.

The Baroness Juliet is indeed a 'Study in Scarlet' with her startling red dress (no dowdy heavenly white robes for her), high-fashion halo, and gorgeous face and figure. She and her otherworldly dog, Pookie, wearing a matching red bow around her neck, entered the antiseptic atmosphere of the hospital and took up a position next to Doctor Watson's bed. Sherlock Holmes and Watson's tearful new wife were standing by the unconscious figure. Mrs. Hudson stood off to the side, head bowed. Inspector Lestrade had just left. A constable was stationed outside the door.

She looked at Holmes, who alone could acknowledge her presence, and directed her inevitable question towards him: *How is he?*

The doctors are cautiously optimistic, Milady, he replied telepathically. *The next few hours will tell the tale. The wound is near his heart, and he's lost a great deal of blood. I see the celestial authorities have removed their restrictions to allow you to be present.*

Raymond is a sympathetic figure, for all of his bureaucratic fussiness.

One day I would like to meet him.

Perhaps that can be arranged. I don't suppose it would be possible for me to converse with the doctor's wife?

Holmes winced. *Probably it would involve more explanation than it's worth.*

What happened, Mr. Holmes?

As best as we can tell, he's the victim of a gunshot fired from a passing cab. Several witnesses saw the incident. Lestrade has gone to interview them. Unfortunately, a road accident delayed the ambulance, and he bled heavily before he was treated.

I have never met Inspector Lestrade. Is he as offensive as Jones and Gregson? asked the Baroness, recalling several provocative episodes she had endured involving those two worthies.

He's an old friend. Bit of a plodder, but dependable and committed. Not brilliant, but sensible. We have worked well together in the past.

That would be a welcome relief. Watson seems to have enough feminine assistance in attendance at the moment and I, as well as Pookie, am on a short leash, so... shall we take steps to flesh out the story? Sorry, a terrible metaphor, considering my unearthly condition.

Holmes found it increasingly difficult to endure Lady Juliet's questions while Watson lay bleeding before him. *Let me take my leave of Mrs. Watson and Mrs. Hudson,* he thought, *and we can go and join Lestrade at the scene of the crime.*

Which is where?

Queen Anne Street. Just outside Watson's consulting rooms. We believe he was just going for his post-appointments stroll to blow off the day's problems.

Do you think it was a disgruntled patient or relative who shot him? Doctors have that liability. As do actresses married to simple-minded barons...

137

Holmes sighed. *That's what Lestrade believes. I am withholding judgment. Shall we go?*

In deference to our partnership, Mr. Holmes, Pookie and I shall ride in the cab with you, although I detest the things. I'd much rather flit. But then again, I don't know where I'm going.

Do you ever, Lady Juliet?

WHAT?

*****

The gawkers had long since disappeared in front of Watson's surgery, leaving Inspector Lestrade and two constables to survey the vicinity. The cab containing Holmes and the invisible Baroness/canine combination pulled up, and deposited Holmes on the sidewalk. Pookie jumped out and initiated a sniffing ritual, beginning with the constables, and then the Inspector. Lady Juliet, floating casually, looked carefully at Lestrade.

He's short, isn't he? Strange face. Reminds me of a ferret.

Holmes unleashed a transcendental chuckle. *You are not the first to make that observation.*

"Hello, Mr. Holmes. I was wondering when you'd arrive," said Inspector Lestrade.

"Inspector," acknowledged Holmes. "The hospital staff tells me that Mrs. Watson, Mrs. Hudson and I just missed you at Watson's bedside. It was kind of you to visit him."

Inspector Lestrade nodded curtly. He wanted to relay his information to Holmes as quickly as possible. "As you can see, Holmes, the blood stains are pretty profuse. No spent cartridges. I assume the casings landed in the floor of the cab." He swept his

138

hand over the crime scene. "We waited for you before ordering a cleanup. Although, I'm sure the good doctor's wife is highly distressed, and would appreciate all the evidence being removed. My constables tell me she knows nothing, and has no idea who would want to shoot the doctor. By the way, do you know her name?"

Holmes frowned at the Inspector. "I simply call her Mrs. Watson."

Typical males, thought Lady Juliet. *I shall call you Mr. Detective and Mr. Inspector. So there!*

Holmes ignored the Baroness. "I understand there were several witnesses."

"Yes," said Lestrade, referring to his notes, "...two neighborhood women... and a young lad. They claim they heard one shot. The ladies were too shocked to remember anything else. They ran to call a constable, who summoned the ambulance."

Why are women always shocked? I'm never shocked. Sometimes shocking, but never shocked!

Holmes continued to ignore Lady Juliet. "Did you get the identification number of the cab?"

"Yes, the boy used his head and tagged the cab. We tracked down the growler. The owner claims it was stolen. We haven't examined it yet. No doubt you will want to."

Mr. Holmes, ask Lestrade if the shooter was a man or a woman.

"Was the shooter a man or a woman?"

"A woman? Er... the boy says a man, and the two ladies say, 'I don't know.' The driver was definitely a man. No description worth anything. Face covered. Heavy coat. Slouch hat."

Observant bunch! thought Lady Juliet. *Oh, I suppose the child did alright. You may want him as one of your Irregulars, Holmes. Oh, here I am being snide when poor Watson is at death's door. Excuse me, and I'll check in with Raymond. He'll have a status report.* She went blessedly silent.

Holmes asked the Inspector, "So there were two of them. Both are far away by now. Probably professionals. Where is the cab now?"

"The horse had brought it back to the cab rank. We have it in custody at the Yard's stables."

The Baroness returned. *Mr. Holmes! Raymond says there has been no requirement for a mansion. Watson's still alive. Oh, by the way, Inspector Pookie wants to interview the horse.*

It took a supreme effort, but Holmes remained stone faced. *Very funny!* he thought. *I wish she could. We might actually hear something useful.*

He glanced at Lestrade. "I'll just have a look around here, although anything of value has probably been obliterated by those nosy parkers, or your lot."

Lestrade frowned. "That's a familiar complaint. The constables and I have been very careful not to disturb the surroundings."

"Thank you for that," said Holmes. He took out his glass, walked around the perimeter, leaned over and picked up what looked like a suit button, placing it in one of his ever-present small envelopes. "This may have nothing at all to do with our

villains. In fact, it may be Watson's, or totally unrelated, but…
we shall see.

"Well, Inspector, we have the means and opportunity
defined. We'll need to establish motive before we track down the
potential killers. It may even be mistaken identity. We will have
to wait until Watson regains consciousness to make any progress
on that front. Meanwhile, let's go and examine the cab."

Then, telepathically, *Milady, I need you to swoop back to
St. Mary's and see if you can gather any more useful information;
and then join me back at Baker Street.*

Righto, Mr. Holmes! she thought. *I was getting tired of
just tagging along. Any messages for the good doctor or his wife?
Not that I can speak to her, of course. Maybe Watson will be
conscious, although they've probably sedated him hard and
heavy. Time for another flit, Pookie. No horse interview. Sorry.*

*****

Except for the sleeping patient, Doctor Watson, the
antiseptic room at St. Mary's Hospital was empty.

Doctor Watson! Doctor John Watson!

A female voice and the sound of a snuffling dog. The
doctor, no longer sleeping, couldn't open his eyes. The pain had
disappeared, but he couldn't move.

Where am I? he thought. *Who is talking to me…? Wait!*

He recognized the distinctive, musical voice.

Doctor Watson, repeated the voice. *Hello!*

He was hearing the voice from inside his brain, not with
his ears!

Lady Juliet? he wondered.

Yes, and Pookie!

Am I dead? Am I a ghost, too?

There was a tinkling laugh. *No, you're still very much alive. I have that from the Highest Authority. It's just that you're heavily sedated and unconscious. However, your subconscious is churning away and that's how we're communicating. You can't use your voice or your ears, but you can use your brain. I know that doesn't make much sense, but you're a physician. Live with it.*

She laughed again. *I meant that literally. Pookie, get down, girl.*

Lady Juliet, where am I?

St. Mary's Hospital. You've been shot. I know what that's like. Killed me! Fortunately, you're going to pull through. I do hope Raymond's right! Your wife, Mr. Holmes, the police, Mrs. Hudson, and the hospital staff have been all over you. Now it's my turn.

Forgive me, Baroness, but this is damned uncomfortable and inconvenient!

Yes, doctor, I know. It'll be over soon. Let's talk. Any idea who shot you, or why?"

No! Not all... Wait, I have one idea. It may mean nothing.

You, of all people should know about clues, doctor. Tell me!

Doctor Watson struggled to explain: *Yesterday, I had just exited from Cox and Company, the bank on Charing Cross where I have my accounts, and where I have several tin dispatch boxes in their safe. That's where I keep my unpublished manuscripts. As I turned up the street, I was accosted by a tall, unshaven ruffian who asked me if I was Doctor Watson. I admitted that I was, and he said, 'I have a message for you. You're not going to publish that story!' That was it. He stalked off before I could intercept him. You know, this sub-conscious thing is very difficult.*

I agree. It's not easy for me, either. We just have to concentrate. Did you recognize that man? Do you know what story he was talking about?

No, to both of your questions, he replied. *It was obviously a threat related to one of Holmes's adventures, but I don't know which one. I had just put three new stories in the boxes, but he could have been talking about any of them. There are over twenty altogether. I don't know who he was. I don't think he was acting for himself. He seemed like he was a hired hooligan.*

Hmmm... thought Lady Juliet. *I think his threat, and your being shot, are certainly related. It sounds like whoever hired him wasn't going to rely on your being intimidated, so they decided to take a more drastic step. He or she is probably trying to figure out how to get their hands on your dispatch box. We have to get there first. Where is the key? We'll get Lestrade to obtain a warrant and fetch the latest box from the bank and open it. I'll flit back to Mr. Holmes right now.*

My wife can give Holmes the keys to the deposit box and the dispatch box, Lady Juliet. I keep them in our own safe. She has access to it. Do you think Holmes is in danger?

Yes, Doctor, I do! Now, just relax. These sub-conscious conversations can be exhausting. Get well... quickly. I'll be back after I see the Great Detective. Come, Pookie. Let's go to Baker Street.

What's What Watson?

*****

Sherlock Holmes had just returned from a fruitless examination of the cab used in the shooting. He and Inspector Lestrade had found nothing in the vehicle, and the owner was glad to get it and the horse back, even with the possibility of it being impounded as evidence. He knew nothing useful about the theft. He had stepped away from the cab rank for a few moments and returned just in time to see horse and vehicle being spirited away. His colleagues were equally clueless. Data! Data! Holmes needed data and nothing was forthcoming until…

Lady Juliet swept into the room. *Mr. Holmes, I just left Doctor Watson. He's comatose, but we had a sub-conscious brain to brain conversation. You should try one. I have information for you, but we have to act quickly.* She proceeded to tell him about the hoodlum, and the threat, and the dispatch box. She finished off breathlessly (of course, as a ghost she was always breathless): *You're in danger. Someone wants to eradicate all evidence of one of your adventures, including you and Watson.*

How is Watson holding up?

Raymond tells me he is not expected at the Pearly Gates any time soon. His information is quite reliable.

Holmes replied, *Good! Cox and Company will be closed for the evening, but I will contact Lestrade, bring him up to date and have him obtain a warrant to open the safety deposit vault and retrieve Watson's tin box. We'll go there first thing in the morning. I'll need to get the keys from his wife. Thank you, Baroness. I doubt if this ruffian is a principal. Someone important is intent on expunging evidence. Unfortunately, I can think of several dozen who would fit the bill, although not too many who are desperate enough to kill.*

Do you suppose they might try to break into the bank tonight if they are that determined?

A good thought. I'll alert Lestrade and ask him to post extra protection at Charing Cross.

*****

Lady Juliet's warning proved prophetic. During the night, two hooligans were collared trying to break into the vaults of Cox and Company. They steadfastly refused to give any information about their mission or who had issued their commission.

The next day, on their way to Queen Anne Street to collect the keys from Watson's wife, Lestrade updated Holmes on the attempted break-in. Holmes remarked, "Well, our opponent seems capable of inspiring fear in his minions and has probably compensated them well to keep their silence. He, or she, is no doubt quite powerful. That may narrow our selection a bit."

Lestrade nodded and the Baroness, uncomfortable in the cab (in which she and Pookie took up no space), wondered telepathically, *It sounds to me like a horrendous scandal or traitorous disgrace is at the heart of this. Or possibly an international incident. The continent is on tenterhooks. Governments don't play gently under those circumstances. I keep up to date, by the way, if you thought I was a feather-brained nincompoop.*

Holmes smiled. *Hardly that, your ladyship,* he thought.

Much as I dislike the prospect or him, this may be a time to revisit your brother.

A similar thought occurred to me. We will beard Mycroft in his den armed with Watson's dispatch box. Holmes looked out of the cab's window. "Here! We have arrived at Queen Anne Street," he told Lestrade. "It will only take me a moment to secure the keys, and we can head to the Bank."

Watson's wife was puzzled at the request, but immediately acquiesced. She opened the personal safe and passed the keys to Holmes. "I really don't understand, Mr. Holmes. Has John's writings any bearing on his shooting?"

"We don't know, but it seemed prudent to secure them in a more closely protected environment. An attempt was made last night to break into Cox and Company. I doubt it was a coincidence."

"My goodness. This is all so distressing, but I mustn't upset John. I am leaving now for the hospital. I hope he is conscious. The doctor was encouraging when I left."

"Watson is made of sterling stuff. He has survived bullet wounds before. I am most hopeful. Thank you again, Mrs. Watson. We shall take good care of the keys and the dispatch box."

Lady Juliet, who had tagged along with Holmes while he made his brief visit, commented: *She seems quite simpatico. A good marriage. You should try it, Holmes.*

Thank you, no. How could I consort with you if I were married? My wife wouldn't stand for it.

Touché! Well, on to Cox and Company and then the commodious and hospitable Diogenes Club. Pookie and I will fly ahead. See you at the bank.

Holmes informed the Inspector of his (and without mentioning her, Juliet's) concern that this was an international incident in the making and his intent to consult Mycroft. Lestrade, as usual, was dubious but agreed, nonetheless. He was not fond of Mycroft, either.

The managers at Cox and Company were duly upset at the abortive attempt to enter their premises but relieved that the effort had been thwarted. They too, were puzzled at the request to empty Watson's safety deposit box, but Lestrade's warrant calmed their fiduciary concerns while sharpening their curiosity. Holmes took the tin box and without opening it, thanked the officers and left, Lestrade trailing behind.

Holmes quietly concentrated: *Baroness, you and your dog travel speedily. Can you go to St. Mary's Hospital and check on Watson's condition, and then meet us at the Diogenes Club?*

No need, Mr. Holmes. I will just get a status report from Raymond.

The Senior Heavenly Director was a bit nonplussed to find Juliet and Pookie suddenly manifesting in his office. "Lady Crestwell, it is highly unusual for us to be keeping tabs on a mortal who is not under our supervision. However, I have found in your case, resistance is futile. Give me a moment!"

He paused, focusing, head bent down. "He is recovering and has regained consciousness for short periods. I have told Real Estate to cancel the order for his mansion, at least for the time being. I trust we will be seeing you back here shortly. Your angelic understudy at the Saintly Spectaculars is doing well, but her wings have resulted in a few costuming difficulties."

"Raymond, you are a sweet old fuddy-duddy."

Did he actually blush?

"Thank you. Pookie and I shall return anon."

She returned to the world of the living, relayed the news to Holmes, and then flitted to Pall Mall and the Daunting Diogenes. The prune-faced Majordomo and his equally dour footman occupied their usual places as she sailed past. *Ah, the Sunshine Boys!* she thought. *Bringing joy and excitement wherever you go! Don't disturb yourselves. I'm sure ethereal ladies and dogs are always welcome, and I know the way to the Stranger's Room. But first, while I wait for Holmes and Lestrade, a stop or two to see if any of the members passed away during the night. Difficult to tell. But of course, I'll know a ghost when I see one.*

Rather than make his usual grand entrance, Mycroft had already made his way to the Stranger's Room and was settled in an oversized chair, demolishing a stack of hazelnut Turkish Delights (*or 'lokum,' to the knowledgeable aficionado*).

Holmes and Lestrade entered the meeting place, followed by the Baroness and her dog. She had been entertaining herself making faces at the stolid members. Pookie was immediately taken up by the Turkish Delights, but sorely disappointed that she couldn't take a bite out of them.

Lady Juliet sympathized. *Don't worry, love. I'll get you some Heavenly Chewies shortly. They're much better for you. Look how fat Mr. Mycroft is! We don't want that to happen to you.*

Mycroft rumbled, "Well, gentlemen, what dire circumstance requires my attention? Is the Empire still safe?"

Holmes replied, "You would know that better than I, brother dear. But you may have hit upon something. We are involved in a most peculiar situation involving Watson and his scribblings." He held up the tin box. "The Empire may indeed be at risk."

"How is Watson? Inspector, have you caught his attackers?"

"He is recovering, Mr. Holmes, and no, we have not run *them* in yet," said Inspector Lestrade. "We believe they were hired assassins employed by some ruthless and powerful individual. Doctor Watson was warned not to publish one of his stories but then was shot, anyway. Someone wasn't taking any chances. And then last night, an attempt was made to break into Cox and Company, the bank where Doctor Watson kept his manuscripts in the dispatch box your brother is holding. We believe the box was the target. They failed, and we have the two in custody. They won't talk. I don't believe they are the same villains who assaulted Dr. Watson. We know these two as break-and-entry specialists. Killing is not part of their act."

Mycroft looked at Sherlock and said, "So the solution would seem to be in that pile of paper that I assume is in the box. Is Watson conscious enough to lend some help in sorting this out?"

"We don't know yet. We've come to you to see if there are any rumors of an international nature that may have a bearing. We need to pore over the manuscripts. Of course, it could be something altogether different. A husband trying to protect his wife's reputation or his own."

The Baroness chortled, *That's far more likely. It may be the wife, herself. Remember the murderous Selma Fairfax! Society ladies are so genteel.*

Mycroft paused. "The Russians are active again, stirring things up on both sides of the Channel. They are once again attempting to suppress the Polish Nationalists and seeking to involve the British. Count Volkov is back at it. Do you remember, Sherlock? You faced him down when he attempted to subvert the Foreign Office the last time?"

This got the pair's attention. Lestrade said, "I thought he had gone to ground."

Mycroft chuckled, "So did we. He's a persistent blaggard. As you know, he escaped back to St. Petersburg, but our operatives believe he has returned, well-disguised and no doubt, vengeful. He may be your man, although I wonder what Watson may have written about him to inspire this reaction."

Holmes asked the Baroness telepathically, *He was involved with Lady Selma in picking your husband's brains, was he not?*

That was Von Meyer, though Reginald's brains were easy picking, the idiot.

Unfortunately, we can't question Lady Selma. She kept her appointment with the hangman for the Baroness' killing.

Juliet couldn't resist, *Well, that's a dead end!*

Holmes frowned. *A little less whimsy, Milady.*

Sorry, Mr. Holmes, I'll behave. It's actually Pookie. She's the comedian, not me. The dog rolled over in response.

Holmes turned to his brother. "Mycroft, if we leave this box in your scrupulous care, will you have one of your specialists analyze the contents for items that could be embarrassing or dangerous to Volkov, or to some other international outlaw? We will go to Watson and see what recollections he can conjure up. As I said, it could be something totally different. A domestic scandal, or a criminal trying to cover his tracks."

"All right, Sherlock! I'll see to it. The box will be carefully guarded and its contents meticulously examined. I wonder how Watson will feel about that! May I advise you to watch your back carefully. If it is our Russian adversary, he bears you a great deal of ill will."

Holmes remarked, "I defeated Volkov once, but obviously, not completely. Regardless of how this particular adventure turns out, I must deal with him again. Your advice is taken to heart, dear brother. We'll await your office's conclusions and will take special precautions, won't we Inspector?"

Lestrade nodded. "No mistake, Mr. Holmes! I'm heading back to the Yard and then to Wormwood Scrubs Prison. I want to see if those two cracksmen have decided to spill their guts. They'll probably claim they don't know who they're working for, or why the box was so important, but maybe we can get a few hints if we get them talking to each other."

Holmes agreed. He closed his eyes, and thought, *Baroness, how would you like to listen in on the conversations between those two 'yeggs?' If they think they're alone, they might say something interesting.*

Ooh, Juliet the Spy! She beamed. *And Pookie, her faithful sidekick. Sounds like great fun! I'll travel along with the unsuspecting Inspector. I always wanted to ride in a police van. I almost did, once when a show I was in was closed by the Lord*

Chamberlain. The stuffy git. Give Watson my love. Come, Lestrade! Intrigue awaits.

She flitted past the Diogenes Duo who were grimly ensuring that the outside world did not impinge on the Silent Sanctum. *"Goodbye, boys. Control your enthusiasms but keep smiling! See you again! Come, Pookie! No, you can't bite them. A pity! Come on, let's follow the Inspector.*

Holmes walked out into the street and blew a whistle, a signal for the Irregulars. He was almost instantly surrounded by a band of ragamuffins, eager to earn a shilling or two or even half a crown. He jingled the change in his palm and said, "Find Shinwell Johnson and ask him to meet me at Baker Street at 2 o'clock." He tossed them the coins, hailed a passing cab and headed for St. Mary's Hospital.

He ran into Mrs. Watson and Mrs. Hudson in the corridor as they were exiting the room. "Oh, Mr. Holmes," said Mrs. Hudson. "He is recovering. The doctors are very optimistic. Please don't tire him. I'll be back later."

Holmes smiled. "Thank you, Mrs. Hudson. You are truly a gem. I'll be back at 221B at about one o'clock. A bit of lunch would be most welcome. Then, at two, I am expecting Mr. Shinwell Johnson."

"Oh, Mr. Holmes! That reprobate!"

"Yes, but a very useful reprobate, Mrs. Hudson. You should be used to my peculiar associates."

She frowned. "I am indeed. Much to my sorrow." She sniffed and marched off, with Mrs. Watson in tow.

Holmes entered the room, and was pleased to see his friend awake, and propped up on pillows. A nurse had just finished his ablutions and had withdrawn the curtain surrounding the bed.

"Well, my old comrade. Another bullet to keep your Jezail company."

"No, they removed this one. It came from a Short Enfield. Only a few thousand of them in circulation. So much for ballistics analysis."

"Do you feel up to a quick conversation?"

"I just had an exhaustive session with the ladies, but I'd welcome a little masculine dialogue. Speaking of ladies, did I have some kind of sub-conscious session with Lady Juliet, or was I dreaming?"

"You were in a dream state, but our glamorous ghost was indeed in contact with you. She is quite remarkable. The two of you agreed that your attack was prompted by someone who didn't want one of your stories made public. Unfortunately, you were unable to identify the individual who threatened you, or the two men who shot you. An unsuccessful attempt was made to steal your dispatch box from Cox and Company. We have those rogues, but they're not talking. The box and your manuscripts are now in Mycroft and his staff's capable hands. He believes your assault was inspired by the Russian Count Volkov. Remember him?"

"That blaggard. I thought he had escaped to St. Petersburg."

"It seems he's back, doing the Grand Duke's bidding once again."

"But what would he want with my stories?"

"That's what we intend to find out."

"Are you sure he's responsible for my near-death experience, Holmes?"

"No, I'm not. We're pursuing alternatives as well. We could use your help, Watson. Spies, blackmailers, extortioners, jealous husbands? Possibly resentful wives, disappointed heirs, vengeful relatives? It might even have been crooked police, military or politicians, thieves, or insane killers."

"You just listed off the complete cast of characters in my manuscripts! It could be any of them if they felt I was threatening them."

"It was probably one of your more recent stories that triggered the attempt on your life. Either that or it's the first opportunity that he, or possibly she, has had to deal with you. That brings us back to Volkov, if he has just recently returned to England."

"There might be one tale in which he is a dominant character but unless his colossal ego, chafing at being defeated, is the cause, I don't know what would inspire him to such violence."

"Perhaps it's something of which you're not aware."

"Good Lord, Holmes, I'm the author. I know what I wrote."

"Do you? We'll see. I have an appointment. I'll return later in the day."

*****

Lady Juliet Armstrong, Baroness Crestwell had never been inside a gaol. Nor had Pookie, although in her former life she had escaped from the Royal Dog Catchers once or twice while

154

running loose. Their trip to Wormwood Scrubs Prison was a new, but not very pleasant, experience. The Governor welcomed Lestrade and led him back to the Class B wing, housing felons who are a public risk, but may not require maximum security. The Cox and Company cracksmen qualified. The two ghosts tagged along.

The two suspects were brought into a small room where Inspector Lestrade was waiting for them. Lestrade led off, "All right, my lads. Let's get the situation straight. You two have been caught dead to rights trying to break into a highly respected financial institution. That will not sit well with the Crown Prosecutor. I suspect your trip to the Old Bailey will be short and conclusive and you'll be returned here to serve out a lengthy sentence. I can't do much about the sentence itself but I can have some influence on the length. But I need your cooperation. You tell us what we want to know and I'll tell the prosecutor that you cooperated. Do we have a deal?"

"Get lost, rozzer," one of them spat. "We don't have anything to say to you. We have a solicitor coming who's going to get us out of here double-quick. Our employer is a powerful individual, don't you know? We don't need any help from a Scotland Yard Inspector, but thanks for your consideration." They laughed.

"Oh Pookie," said Juliet, unheard and unseen by the room's occupants, "these are a pair of hard cases, but I don't think they have much in the brains department. As soon as the Inspector leaves in frustration, we're going to listen in as these two convince themselves that they'll be back at their neighborhood pub before sundown. Then we'll report back to Mr. Holmes."

What's What Watson?

The Baroness had it spot on. The prison governor had let the two of them stay in a cell together and posted a guard nearby to take in their conversations. Unfortunately, they knew the guard was listening, so they kept their voices low and spoke in whispers. The guard was frustrated. Lady Juliet was not.

"That Rooshan isn't going to let us stay here in the clink," one of them whispered. "We know too much, and he's worried that we'll peach on him."

"I don't know, George. He may just leave us to face the music. I'm worried."

"Don't be a silly git. He'll get us out of this real smart. Now just shut up."

"Did you hear that, Pookie?" said Lady Juliet. "They said, 'that Rooshan.' Sounds like Volkov to me. Let's flit back to Sherlock Holmes."

That afternoon, the bodies of suspected criminals George Simmons and Percy Williams were found poisoned in the Class B cells of Wormwood Scrubs. An investigation was immediately launched, but nothing of significance was discovered.

Learning of this, Holmes conferred with Lestrade. "Our opponent is quite serious, Inspector. He's not leaving any part of his trail uncovered."

He did not reveal the evidence provided by the Baroness. She, in turn, decided to stage a one- woman defense of Watson and Holmes, albeit a ghostly defense. Nobody, especially Count Volkov, would get away with murder. It was The Baroness vs. The Count.

*****

However, all that would be future tense. At the moment, Sherlock Holmes had a 2 o'clock appointment with his sometimes co-conspirator and informant, Shinwell Johnson. Lady Juliet and Pookie arrived at 221B Baker Street just as Johnson was plodding up the seventeen steps behind Mrs. Hudson. The landlady tapped on the door and in a loud voice announced, "Mr. Johnson is here to see you, Mr. Holmes." With a disapproving frown, she turned on her heels and strode down the stairs to her rooms.

Shinwell entered, muttering, "Gracious ol' bat! Hullo, Mr. Holmes. Your brat army tracked me down. You should register them with the Home Office. They make Scotland Yard look a bunch o' bleedin' amachures."

The Baroness took up a comfortable position, nodded at Holmes and mentally said, *I have some important things to tell you.*

He replied telepathically, *This won't take long. You may find it interesting.*

A celestial pout followed by, *Oh all right.*

Johnson continued. "I assume you want to do some business?"

"I do, indeed. Information! Our usual rates."

"It so happens, I am available."

"Good, I need the identity of a couple of killers."

"Killers in London, Mr. Holmes? Hardly possible."

"These two shot Doctor Watson in the street, while driving by in a stolen cab."

"I heard about the doctor. Is he dead?"

"No. Although, I would like certain people to think so. We believe these miscreants are tied up with Count Volkov."

"Is he back in town? I thought he skipped."

Juliet snarled, *He's back, all right. But he might not be for long.*

"We have strong suspicions that he's here heavily disguised. He seems intent on stealing Watson's manuscripts. We don't know why. I want you to find those two would-be assassins. Lestrade and I want to put them out of business. They may also lead us to our Russian friend."

The Baroness mentally shouted (in a ladylike fashion), *I can find him sooner!*

"How is Chief Inspector Lestrade?" asked Shinwell. "Give him my best regards. All right. I assume this is a rush job?"

"Speed would be greatly appreciated."

"Bob's yer uncle, Mr. Holmes. Back to yer in a twink." He rose and strode to the door.

Lady Juliet watched him leave, shook her head and smiled. *You have some rare associates, Holmes. Anyway, our two cracksmen tagged their patron as a Russian. Pookie and I are going to the Russian Embassy. He may show up there.*

*****

It's not clear whether her stay in Heaven had bestowed the gift of prescience on Lady Juliet, whether she was lucky, or whether she was just plain smart, but at that moment, Mijn Heer Josef Schnell, diamond merchant from Rotterdam, was entering the offices of the Russian Embassy. He announced himself to the officious receptionist and stated that he was summoned by the Ambassador. He was allowed to wait. A scarlet-clad wraith settled next to him and a transparent little white dog sniffed at his highly polished boots. Naturally, he didn't notice. Finally, an ornate door opened, a tall, uniformed officer clicked his heels and said, "Mijn Heer Schnell, the Ambassador will see you now. Follow me!"

He entered an opulent anteroom, followed by his celestial hangers-on, and proceeded to an even more opulent office. The Ambassador was seated behind a massive desk but did not rise at the diamond merchant's entrance. "Count Volkov, please be seated."

Lady Juliet gaped. *Volkov!*

"Your activities here over the past few weeks has been reported back to the Grand Duke. He is not pleased. In fact, he has requested your immediate recall to St. Petersburg.

"Our relationship with the British Empire is tenuous at best. The revolutionaries are not helping. But we cannot permit you to go buccaneering about, staging your own private wars. You will be ready in three hours to leave the country. You will be provided with an escort all the way to Rotterdam, where you will be met by members of the Grand Duke's staff and brought to his offices in St. Petersburg. I do not know what will follow."

The Count was shocked and belligerent. "Gospodin Ambassador! I am not accustomed to being treated in such a cavalier fashion. I am a member of the aristocracy, entitled to all the perquisites of my rank. I will not be shipped like baggage across the channel and into the hands of the Grand Duke's thugs."

The ambassador was unmoved: "I suggest you post a protest with the Grand Duke when you see him. In the meantime, I will await a report from my staff confirming that his orders have been carried out. Do svidaniya, dear Count. Have a good journey. Klaus, please go with the Count."

Volkov turned on his heel and stalked from the office, suitably accompanied.

Baroness Juliet took her leave and swiftly returned to 221B Baker Street. "Mr. Holmes," she cried, "Volkov is getting away with murder! The Russian Government is shipping him back to St. Petersburg with an escort. I want him caught and punished here!"

Holmes quickly grabbed his hat and coat. "I'll contact Mycroft. I doubt he'll want to create an international incident, but we shall see. Let's go to his office. He'll be there instead of the club. I'll send a message to Lestrade, as well."

*****

Juliet was beside herself in exasperation. That fiend was going to escape to Russia and nobody was going to do anything about it. She took out her annoyance on Holmes who, of course, was the only one who could see or hear her, since Doctor Watson was still in the hospital. Pookie joined in the frustration by growling, thrashing her tail and stamping her paws. "Your brother is the consummate bureaucrat. He'll just hem and haw while Volkov leaves."

"Patience, Milady. If what you say is true, I don't believe the Russian authorities will be particularly gentle with our noble adversary. The Grand Duke is rather intolerant of failure and lack of discipline, both of which Volkov has demonstrated in spades. We still have Watson's assailants to find and deal with. I expect we will be getting positive results from Shinwell Johnson. Here we are at Whitehall," he said, as the cab slowed to a halt. *Please remember to use telepathy from this point forward. Lestrade will be joining us shortly.*

Mycroft Holmes's role in the British government is shrouded in mystery. His brother claims that, occasionally, Mycroft *is* the British government. In the guise of Chief Auditor, he tugs on the threads attached to most of the ministries and departments under the purview of the Prime Minister. He has been mentioned as most helpful by His Majesty. He does all this by sheer dint of intellectual prowess. Physical exertion, nay even unnecessary movement, is anathema to him.

His office was spartan but engineered to minimize movement or discomfort of any sort. Mycroft smiled, but did not rise, as his brother walked in with his unseen companion. "So, Sherlock, our bird is about to fly the coop. I suggest we let him go. We have operatives in St. Petersburg who are quite capable of dealing with him, without our having to explain his fate here in London. Our delicate relations with the Tsar can use a little relief. May I ask how you know of his imminent departure?"

"Like you, Mycroft, I have my sources." He gave the Baroness a telepathic wink. She pouted in return, dissatisfied with Mycroft's conclusion.

Just then, Inspector Lestrade entered the office. The two Holmes brothers quickly filled him in on the latest details. Lestrade was unsatisfied. "We still have those two riflemen to deal with, and those safecrackers as well," he said, unaware of the fate that befell the two prisoners in Wormwood Scrubs.

Holmes smiled. "I believe I have that in hand. What have your specialists discovered from their analysis of the dispatch box, brother?"

"Exactly nothing. There is not one iota or scintilla of mention of Volkov in the entire array of manuscripts. I suggest you look elsewhere for your smoking gun, as it were. I will return the box and its contents to you. If the Count is taking leave of our shores, I don't believe the box is in jeopardy any longer. Return it to Doctor Watson."

"I will, but first there is the matter of the two would-be assassins to be resolved. Come, Inspector, join me back at Baker Street. I believe I may have some news for you."

Telepathically, he said, *And you too, Milady, as if you need an invitation.*

She stuck out her tongue, and she and Pookie both flitted before Holmes could make any comment.

*****

Once again, Shinwell Johnson proved his reliability and competence. He greeted the Inspector who grudgingly acknowledged him. "Gents, the lads you want are in a Manchester nick. Fight in a pub with drawn knives. Nasty pair. Ernie Caldwell and Joey McPhail. They did some work for your Russian Count in the past. Anonymous shootings are their specialty. Dumb as rocks, but vicious. You didn't hear about them from me. I'd appreciate payment in small bills. Always a pleasure, Mr. Holmes, Inspector."

What's What Watson?

"Thank you, Shinwell, your secret is safe, isn't it, Lestrade?"

"Hmm? Oh, yes, right. Good work, Johnson"

When the brief financial transaction was completed, Lestrade asked Holmes if he could use his newly installed telephone to call Manchester. An attempted murder charge by Scotland Yard trumped the local complaint. He arranged for the two heavies to be transported back to London.

Lady Juliet looked at Holmes. *Isn't it time we visited our partner?*

In due course, Baroness. I have an errand to perform first at a newsagent.

A newsagent? There are times when I don't understand you, Mr. Holmes.

You are not alone.

Holmes turned to Lestrade. "What say you, Inspector? Shall we visit the wounded?"

"Let's go. The police van is at the curb."

Lady Juliet and Pookie passed on the privilege of riding in the police vehicle and so missed Holmes's brief sojourn, stopping the van in front of a perplexed young boy selling the latest newspapers. Holmes sifted eagerly among the papers and magazines.

"Aha, I've got it," he shouted at the confused news seller. "Thank you, good sir. You keep a bountiful inventory."

"If you say so, Guvnor. Twenty pence, please."

The Baroness and her dog had swooped into St. Mary's and were in the act of being solicitous over Watson's condition.

Mrs. Watson had just left again, and Mrs. Hudson, after bringing in her Dundee cake, had returned to Baker Street.

Juliet brought the doctor up to date on the goings-on, expressing her frustration that Volkov was being returned to Russia. Watson was somewhat more sanguine. "I think I agree with Mycroft. The Russian government can be quite stringent when it comes to discipline. I wouldn't want to be in the Count's boots right now."

Holmes and Lestrade entered the room. "Watson, old friend! How are you? You're looking much better."

"I am, in fact. Hello, Lestrade."

In order not to confuse the Inspector, who hadn't a clue about the Glamorous Ghost, Holmes repeated what she had already told Watson. He also told Watson about the deaths of the two safecrackers which had just come to light, courtesy of the newspapers.

The doctor turned to Lestrade. "My attackers have been found?"

"Found, and on their way back to London to stand trial. They'll probably accuse Volkov in an attempt to avoid the gallows."

"You're sure the Count was the instigator of all this?"

"Absolutely!" remarked Holmes. "As you know from our previous history with him, he is a hot-headed swine intent on vengeance against the two of us. I'm sure I was to be his next intended victim. By the way, I have your dispatch box. The experts found nothing suggestive."

"What made him think there was a story about him in the dispatch box?"

"You told him, Watson!"

"What? Holmes, I did no such thing. I have had no contact with Volkov since he escaped to Russia the first time."

"Perhaps not, my dear chap, but you told him, nonetheless. We have been searching in the wrong place for our solution."

Watson wearily shook his head. "I don't understand."

Holmes handed him a copy of the Strand Magazine from several months ago. "You have a story in this issue."

"Yes, but it's about a series of jewel thefts!"

"Read the opening paragraph!"

He took the magazine and read aloud:

"I have had many strange adventures with my good friend, Sherlock Holmes. There was the bizarre episode of the Crumbling Inn; the mysterious disappearance of Lord Severill; the unspeakable horror of the Cornish Caves and the dastardly intrigues of the international scoundrel, Count Volkov. All of these stories will be consigned to my tin dispatch box at Cox and Company where they will await the future passing of the principals involved or in the case of the Count, a relaxation of the Official Secrets Act."

"But I never actually wrote that story. I gave up. Too much trouble with the Foreign Office."

"He didn't know that, Watson. I assume that on returning to England, he saw your name on the cover, bought a copy to see what his arch-enemies were about, and read that paragraph."

"Good Lord, two men were poisoned, and I was shot, over a manuscript that never existed."

The Baroness had the last word: *It was a ghost story, Doctor!*

Wearin' of the Green

Paradise time: *Perpetuity*   *Earth Time*: *March 1902*

Lady Juliet Armstrong, the erstwhile Baroness Crestwell, now deceased, was on her way to take her ephemeral dog Pookie to the Galactic Groomers for her bath, comb and fluff. The dog, that is; not the Baroness.

Whenever their earth-based owners passed on and crossed over into the Heavenly climes, their animals who had preceded them (and were waiting patiently) could cross the Rainbow Bridge and rejoin them. The reunions beyond the Pearly Gates were always joyous and noisy. Such was the case with Juliet and Pookie, a frisky and opinionated white Bichon Frisé. Pookie felt she could do without the grooming, but the Baroness had her reputation for glamour to uphold. A former superstar actress on London's musical stages, married to a dim-witted, but rich, nobleman, she had been shot to death at the behest of a nasty rival.

She and her dog had since turned Heaven on its celestial ear, defying traditions, acting, singing, dancing, causing aeronautical upsets and wearing daring scarlet gowns in lieu of standard "dowdy" cosmic white robes. Even her haloes were "dernier cri." She also had made several return appearances on earth in the company of Sherlock Holmes and Doctor Watson, helping to solve or prevent crimes.

Wearin' of the Green

Before the Baroness or her canine companion could venture forth, she found herself facing an impressive, tall, white-bearded figure clad in a green robe and equipped with an elaborate staff and a white pointed crown (a crozier and mitre, as she was to learn). Not sure how to react, she bowed to this extraordinary entity. He bowed in return.

"Am I addressing Lady Juliet Armstrong, Baroness Crestwell?" he inquired.

"You are, indeed, sir. May I inquire who you are?"

"I am Padraic, Bishop of Ireland."

"St. Patrick? I am overwhelmed, sir... your grace, your excellency. I'm sorry. I don't know the appropriate address for a saintly bishop. Do tell me. Did you actually drive the snakes from Ireland?"

"Patrick will do well enough, milady. And no! There weren't any snakes there to begin with. The story was started by an overly eager acolyte of mine. However, I do have a request."

"What may I do for you, bishop?"

"If you pay any attention to the calendar on Earth, you know that my feast day, March 17, celebrated globally, is fast approaching. It is usually a jolly experience. Often too jolly, if you take my meaning, bordering on the riotous in some quarters. However, there are, in addition to the usual ecclesiastical proceedings, a few traditional events I heartily enjoy. Parades, concerts; feiseanna featuring talented performers. Unfortunately, one of them will be impeded this year. A world-famous organization called McNamara's Band is missing one of its primary artists and may not be able to play. This is a terrible shame.

167

"Here is my request. Would you and your faithful dog be willing to make another descent to Earth and persuade Mr. Sherlock Holmes and his medical associate to search out this lost musician and restore him to the band? I have gotten Senior Director Raymond's permission for you to go. Perhaps, artist that you are, you could perform on March 17 while on Earth. Of course, only we incorporeals would be able to appreciate it."

*****

From the journals of Doctor John H. Watson...

Holmes was in another one of his moods as we sat in his Baker Street room, brandies in hand; and he was filling the atmosphere with enough pipe smoke to cause pulmonary damage to our landlady, the saintly Mrs. Hudson. Fortunately, she was in her own quarters on the floor below at the moment and did not have to endure our induced fog. The March weather provided enough haze and miasma to shroud London in thick mist on a daily basis. It required no assistance from us.

"Boredom, my dear Watson, is the curse of the intellectually gifted."

I ignored his lack of personal modesty and riposted, "Holmes, you have been busy to the point of frenzy. How can you possibly be bored? You have been inundated with clients and cases."

"But they are all the deadly same, old man. Yet another socialite with missing jewels. Amateurish embezzlement. Blackmail. Missing husbands. One more violent death. Not a truly interesting or novel item in the lot. But one must make a living, I suppose, and so I accept what comes our way unless it falls well below my rather lenient standards. No divorces or lost cats."

I shook my head in mock despair. "What would satisfy your requirements for excitement? Who or what would provide an interesting challenge? Another Moriarty or Moran?"

"I don't know. I'll recognize it when I see it."

"Hello, Holmes! Hello, Doctor!" called out a spirited, high-pitched voice.

"Arf!"

The 'interesting challenge' stood in our midst with her formidable little canine by her side. Baroness Juliet and Pookie had returned. They were visible and audible only to the two of us. This sometimes led to complications, but she was an impressive colleague, capable of imperceptibly going places and seeing things that we could not. She could also 'flit' immediately from place to place while we struggled with earthbound conveyances. An amazing partner, but unfortunately, dead.

I said, "Milady, welcome back. Delighted to see you again! But wait, something is different! I have it. You've traded your scarlet gown for an emerald green confection. And Pookie has a matching bow. Very attractive. Don't you think so, Holmes?"

"Indeed! So, Baroness, what brings you to our humble abode? Another heaven-inspired conundrum?"

"Yes. Oh, this room is deadly," she said, waving her arm through the smoke. "You'll smoke yourselves to death, and then we'll all be ghosts. Would you believe I'm here on behalf of St. Patrick himself? Hence my green dress. I'm glad you like it.

You'll very shortly have a distinguished Irish gentleman at your doorstep with an interesting dilemma. I'll let him tell his story, but the ancient Bishop of Ireland would greatly appreciate our combined efforts to solve the problem before his feast day on March 17. You'll see why in a few moments."

I looked at Lady Juliet. "How do you know that this gentleman will appear?"

"Oh, Doctor. Trust me, or rather, trust St. Patrick. He has his ways, doesn't he, Pookie?

I swear the dog barked with an Irish brogue.

At this point, Holmes's page Billy risked smoke inhalation and knocked on the door in a pattern we both recognized. I rose and opened the portal just enough for him to hand in a tray with a calling card lavishly decorated with shamrocks. "A Mr. McNamara, Doctor Watson. He does not have an appointment but says it's important; and he requires a wee moment with you and Mr. Holmes."

Billy hesitated before continuing, "He's Irish."

"Just a moment, Billy." I turned to Holmes who looked up at the cloud-covered ceiling, rolled his eyes at Lady Juliet and with a wave of his hand, agreed to see our Celtic visitor.

I turned back to Holmes's pageboy and said, "Wait a few minutes, then show him up." I closed the door and threw open the windows to dispel the tobacco smog. Holmes donned his jacket and settled back, under the careful scrutiny of our ghostly associate and her dog. She sat on a table and Pookie joined her.

We had extinguished our pipes and cleared the atmosphere sufficiently to allow a face-to-face conversation when the sound of footsteps echoed on the seventeen stairs leading to Holmes's rooms – first Billy's familiar tread, and then a strong, almost martial strut. Before I could open the door to welcome our guest, he opened the door himself and strode into the room, hand extended with a glittering mustachioed smile. He wore a muted dark green suit, a matching top hat and a spray of shamrocks in his lapel. In a resonant voice he proclaimed: "Ah, Doctor Watson and Mr. Sherlock Holmes. Top of the mornin' to you. Fergus McNamara at your service. I hope that shortly you will see your way clear to be at my service."

He chuckled. "I have a problem that I think can be a challenge for your formidable skills."

He spoke with a distinctive but quite articulate and cultured brogue. At first glimpse, I suspected he was military, but that was quickly disproved. "I am sure you are familiar with my organization - as fine a marching musical troupe as has ever been gathered together. A true collection of virtuosos who collectively produce sounds unrivalled throughout the world. McNamara's Band!"

When we failed to immediately respond in recognition, he momentarily frowned but then recovered his infectious smile. "Ah, well! We Sons of Erin are accustomed to going unrecognized by our English cousins. Not so for other countries like America." He burst into song. "When General Grant to Ireland came, he took me by the hand. Says he, 'I've never seen the likes of McNamara's Band...'" He doubled over in a booming laugh. We looked on in puzzlement.

"However," he said, "enough self-admiration. I promised to be brief and, sure, I will be. I am involved in a major international incident and it's not with England."

171

Since McNamara had already identified and characterized himself, and his dress and brogue supported his claim, Holmes skipped his usual personal identity parlor game and went immediately into his formulaic introduction, glancing in Lady Juliet's direction. "Please briefly elucidate your problem, sir, leaving out nothing, however insignificant."

This always struck me as a bit of a contradiction, Lady Juliet telepathically announced. *Highly detailed brevity. Ah, well!*

Holmes ignored her. "First off, what brings you and your ensemble to London?"

Unaware of Juliet's presence, he replied. "Why, bless you, Mr. Holmes, we are on tour, performing for the English public as well as the royal and aristocratic great and good. Our reception has been phenomenal, if you'll pardon a bit of braggadocio. 'Right now, we are rehearsin' for a very swell affair. It's an annual celebration. All the gentry will be there...' St. Patrick's Day, ye know. As soon as it's over, we'll be returnin' to Erin. That is, we will be once we solve our problem. You see sir, one of our key performers has gone missing."

Holmes wearily raised his eyebrows. "I assume you have reported this to the police. Tracking down missing persons is their province."

"I have indeed, but there are jurisdictional complications. You see, we are not sure whether he disappeared here, or in Ireland; and to further compound the issue he is a Swedish national. His name is Yulius Eriksson. He calls himself Uncle Yulius and he beats the big bass drum in our band. Both he and his drum are missing. Neither Scotland Yard nor the Irish Garda are providing much help. We have also contacted the Swedish

Police Authority, but since it is unlikely that he was in Sweden when he vanished, they have not taken any steps as yet.

"I should tell you that Yulius is quite eccentric, but he has a magnificent sense of rhythm, and is strong as the proverbial ox. He has to be, in order to handle that huge drum. Oh, one other thing. He is indeed an uncle. His nephew is Sweden's King Oscar II. Yulius may be being held somewhere for ransom, but we and his family have not received any demands for his release."

This last bit of news linking the missing drummer to the Swedish Royal House got Holmes's attention. "I assume you wish me to locate Uncle Yulius."

"And the bass drum. It is highly unusual, very valuable and bears a McNamara's Band imprint, a map of Ireland, an Irish flag and clusters of shamrocks. Right now, we're making do with a smaller drum and a replacement drummer. But they are no substitute for Yulius and Drusilla."

"Drusilla??" I blurted.

"Yes, Doctor! That's the drum's name. Yulius is quite taken with her. "

"When did any of you last see Uncle Yulius?" asked Holmes.

"That's the thing of it, Mr. Holmes. There are several answers to that question. Which version would you like?"

"I always prefer the truth, Mr. McNamara. It makes my task that much easier."

"Well, the truth is, we don't exactly know. Ye see, we had just finished a concert in Dublin and were on our way to London via Holyhead. It was to be the beginnin' of our Grand Tour in England culminatin' on St. Patrick's Day. We were booked on the overnight mail ferry across the Irish Sea. The band traveled together. We stored our luggage and instruments in our shared cabins. All except Yulius. Drusilla was too large to keep in our livin' space, ye see, and he wouldn't let the drum out of his sight. So he said he would be beddin' down in one of the storage holds with Drusilla. He said he'd rejoin us after we landed."

"Did he?"

"No, and none of the band saw him get on or off the boat. He would have had to use a different gangplank to get to the storage hold. None of the boat crew remembered seeing him or the drum.

"The boat ran into some weather and arrived late at Holyhead. We were in a great rush to catch the train to London and everything was helter-skelter. We boarded the train just as it was gettin' ready to pull out. Once we were under way, I walked through the cars and took the roll. Everyone was present and accounted for with instruments and luggage – except Yulius. I thought he might have gotten aboard one of the mail cars with his drum and so I wasn't all that concerned.

"I talked one of the conductors into taking me to the post office and storage cars. The postal staff said they would have remembered a big ornate drum and when I described Yulius, they couldn't recall seeing him either. Long story short, Uncle Yulius wasn't at the station to greet us when we arrived in London. That was two days ago. Since then, I've been searchin' and contactin' the police forces as well as the ship line and railway authorities. Nothing. That's why I'm here."

I shook my head. "A large, older man with a huge, decorated drum can't just disappear like that."

Holmes replied, "Unless he never got on the ship in Dublin or went overboard on the journey. He might also be somewhere in Holyhead. There are possibilities, and as you know, Watson…"

"Yes Holmes, I know. Once you eliminate the impossible, whatever remains, no matter how improbable, must be the truth." I could recite that in my sleep. Juliet laughed and clapped her hands. Pookie wagged her tail furiously.

McNamara stared at us. "Well, Mr. Holmes, are ye goin' to take my case?"

"Yes, Mr. McNamara," he replied, receiving a telepathic cheer from Lady Juliet. "I find this quite interesting. But first, I have some research to perform. One other question. Does the King know his uncle is missing?"

"I haven't informed him yet. I doubt if the Swedish Police have spoken to him, either. Queen Sophia doesn't approve of me or my organization. She and the Court think Yulius is somethin' of an embarrassment."

"A pity! He seems like someone I'd like to meet. Another musician. I'll try to make that happen. Where and when may I contact you?"

"We have a number of performances over the next few days in different London venues. I have an agent here in the city. He will know where I am and how to reach me. Here is his card. I hope you find Yulius alive, safe and well. Thank ye. McNamara's Band isn't the same without him and Drusilla."

When the Hibernian Impresario had descended to the ground floor under the amazed stares of Mrs. Hudson and Billy,

I turned to Holmes. "So your interest has been ignited. What is the research you have to perform?"

"I need to enquire further about this band. Who is McNamara? Could they be leftovers from the Fenian movement? Are they strictly musical entertainers? What is a Swede doing in the group? Especially a Swede who is also a member, however removed, of the royal family? I think a visit with brother Mycroft is called for. There may be a little international intrigue afoot here."

"Really? I thought Yulius might be a royal pariah, from what McNamara implied."

"Perhaps, old man, perhaps!"

A visit to Pall Mall or the Diogenes Club seemed to be on the agenda. Always a unique experience.

The Baroness had several sessions in the past involving Mycroft and the Diogenes Club. He was not one of her favorite people and she went out of her way to show her disdain for the staff and curmudgeons who inhabited the club. However, she shrugged and said. "Pookie and I will flit over there. I'll find you in The Stranger's Room after I get past the prune-faced majordomo. Always such a delight and so is your brother." She left humming "Kathleen Mavourneen."

*****

I have written about Mycroft Holmes in the past. The brothers make an interesting pair. Both are supremely intelligent - a fact they are at pains to continuously demonstrate to each other as well as the world at large. Mycroft holds a shadowy position of great influence with the British government. He hides its true nature behind the title of Chief Auditor or some such.

While Sherlock is a limitless reservoir of nervous energy, Mycroft has raised lethargy and self-indulgence to a major art form. Older, taller and definitely heavier than Sherlock, Mycroft seldom bestirs himself beyond his fixed routine. He lives in rooms in Pall Mall. He regularly walks around the corner each morning to his offices in Whitehall and in the evening, walks back to Pall Mall. A dedicated and knowledgeable gourmet/gourmand, he then dines at the Diogenes Club from quarter to five until twenty to eight. The Club is located across from his lodging. He seldom breaks this routine or goes anywhere else.

Holmes describes the Diogenes Club as follows: "There are many men in London, you know, who, some from shyness, some from misanthropy, have no wish for the company of their fellows. Yet they are not averse to comfortable chairs and the latest periodicals. It is for their convenience that the Diogenes Club was started, and it now contains the most unsociable and unclubbable men in town. No member is permitted to take the least notice of any other one. Save in the Stranger's Room no talking is, under any circumstances, allowed, and three offences, if brought to the notice of the committee, render the talker liable to expulsion. My brother was one of the founders and I have myself found it a very soothing atmosphere."

I had been to the Diogenes Club several times and had come close to being ejected and permanently barred for talking outside The Stranger's Room. When we arrived, the dour and stiff-necked doorman greeted Holmes and frowned in my direction. Making an exception to the silence rule, the reception clerk summoned Mycroft and pointed us at the empty Stranger's Room. Empty that is, except for a feisty white dog and her feisty green-clad mistress. Mycroft was in the process of finishing off his substantial evening meal, and it was some time before he made an appearance.

"To what do I owe this visit, brother mine? I cannot believe it is strictly a social call."

"No, it is not. Once again, I would like to drink at your infinite fountain of information."

"I suspected as much. A new case?"

"Yes and a rather strange one. But first, a few questions. Are you familiar with an Irish marching ensemble called McNamara's Band? They are in London on a Grand Tour."

"This not the first time they have appeared in London or Great Britain," recalled Mycroft. "The Home Office investigated them on their last appearance. They pronounced them to be harmless entertainers, quite good actually, but totally apolitical. Do you think otherwise? Has their membership changed?"

"Not that I know of, but I have been approached by their leader, Fergus McNamara, to help find a missing band member. An unusual bass drummer and his equally unusual drum. Both have disappeared." As expected, he said nothing about Lady Juliet or St. Patrick.

"As usual, I assume the police have not been of any assistance."

"Not Scotland Yard, the Irish Garda or the Swedish Police Authority."

Mycroft tapped his finger thoughtfully. "Why are the Swedes involved?"

"The missing drummer is Swedish. The only non-Irish member of the band. His name is Yulius Eriksson. He is something of an eccentric, but very popular, especially with the ladies."

I smiled and added, "The drum's name is Drusilla. Lavishly decorated, huge and very valuable!"

Holmes spoke up. "He calls himself Uncle Yulius. He is the uncle of the Swedish King Oscar II."

Mycroft winced. "Now I see why you approached me. You are no doubt aware that there has been a long-lasting state of dissension between Norway and Sweden. Nothing official, mind you, but occasional flareups staged by malcontents on both sides."

I said, "Not unlike our relationship with the Irish."

Mycroft paused. "Yes, Doctor, I am sorry to say. Where did this individual vanish?"

"That is part of the problem. Somewhere in transit between Dublin and London. It could be the Dublin docks, the Irish Sea ferry, the Holyhead docks, the mail train to Euston or the station itself. No one claims to have seen him at any of those venues. By the way, he travels constantly with the drum. Won't let it out of his sight. It is painted with the band's title, the Irish flag and map, shamrocks and I think the drum's name, Drusilla. He was probably wearing his green marching uniform. He is large, white hair, very strong and still handsome for a man his age. "

Mycroft laughed. "Could anyone look more unusual? Really, Sherlock, what is the problem? A thorough police search would seem to be in order. "

"In all three countries? What would the Home Office say to that? I need to know more about the Swedish situation. It seems their Queen is not pleased with the King's uncle. Do you think a member of the Court decided to remove the Royal Irritant?"

"Possible... but improbable!"

I guffawed. Both Holmes brothers stared at me.

"Mycroft," said Holmes, turning back to his brother, "can you arrange an interview with the Swedish Ambassador?"

"Count Carl Lewenhaupt? Yes, we've met at several diplomatic bun-fights. I hate those things. The conversation is dull. The issues petty and the food inedible. The Ambassador, however, is a rather likeable chap, and our countries have lived cooperatively over time. I'll contact him for you. What did you say the missing person's name is?"

"Yulius Eriksson. Uncle to the King."

"Ah yes! I shall send you a wire with an appointment."

*****

Our visit was agreed and scheduled for ten o'clock next morning. The Swedish Embassy is a modest building near Marylebone Street, well-furnished, but hardly in the pretentious class of the continental superpowers. The Ambassador's aide met us in the reception area, identified himself as Lars Gustafsson, and invited us to follow him to the office of the envoy. Count Lewenhaupt smiled, rose to greet us and extended his hand in welcome. Unseen by all but Holmes and myself, Lady Juliet took a seat and the dog climbed under a chair.

"Mr. Holmes, Doctor Watson. Delighted to meet you! I must confess, Doctor, that I have a passion for your stories. And of course, Mr. Holmes, I am fascinated by your formidable detection skills. Doctor, when is your next story coming out?"

"Shortly, sir. I shall see that you receive a signed copy when it is released."

"I would be most grateful. Now, how can I be of service to such distinguished company?"

The Baroness chuckled. *You don't know the half of it,* she said telepathically, her voice directed towards Holmes and me. *I'm distinguished, too.*

Holmes replied, "We are in search of one of your countrymen who disappeared a short time ago."

"Goodness, is he accused of some misdeed?"

"No sir, at least not as far as we know. He may be the victim of foul play, but even that is doubtful."

The envoy replied, "Men and women vanish all the time. I am occasionally called upon to assist in the search. What makes this individual and his situation worthy of my attention?"

"He is the King's Uncle, Yulius Eriksson."

Lars, the Ambassador's aide smiled. "Ah, the Irish Drummer! He's a member of a marching band. McGuiness, is it?"

I replied, "McNamara, Mr. Gustafsson. Mr. McNamara is our client. Uncle Yulius disappeared along with his highly unusual bass drum while enroute from Dublin to London. No one seems to know exactly where or when. We have been commissioned to find him. The police have jurisdictional concerns and have not been forthcoming. That includes the Swedish Police Authority."

Holmes joined in. "Since he is a member of the Royal family, we thought it would be wise to consult you."

The Ambassador nodded. "Quite reasonable. Well, his predilection for beating a bass drum has not endeared him to the Queen and other members of the court. His nephew, the King, is fond of him, however. His self-imposed exile in Ireland seems to render moot his status as a Royal; he's seen more as a *persona non grata*. Thus far, the band has not attempted to perform in Sweden. I suspect the Queen would prevent that from happening. A pity. I hear they are quite good. I may go to one of their concerts while they are here in London."

"What can you tell us about him and his own family?"

"Well, if he ever decides to retire his drumming, he can take up the title of Count Yulius. His wife died several years ago. He has two children of his own – a son in Stockholm, who shares the Queen's embarrassment at his father's musical endeavors; and a married daughter, living, oddly enough, in Ireland. Lady Astrid, the wife of Lord Pendleton, an Anglo-Irish peer and member of Parliament. They have substantial holdings in Roscommon. I think it was she who got Yulius interested in McNamara's Band."

"Does he live with them?" I asked hopefully.

"I don't think so. I'm not sure where he lives. I suppose he visits every now and again. Shall I contact her for you? She will be disturbed by his disappearance."

"That would be most helpful. We wondered if there was a chance he had been kidnapped by Norwegian dissidents."

The Ambassador looked at his aide. "Have we received any indication of foul play, Lars?"

"No, sir. No demands for ransom or political action. I've heard nothing from the Court, either."

Holmes pointed out, "I don't know if the King is aware of his uncle's disappearance."

"He probably is, Mr. Holmes, if McNamara approached the Swedish Police Authority."

Holmes shifted in his chair. "No one seems very excited about it."

The Ambassador chuckled. "It's not the first time Yulius has gone missing. I suspect he and his drum will reappear when he is of a mood."

"I'm told he was quite excited about making this Grand Tour. Deliberately vanishing without telling anyone would seem a bit strange."

"Yulius _is_ strange. I shall send a message on to Lady Astrid. Give Lars your address… and please don't forget to send me your next book, Doctor."

*****

When we returned to Baker Street, the Baroness was intrigued with the prospect of meeting another member of the female nobility. "This is getting more and more interesting, Holmes. My money is on Queen Sophia having Yulius kidnapped. Maybe this Lady Astrid is involved. What do the two of you think of that?"

"Data, data, Milady. It is much too early for surmises."

Wearin' of the Green

We had a message from Fergus McNamara inviting us to a late lunch. No doubt, he was looking for a progress report. My stomach was issuing a 'no progress' report, so I cast a vote in favor of a hearty meal. We met at the Old Horseshoe which featured Irish fare. Lady Juliet doesn't eat, but Pookie does. The Baroness fed her a 'Heavenly Chew' snack which she greedily wolfed down. I was dubious about Irish cuisine but was pleasantly surprised by a savory Guinness beef stew. Clearly, McNamara was trying to impress us with Celtic cookery and culture.

"The Band is holding a concert this evenin' at the Garrick Theatre, gentlemen, and I would be powerfully pleased to have you as my guests. You will see and hear what all the ravin' is about. We are sold out. Of course, we are not at our very best without Yulius and Drusilla. But 'twill do, 'twill have to do till they return. Do you have any news?"

Holmes smiled, looked at me and said, "Doctor Watson and I would be pleased to join you and the band this evening. As to news, we are performing our due diligence. We met this morning with the Swedish Ambassador. He confirmed the feelings of the Queen toward Yulius who, by the way, would be a Count if he abandoned his drum-thumping. The world of music would no doubt suffer, however."

I interjected. "There are no indications that political dissidents are at work, although one can't be sure. We leave tomorrow morning for Roscommon to meet his daughter, Lady Astrid. I understand you know her."

"Lady Astrid? A wonderful lass. Not a lass at all. A grand mature woman. Met her at a fête in Galway. Her husband, Lord

Pendleton, is a bit of a social climbin' snob, and her brother is a Scandinavian twit, but she's the salt of the earth. 'Twas she who introduced me to Yulius, her father. He was stayin' with her, much to her husband's annoyance, and playin' drums with a small village group. I heard him and offered him a place with the band. Yulius was reluctant until he made the acquaintance of Drusilla. She can be a very persuasive and dramatic drum. Give Astrid my very best regards, although what she can tell ye about Yulius' whereabouts, I just don't know. See ye tonight at seven at the Garrick." He paid the bill and exited whistling an Irish tune I couldn't identify.

*****

We spent the rest of the afternoon back at Baker Street preparing for our hoped-for jaunt to Roscommon. We were unsure as to whether or not we would have the opportunity, since we had still not heard from Lady Astrid. Our journey was in a state of suspension.

Holmes was paging through a thick brochure and looked over at me.

"Watson, what do you know about Irish Dance?"

"Precious little, Holmes. Why do you ask?"

"It seems McNamara's Band offers an exhibition of Irish Stepdance as part of its concerts. Lady Astrid is one of their group's sponsors. She was a hard shoe dancer herself, in her earlier days. She probably inherited her rhythmic skills from her father."

Juliet squeaked. "A dancer! A kindred soul. I must see her. Did you know Pookie can dance on her hind legs? Show them, Pook!"

The dog reared up, did a series of graceful turns and I swear, bowed to us.

Holmes, nonplussed, continued, "Her husband met her at a feis and, as many males would, pursued her. Strange that he is no longer enthralled by Irish music and dance. Ah well, now that he is an aspiring MP, such frivolity must be deplored. A pity. However, Lady Astrid seems to be an independent soul, if McNamara is to be believed. Like you, Baroness, I have a suspicion that she is somehow involved in Yulius disappearance."

"On what grounds, Mr. Holmes?"

"At the moment, none. As usual, I need data. It's my intellectual lifeblood. However, let us settle for a bit of Hibernian entertainment. Shall we repair to the Garrick?"

*****

The lobby of the theatre was beginning to fill when we arrived. Fergus McNamara, resplendent in his bright green uniform. had been waiting for us. He waved his arms vigorously and rushed over, pieces of cardboard and a cluster of shamrocks in each hand. "Gentlemen, it's good to see ye. Here are your tickets – best seats in the house. There is someone I want ye to meet."

He took us by the arm and marched us to an alcove where a mature, but highly attractive, woman stood with a young man. "Lady Astrid Pendleton, may I introduce Mr. Sherlock Holmes and Doctor John Watson? They are working with me in trying to find Yulius."

She smiled and extended her hand, "Mr. Holmes, Doctor Watson. Such a pleasure! Your fame precedes you. This is my son James. He is an aficionado of Irish music, much to his father's chagrin."

The Baroness eyed James very carefully and then turned her attention to Lady Astrid. She approved.

The youth shook our hands enthusiastically. "An honor to meet both of you. I am also a devotee of your stories, Doctor and it's a privilege to meet the Great Detective in person."

I bowed and Holmes took the introductions in stride. "Lady Astrid. Delighted to make your acquaintance. You have just saved Doctor Watson and me a great deal of time, effort and expense. We were prepared to leave for Roscommon to meet you tomorrow. Perhaps you received a message from the Swedish Ambassador requesting an appointment? As Mr. McNamara told you, at his request, we have been engaged in a search for your father."

"Oh, Mr. Holmes. I am so sorry, but I have been here in London all week, and probably not getting all my messages. I hope I have prevented you from going to Ireland on a fruitless wild goose chase. What is all this about Yulius?"

McNamara blurted, "He's missing, Astrid. Him and his drum Drusilla. He's a mainstay of McNamara's Band. We are making do without him on this tour, but just barely. Do you have idea where he might be?"

She looked puzzled. "None at all. Did you think he might have been at Roscommon?"

I replied, "The thought had occurred to us."

Lady Astrid frowned. "Well, he wasn't."

James stared at her. "Yes, he was, Mother. I saw him. Well, not him really, but his drum, and you know they are inseparable. It was in the gatehouse when we were leaving for Dublin and the ferry. I assumed you knew."

Before this conversation could go any further, the theatre manager interrupted. "Mr. McNamara, it's time. Your band is assembled behind the curtain. The audience is seated. May I ask you gentlemen and the lady to take your places so we can begin in a timely fashion?"

We agreed to resume the conversation at the interval of the performance. McNamara ran off to be with his charges. We rushed down the aisle, pleased to find that our seats were indeed the best in the house. Juliet and Pookie, invisible to all, took places at the side of the stage.

No sooner had we sat down, when the curtain opened with a blaring fanfare.

The festivities began with the customary "God Save the King." The anthem was well performed. His Majesty was not in attendance. No surprise. He was still in mourning for his recently deceased mother.

I directed my thoughts towards Lady Juliet. *Have you met the Queen? Surely she is in Heaven.*

She is, Lady Juliet replied, *but she has been taken up with her reunion with Prince Albert, and not appearing in public.*

McNamara then stepped forward onto the apron of the stage. He bowed to the loud and lengthy applause. "Good evenin', everyone." Over a soft underlying rhythm section, he half-sang, half spoke:

"Oh, me name is McNamara, I'm the leader of the band.

Although we're few in numbers, we're the finest in the land.

We play at wakes and weddin's, and at every fancy ball,

And when we play at funerals, we play the March from Saul."

He continued into a chorus, supported by the appropriate instruments:

"Oh, the drums go bang, and the cymbals clang, and the horns they blaze away,

McCarthy pumps the old bassoon while I the pipes do play,

And Hennessey Tennessey tootles the flute, and the music is something grand,

A credit to old Ireland is McNamara's Band!"

The band swept in with a full burst of sound, and applause echoed throughout the hall. There was a spontaneous standing ovation and the waving of Irish flags. I raised my cluster of shamrocks and Holmes even smiled. Lady Astrid was beside herself, as was James. The evening was beginning with a true Hibernian "bang."

The program carried on with a series of Irish marches, folk music and love songs for which the sons and daughters of Erin are rightfully famous. Several times, Lady Juliet rose from her perch and swayed to the music. Pookie joined her. At last we reached the interval.

McNamara had ordered tea for all of us although I am sure something stronger would have been preferred. James and I went off to visit the facilities, creating a conversational vacuum.

When we returned, Lady Astrid picked up the discussion. "No, James. I did not know the drum was there. In the gatehouse, you say? I suppose it was Drusilla. There's no mistaking that ornate instrument. But where was Father? Was he staying in the gatehouse? What was he doing for food and drink? I suppose he was wearing his band uniform?"

"Cook has a soft spot for Grandfather. If he revealed himself to her, I'm sure he was well supplied."

I asked, "But where is he now? Is he still in Roscommon?"

Holmes replied, "I suspect he is a lot closer."

I looked quizzically at my friend. I got an enigmatic smile in return. "You see, Watson, but you don't observe!" How many times have I heard that?

The band had returned and were moving to the rear of the stage, leaving a large open space for the dancers.

Lady Astrid clapped her hands eagerly like a little girl. "It's time for my protégés." The band broke into Stepdance music, and a flight of lovely young women skipped out, one after another, to the center of the open space. Hard shoe reverberations echoed as each girl jumped, spun and stomped on the floor. The sounds were reminiscent of my time in the military, but never with such beautiful companions. They then formed into a unison body, and the sound was precise and intense with the Band and the rapid-firing feet. Tap, tap, tap, snap, snap, snap!

Eventually they ended their highly entertaining routine, as did Lady Juliet who had invisibly joined them. The retinue bowed to intense applause and skipped off. And then… Boom! Boom! Boom! From the wings, stage right, came the unmistakable sound of Drusilla joining in the joyful noise.

Yulius, decked out in vibrant green, festooned with shamrocks, and marching in exact time with the other percussionists, had come back. Applause erupted from the audience, the dancers and even the band. McNamara was beaming. Yulius took over the center stage, carefully lowered Drusilla to the floor, smiled at the band, waved his drumsticks and over a subdued rhythm, sang out:

"Oh, my name is Uncle Yulius and from Sweden I did come.

To play in McNamara's Band and beat the big Bass Drum. *(Boom, Boom)*

And when I march along the street, the ladies think I'm grand. *(Boom, Boom)*

They shout, "There's Uncle Yulius playing with an Irish Band. *(Boom, Boom)*

Oh, I wear a bunch of shamrocks and a uniform of green. *(Boom, Boom)*

And I am the funniest looking Swede that you have ever seen. *(Boom, Boom)*

There's O'Briens and Ryans and Sheehans and Meehans, They come from Ireland. *(Boom, Boom)*

But, by Yimminy, I'm the only Swede in McNamara's Band." *(Boom, Boom)*

This inspired gales of laughter and applause, and the band started up a rollicking rendition of their theme, *Ta-Da-Da-Da-Da-Da-Da-Da-Boom,Boom,* as they marched off the stage with Yulius and Drusilla in the lead. McNamara walked out on the apron, waved his hand for silence and said, "Ladies and Gentlemen! There are several guests I want to innerduce. First is Lady Astrid Pendleton, daughter of our own Uncle Yulius who, incidentally, is a real uncle, to the Swedish King Oscar II himself." This brought gasps and mumbles from the audience. "She is the sponsor of our wonderful Irish Dancers who, I hope, ye enjoyed this evenin.'" He called out, "Lady Astrid!" over the applause. She rose and waved.

"Also in our audience is the legendary consulting detective, Mr. Sherlock Holmes, and his famous associate Doctor John Watson, who writes those wonderful stories about Mr. Holmes. Gentlemen!" I rose, blushing, and took a very curtailed bow. Holmes stayed seated but deigned to wave listlessly.

McNamara continued, "Thank ye all fer comin' tonight. I hope ye really enjoyed yerselves. We are on a Grand Tour here in England through St. Patrick's Day, and appearing in many venues, and on marches. There are brochures in the lobby describing our itinerary. Please visit us again and bring your family and friends. Good evenin' to ye all."

The crowd started to move out. Lady Astrid was surrounded by well-wishers. Holmes raced for the doors, almost knocking over a geriatric music enthusiast and leaving me to contend with the mob. I ended up signing concert programs for a number of fans of the Great Detective.

McNamara came up to me. "We are having a wee party in the Groundlings Pub across the street. Please join us. I want to also corner Yulius and find out what his 'now you see me, now you don't' act was all about."

I concurred. I also needed to track down Holmes, who I knew would not be far away.

He was sitting in a corner of the Groundlings pub, nursing a brandy, waiting for me, and watching the band members and dancers streaming in and heading for the Fife and Drum Room and the festivities. The musicians were not wasting any time lubricating their pipes, and the dancers were massaging their legs and feet while soaking up ales and gins.

"Sorry to have abandoned you, Watson, but you know how I feel about pressing crowds."

"Well, I did develop a case of writer's cramp. Look, here comes Lady Astrid and James. She looks a bit flustered."

She spotted us, smiled and wove her way to our table. "Gentlemen, will you be joining in the merrymaking? James is awed by the musicians and show people. This place celebrates all the theatrical greats who have trod the boards at the Garrick. My husband would never approve of my being here, so let's not tell him, shall we? He doesn't like my dancers, either. Have you seen my father?"

*****

Almost in response to her question, the pub doors opened yet again, and an ornate bass drum entered with drummer attached. Yulius had made his way across the road, still resplendent in his uniform while struggling to manipulate Drusilla, manage the pub doors and work his way through the crowd. He saw us and nodded. His hands and arms were fully occupied. James rushed to give him a hand as McNamara arrived on the scene. We all went into a smaller room away from the crush of the revelers. McNamara sent a waiter off for drinks. Then he turned and asked:

"Yulius, you old rascal, where have ye been? The band doesn't sound the same without you and yer drum. I've had the police lookin' for ye… and this is Sherlock Holmes the Great Detective and Doctor Watson, his associate. They've been on your trail."

Lady Astrid joined in. "Yes, Father. We thought you were kidnapped, murdered, or even worse!"

He replied, "I'm fine, Astrid. I've been hiding in Roscommon. I just arrived in London today. I fought off a pair of toughs in Dublin who were trying to steal Drusilla. One of them now has a black eye from my drumsticks. What would the vandals want with my drum? I don't know why, or who sent them, but I decided to stay in the gatehouse until I was sure there would be no repeats. Do you have any idea, Mr. Holmes?"

"I have suspicions, Uncle Yulius, but as yet, insufficient evidence. I will continue to follow up."

McNamara breathed a sigh of relief. "I'll continue to pay your fees and expenses, Mr. Holmes, and yours as well, Doctor. We can't let this happen again."

Lady Astrid agreed. "If I can spend money on dancers, I can certainly call on my income to protect my father."

Yulius smiled at her and Fergus McNamara. "And Drusilla!" he exclaimed.

"And, of course, Drusilla!" said Fergus. "In the meantime, how about a glass of stout? Let's join the band and dancers. Wonderful to have ye back, old boy!"

Holmes turned to me. "It seems we are going to make that journey to Ireland after all."

I replied, "I'm still packed."

Next morning, a messenger came to our door. He had a note from James Pendleton. "Mr. Holmes and Doctor Watson. If you are planning to visit our estate in Roscommon, you should know that only the domestics will be there. My father, Lord Pendleton, is currently in London at a sitting of Parliament and my mother and I will be here for the remainder of the month. Uncle Yulius will be staying with us when he is not taken up with concerts and marches with the band. We are all staying at the Savoy. We stand ready to assist in any way."

I chuckled. "The charms of the Irish countryside are indeed elusive, but I don't bemoan losing a trip over the Irish Sea. What is our plan?"

"I think it's time to interview the Parliamentary member. Let us see if we can arrange a meeting at one of the Savoy's excellent bars."

No doubt at the urging of his wife, Pendleton reluctantly agreed to meet with us at six o'clock. Holmes had managed earlier to reach Seamus O'Hara, an Inspector friend of his in the Dublin Garda, and give him descriptions of the two yobs who had set upon poor Yulius and his fabulous drum. "One of them will be nursing a severe black eye," Holmes told him.

Wearin' of the Green

In the meantime, Holmes tended to another outstanding case and, since we were not going to Ireland after all, I went to my surgery to relieve my locum of his obligations. A bit later, we joined the band once again to observe one of their rehearsals. McNamara had added a team of acrobats to participate in the theatre performances, although they wanted to perform in the streets as well. He was indeed a true impresario.

When we returned to Baker Street, a message from Inspector O'Hara was waiting for us. He had tracked down two perennial miscreants who practiced violence for hire. They protested that the black eye was the result of a pub-related incident. Presented with the reports and descriptions by Holmes and Yulius, however, they finally caved and admitted they were paid to steal the crazy-looking bass drum. The bloke that hired them spoke like a swell, they said. They didn't ask for, or get, a name. They were paid in cash. The two of them definitely didn't want to have any further truck with Uncle Julius or "his damn drum."

We then journeyed over to the American Bar at the Savoy to await Yulius' son-in-law, Lord Pendleton. As expected, he arrived late, and looked askance at Holmes and myself. He ordered a "Martinez" cocktail. He produced a vapid smile and said "In the American Bar, order American. Now, gentlemen, what pressing issue requires me to spend my valuable time speaking with you?"

Holmes tossed diplomacy to the winds and said, "We want to know why you hired two Irish thugs to spirit away Yulius Eriksson's bass drum. They failed, by the way."

The Peer looked at us in a rage and nearly spilled his drink. "How dare you! I thought I had heard all the nonsense I could stand for one day in the Parliamentary sitting, but this takes all. Call yourself a consulting detective? Well, mister detective, look elsewhere for your culprit, because I had nothing at all to do with that old fool losing his drum. What does he call it? Scylla?"

"Drusilla! And she is still in Uncle Yulius' possession."

"I'm sorry to hear that. He is a major embarrassment, banging away with that ridiculous marching band. I daresay my wife is far too tolerant of him, and I object to the expense she incurs to sponsor those stomping hussies she calls 'Stepdancers.' And now you two. What are you costing me?"

I replied. "Nothing. Our client is Mr. Fergus McNamara."

"That charlatan! Good! Waste his money, not mine. To be absolutely clear, I categorically deny any involvement with Yulius' disappearing drum." He gulped his drink, coughed and rose from his chair. "I bid you a good evening, and I insist that you have no further dealings with my wife, or her senile father."

As he stalked off, leaving us to pay the bill, I said, "Well, that certainly went well. Now what? Do you believe him?"

Holmes produced his trademark enigmatic smile, "Oddly enough, I do. No flustering or sign of guilt. Just pure irritated snobbery. No! I don't like him… but I believe him. That leaves my actual first choice of offender to contend with. I must contact Mycroft again."

*****

197

Next morning found us sitting in Mycroft's offices in Whitehall where he conducted his mysterious activities for the British government.

"So, Sherlock, your missing percussionist has reappeared. Does he offer any explanation for his absence?"

Holmes shrugged. "He claims two Irish toughs waylaid him in Dublin when he was preparing to travel with the band, and attempted to abscond with Drusilla, his bass drum. He fought them off, reclaimed the instrument and decided to hide at the family estate in Roscommon in case there was another attempt made. No one but the staff was at the house. The family members were all here in London. As you know, Lord Pendleton is a member of Parliament."

Mycroft laughed, "And an offensive git."

I laughed with him, "Indeed, an offensive git."

"But not responsible for ordering the attack," said Holmes. "Anyway, after a few days, Yulius decided the coast was now clear and rejoined the band yesterday. McNamara is delighted. Brother dear, can you get us another appointment with the Swedish Ambassador?"

I looked up, shocked. "Surely, you don't suspect the Ambassador!"

"No, but I suspect a Swede!"

*****

Later that afternoon, we found ourselves back at the Swedish embassy. The Baroness and her dog were with us, floating unseen in the corner. The Ambassador's aide, Lars Gustafsson, greeted us. "Back again, gentlemen? I'm afraid you will have a short wait for his Excellency. One of those diplomatic issues that crop up without warning. Is Uncle Yulius still missing?"

"He has been found. Actually, Mr. Gustafsson, it is you we wish to speak with."

"Me?" He twitched. "Why, certainly; but I don't know how I can help you. Is there still a problem if the King's erratic uncle has returned?"

Holmes stared at him. "He was attacked by a pair of Irish hoodlums who were attempting to steal his drum. He fought them off and disappeared for a few days for safety. The toughs have been apprehended and they confessed."

Mr. Gustafsson twitched again. "Is Yulius alright?" he asked.

"Yes, but one of his muggers is sporting a severe black eye. Yulius is a formidable opponent. He has to be, to carry and play that huge drum."

"Well, I'm glad to hear it. Now, how can I help you?"

"You can tell me whether you hired those toughs on your own, or at someone else's direction."

Mr. Gustafsson appeared shocked; then, trembling slightly, he stuttered: "I-I-I d-don't know what-what you mean."

"I'm afraid you do," said Holmes. "You never told these men your name, so they couldn't incriminate you. But we have a record of you making a quick round trip to Dublin on the day Yulius disappeared. You foolishly used your own name and cited 'ambassadorial priority' for the journey. Now, I doubt you thought this up yourself."

Our floating vision in green laughed. *Of course he didn't! It would have taken initiative.*

Gustafsson recovered his sangfroid. "Alright! I was acting for the Queen's Chamberlain. Her Majesty has been increasingly irritated by Uncle Yulius and his antics. It was the Chamberlain's idea to have the drum stolen. It was my job to make it happen. What do you propose to do about it? This Embassy is Swedish territory and you, Scotland Yard, and the Irish Garda have no standing. I doubt if anyone is going to extradite me on such a minor matter... and besides, your proof is quite flimsy."

Holmes was about to speak when the Ambassador's office door opened and several people filed out.

"Mr. Holmes. Good to see you again. And you too, Doctor Watson. I'm still looking forward to my signed book. Now, how can I be of service?"

"A small but rather important problem, sir. Perhaps Mr. Gustafsson would like to tell you about it?"

Epilogue

March 17th. St. Patrick's Day. Lady Juliet and Pookie were staying on until the festivities were over. They were currently ensconced on the sofa. I was visiting 221B Baker Street, and Mrs. Hudson had sustained us with another of her full English breakfasts, when Billy, the page, came bursting into the room.

"Mr. Holmes, Doctor Watson, Mrs. Hudson! Come quickly to the door. Oh, it's ever so grand."

Wearin' of the Green

We swiftly descended the seventeen steps and emerged from the portal to the sound of blaring trumpets, bassoons and tootling flutes. McNamara had brought his green-clad band to Baker Street and we were to be serenaded. McNamara himself was playing the pipes. He waved and bowed in our direction. Several Stepdancers were tapping on the cobblestones in front of Lady Astrid and James, who stood on the curb. The glamorous ghost and capering canine joined the dancers, laughing and singing. I found myself cheering.

Then the band split into two echelons, and a tall robust figure moved between them, pounding a profusely decorated bass drum. Drusilla had come and she had brought her companion with her. He sang out:

"Oh, my name is Uncle Yulius and from Sweden I did come.

To play in McNamara's Band and beat the big bass drum. *(Boom, Boom)*

And when I march along the street, the ladies think I'm grand, *(Boom, Boom)*

They shout "There's Uncle Yulius playing with an Irish Band! *(Boom, Boom)*

*****

Behind the Pearly Gates, a tall, white-bearded cleric in a green robe, holding an ornate crozier and wearing a modest mitre, stood, eyes twinkling, and broke into a beatific smile.

Good Heavens, Holmes

*Earth time: December 1902 **Paradise time:** Eternity, as usual.*

The Baroness Crestwell, Lady Juliet Armstrong, deceased, was returning from her session at Celestial Flying School when she spotted an unusual figure standing by the sparkling opaline doors of her mansion. She looked down at her little white dog and said, "Pookie, is that who I think it is? What is he doing here? Sherlock Holmes, as I live and breathe! How did you get here? Are you dead?"

"No, Milady," Holmes said, as Lady Juliet landed before him. "Still very much alive and earthly. I am here as a result of an unusual and confidential assignment I received from Senior Heavenly Director Raymond. A very agreeable chap, by the way. He requested our joint services, if you are willing, to work on a cosmic issue that could affect the earthly world, perhaps the universe. Heaven would be exempt, of course. We are to establish another partnership, as usual. Watson will be involved, and of course, Mistress Pookie."

"If I am willing? A new adventure? Certainly!" While recently flitting about with Pookie, the pair of them had a near miss with an Angelic Transport Command chariot bringing new applicants to the Pearly Gates. No damage could be done; they were all ephemeral, after all, but it was damned (oops) embarrassing. Then came the citation from Heavenly Traffic

Control (HTC) requiring the two of them to enroll for Remedial Flight Lessons. Even more embarrassing!

However, the Baroness and her dog were becoming highly proficient fliers. She was learning new maneuvers and Pookie was engaging in aerial dog fights. Juliet's swoop was more refined, and she actually could flit a loop, and land more softly. She grudgingly admitted the lessons were worthwhile.

So much so, she and Pookie were invited to join The True Angels flight demonstration squadron (wingless division). The unit is the oldest formal aerobatic team in existence. Being natural performers, the two of them leaped at the opportunity. What a frolic! What a team! The dog was a sensation. So was Juliet!

Her lessons continued. She had just returned from a session on night flying. Peculiar, since the sun never sets in heaven. Next on the agenda was long-distance Earth navigation. Another strange subject.

"All right Holmes, I still sing in the choir, but there are only so many ways to chant 'Hosanna!' I'll leave that to the Cherubim and Seraphim. I actually miss working on one of those mad excursions we've been involved in. Let me change out of my flight suit—it's scarlet, of course—and into my new frock. All of my gowns are scarlet, you know. I'll fetch my formal halo and we can go. On the way, you can tell me about this colossal problem that we'll be dealing with. Pookie, your halo is askew. You need a new red bow, and you could use another bath; but we'll let that pass. So, Mr. Holmes, what's this huge problem?"

"Hell is freezing over."

"What? Holmes, Watson is right. Your sense of humor goes to extremes."

"A metaphoric turn of phrase, my dear Baroness. Still, an event we didn't deem possible is in the offing."

"That sounds delicious. Is it so important that you got Raymond to admit you inside the Gates?"

"That permission came from... higher in the chain of command. They are quite concerned and have commissioned us to investigate. You, Watson, Pookie and me."

"Well, you should be flattered. Quite an honor. But you are, after all, the world's greatest detective."

Holmes rolled his eyes. "You know how I react to honor and flattery."

"Yes, you are a sour old stick sometimes."

Holmes replied, "You also know how I react to insults."

"I am sorry. Please, don't keep me in suspense. What or whom are we pursuing?"

"I don't know, at least not yet."

"Wonderful, Holmes. I just learned how to fly in the dark. Now I'll be flying blind. Stop being so damned mysterious."

"Language, Milady, language; here of all places. Well, someone is trying to flip the Earth's magnetic poles, and may be succeeding."

"Is that all? I thought this was supposed to be a big problem."

"I see your finishing school did not include a course in geology."

"My 'finishing school' was the chorus line at the Orpheum, and the arena stage at the Palladium. But as you know,

I was a dramatic and musical star. I still am. I am not a dumb chorus girl who married an aristocrat. So why don't you enlighten me, Mr. Super Geologist?"

Holmes silently counted to ten. "My apologies! Let us go to Baker Street and I will inform you and Watson together. I may need your assistance leaving Heaven and getting back there. This 'flitting' thing is not easy on aging human skin and bones. By the way, I am seriously pursuing retirement."

"Retirement? Say not so! All right! I'll share several of my flying lessons with you, but don't try it by yourself. Heavenly Traffic Control frowns on unguided missiles in and out of the atmosphere." She giggled and grabbed his hands.

"Down we go!"

*****

Doctor Watson's wife was off on yet another one of her visits to relatives. *Who's counting?* he thought, finding himself at loose ends. Still recuperating from his recent near-fatal wound from a rifle shot, he gingerly made his way out of his Queen Anne Street residence and surgery and hailed a passing cab with his cane. "221 Baker Street, my good man."

He arrived just as Lady Juliet and Holmes flitted into existence in front of the doorway. "Watson, old boy. How are you? You seem to be recovering well. Come in, come in. Can you manage the stairs? Perhaps the Baroness can give you an assist. She just flew me down from Heaven in the finest traditions of the Heavenly Air Force."

Watson stared. "She... did... *what?* Y-you were... where?"

"Ah, poor Watson. Fear not! All will be revealed. I hear Mrs. Hudson coming to the door. She'll lend you a hand."

The door opened, and Mrs. Hudson peeked her head out to see who was making all the fuss on her doorstep. "Oh Doctor, how good to see you up and around. Here, just grab my arm. This stairwell will be the death of us all." They slowly made their way up to Holmes's (and formerly Watson's) chambers.

"Would you care for tea, Mr. Holmes, Doctor?"

"Thank you, no!"

As Mrs. Hudson left, the Baroness sighed. "Now there, Pookie, is something I miss. An afternoon English tea." The dog remembered snacks stealthily passed down to her from the tea table and whined. "Oh, stop your complaining. I brought along a sack of heavenly chewies for you. You get to eat. I don't. Celestial rules. I may lead a protest. Here! Just one! They have to last."

She turned to Watson. "And now, Detective Holmes has some exciting news for us. Something about flipping magnetic poles. I'm flipping confused."

"Flipping magnetic poles? I say, Holmes, that's a scientific old wives' tale."

Holmes shook his head. "I once thought so, Watson. I no longer do."

"That was supposed to have happened over 42,000 years ago. There's very little proof."

"Will one of you scientific prodigies kindly enlighten me about this magnetic stuff. If not, I'm heading back to Heaven to look up Michael Faraday. He's Mr. Magnetism both ways. He's a genius, and he's pretty good looking, too."

"Sorry, Baroness."

Second apology in five earth minutes, Lady Juliet wondered. *Was Holmes mellowing?*

"Let me explain what this is all about and why it's so dangerous. Then I'll describe our assignment. Are you ready for a short tutorial? "

"All right, Shoot. Oops, sorry Watson. Insensitive of me."

"Holmes, you once told me you didn't care whether the world was round or flat."

"True, Watson, but I have been forced to alter my position as a result of this potential threat that is facing us. To begin, let us stipulate that the Earth can be a gigantic magnet. I found out that the Earth is round and has multiple layers arranged like the skin of an onion. Peel back one, and you find another, with different properties, as well as vast differences in temperature and pressure. The crust of the Earth has some permanent magnetization, and the Earth's core generates its own magnetic field, sustaining the main part of the field we measure at the surface. So we could say that the Earth is, therefore, a "magnet.""

"Fine, Mr. Holmes," huffed Lady Juliet. "I appreciate the increase in my knowledge, but allow me to ask, 'So what?'"

"Patience, Milady," said Holmes. "Earth's magnetic field extends from the Earth's interior out into space. The magnetic field is generated by electric currents caused by heat escaping from the core. Earth's magnetic north and south poles are not fixed like the geographic poles. The magnetic poles wander and wobble and, occasionally, switch positions. This obviously affects our compasses and other things".

"The earliest writings about compass navigation are credited to the Chinese, and date from 11th century A.D. There is evidence of compasses being used in Europe about 100 years later. In 1700 the first magnetic chart, covering the Atlantic Ocean, was produced.

"We now have a device that measures magnetic fields. It is called a magnetometer. It was invented by Johann Carl Friedrich Gauss in 1833 and there have been notable further enhancements in both the 19th and now the 20th century."

"Oh, good. I'll go and look up Gauss." Lady Juliet caught herself: "Sorry, I mean Faraday! I'm still waiting, Holmes. What's our assignment?"

"Someone is attempting to tamper with the Earth's magnetic field. We're being called on to stop him or her."

"Is that all? I thought it was something serious."

Watson sputtered, "It is serious, Baroness. Our world could be seriously disrupted. Telephones and wires interfered with. Compasses gone haywire! You could be seeing Aurora Borealis over London."

"Aurora Borealis? She had an act at the Orpheum. Singing and dancing birds! Didn't care for it. Birds chirped off key."

The doctor smiled patiently. "The Northern Lights, Milady. They are caused by magnetic disturbances. Quite beautiful, but not appropriate for the South English sky."

Holmes stared at her. "Let's be serious, Lady Juliet. You just made a flippant suggestion about seeing Johann Carl Friedrich Gauss. If he's in Heaven, we want to talk with him! Can you flit back and arrange that?"

"I'll try. Let me see if all three of us can have a ghostly conversation long distance. Zoom! There would be no need for traveling. Give me a few moments. I'll see if he's there. Why don't we invite Faraday, too? He's cute."

Holmes shrugged. "Certainly. One more mind brought to bear."

"Fine, I'll be right back. I shall use my feminine wiles to entice them to join us." She and Pookie immediately flitted out of the room.

Holmes turned to Watson, "While she's gone, let's look up these two geniuses." He went to his index and then his shelves, paged through a recent *Who's Who* and said, "Here we are. Listen:

"Physicist Ernest Rutherford states, 'There is no honor too great to pay to the memory of Michael Faraday, one of the greatest scientific discoverers of all time.' Faraday discovered that a varying magnetic field causes electricity to flow in an electric circuit. Faraday had shown that movement could be turned into electricity – or in more scientific language, kinetic energy could be converted to electrical energy. James Clerk Maxwell claims: 'Faraday is, and must always remain, the father of that enlarged science of electromagnetism.' Here's Johann Carl Friedrich Gauss: 'Sometimes referred to as 'the foremost of mathematicians' and 'the greatest mathematician since antiquity'. Gauss had an exceptional influence in many fields of mathematics and science and is ranked among history's most influential mathematicians. He formed "Magnetischer Verein" (The Magnetic Association) which supported measurements of Earth's magnetic field in many regions of the world. He developed a method of measuring the horizontal intensity of the magnetic field which is still in use in the 20th century and worked out the mathematical theory for separating the inner and outer (magnetospheric) sources of Earth's magnetic field."

Watson whistled, "I am duly impressed. Let's see what our celestial ambassador can do."

Suddenly, they could hear a dog's barking echoing through their brains. Pookie!

Lady Juliet flitted back into the room, accompanied by the images of two gentlemen. They seemed to be more transparent than Lady Juliet, and slightly out of focus. "Mr. Holmes, Doctor Watson, we have company," she announced. "May I introduce Mr. Michael Faraday and Herr Johann Carl Friedrich Gauss, speaking to us from a higher plane of existence."

The man on the right, with white muttonchops and an ironic grin, nodded to them both. "Carl Gauss is quite sufficient, Baronin," he said. "Danke. Herr Holmes and Doctor Watson, Guten Tag!"

The man on the left, dressed in a style forty years out of date, also nodded: "Hello, gentlemen. My name is Michael Faraday. This a new experience for me in heavenly communication. Your charming associate says you have need of Carl's and my opinion and expertise."

Holmes replied, "Indeed! First let me say how awed we are to be in contact with such genius. We are grateful that you both could spare the time."

"Ach!" Gauss waved Holmes off. "It has been a long time, celestially speaking, since I have had a good problem to chew on. What about you, Mr. Faraday?"

"Yes, we need something to keep the spirit young, so to speak. What is the issue?"

"Someone is attempting to tamper with the Earth's magnetic field. We're being called on to stop him or her."

Faraday responded, "It's been tried before. What are they doing?"

"We believe they are trying to induce volcanic activity resulting in a shift in the Earth's magnetism."

The Baroness interrupted, "Volcanoes? I didn't realize that. That's awful! Why?"

"We don't know. It could be vengeance... sheer insanity... or it may just be extortion. Bringing the Earth's commerce to its knees is a diabolical challenge."

Gauss coughed. "Have you considered that the magnetic field is not the target? It may be collateral damage."

Lady Juliet choked, "There's that phrase again: 'collateral damage.' When I was killed, Scotland Yard called it collateral damage."

Holmes ignored her and asked, "What do you mean, Herr Gauss?"

"The volcanoes themselves. How much more destruction could a series of eruptions do than shifting the magnetic field!"

Faraday agreed. "Lava streams! Hot, dangerous gases. Ash enveloping the atmosphere. The sun blocked! The oceans polluted! Volcanic eruptions can cause secondary events, such as floods, landslides and mudslides, with accompanying rain, snow or melting ice. Tsunamis and earthquakes! Hot ashes can start wildfires, spewing toxic sulfur dioxide and carbon dioxide. No, gentlemen, magnetic field shift can be disruptive, but a chain of volcanic eruptions would be catastrophic."

Gauss agreed, "Your adversary has more on his mind than disturbances. This person wants the end of the world."

Watson breathed in, "Good Lord!"

"Yes, Doctor, by all means, get His help."

*****

They thanked the two experts profusely and signed off. "That was quite a useful way to communicate. It may become popular but only at a cosmic level, of course."

The Baroness rejoined them after seeing off the two scientists. She flitted in, executing a loop in the process. Her flight instructor would be pleased. "Lovely gentlemen, don't you think? I shall have to follow up on Mr. Faraday. Well, what's next?" Not to be outdone, Pookie landed after performing a similar loop. Cheeky canine!

Holmes said, "As a consulting detective, I find it advantageous to follow as well as give advice. I believe they may be right. Even if they're not, concentrating on volcanoes will also give us a lead on the magnetism issue."

Watson asked, "How many volcanoes are there? And where are they?"

"Our first item of research. There are few in Europe, none to my knowledge in Britain but a very large population in the Pacific Ocean and its environs. North and South America have hundreds on their west coasts. So does Africa, on its east coast. We need to catalog them and plot them out. I would imagine that any clusters would be prime target areas for our opponent."

"So you are convinced we have a foe intent on destroying the Earth."

"No, Watson, but it is the safest assumption we can make. Our heavenly guidance seems to lead us in that direction. So we must answer the questions: Where? When? How? And most important, Who?"

Lady Juliet interposed, "I'd like to know *why*."

"Indeed, Baroness, motive is always key. But over time, there have been a progression of madmen intent on destroying Earth's civilization. Sometimes, to replace it with something they considered better. Sometimes, to dominate the smoking residue. Sometimes, to simply carry out suicide on a grand scale. I assume Hell is full of these monstrous villains. We have no way to check. We can presume some level of insanity, but unfortunately, insane men and women often seem quite normal. Until they break."

Lady Juliet pondered. "Are there such things as volcano specialists?"

"Yes, volcanologists have been around for centuries," said Holmes. "I know of one in Naples. Father Giuseppe Mercalli. He is famous for creating a scale of eruption magnitudes. What say you, Watson? Up for a trip to the Mezzogiorno? Baroness, want to do some trans-European flying? Pookie, Italian dogs can be formidable."

She barked and did a back flip.

*****

The Baroness went back to Heaven with Pookie and took up her long-distance navigation classes. "Don't worry," she told Holmes and Watson, "I'll meet you both in Naples in plenty of time." The trip by ship to Naples was long and uncomfortable. The Mediterranean sun was intense. Holmes and Watson engaged themselves in updating their geological knowledge to the extent they could from the limited ship's library, and the materials they had brought with them.

Holmes had asked Watson to research the world's active and semiactive volcanoes. He came up with a list ranging from Italy's Vesuvius, Stromboli and Etna to Japan's Mt. Fuji and Indonesia's Krakatoa. Five hundred in all. Of course, there were over a thousand of the dormant variety and countless more on the ocean floors. They needed to seriously reduce these candidates. They hoped Father Mercalli would assist in that. Holmes had wired ahead and received a gracious welcome from the priest.

As the ship docked in the Bay of Naples, a vision in scarlet aided and abetted by a prancing white dog was standing there to greet them. She stood at the base of the gangplank allowing passengers and crew to pass through her unnoticed.

Hello, you two, she called out telepathically. *I told you I'd meet you here. I almost didn't make it. My celestial compass threw a fit and I ended up in Milan. But we recovered, didn't we, Pookie? We're certified World Flitters!*

Holmes frowned. He directed his thoughts towards Lady Juliet: *Your compass went askew? Is it still acting strangely?*

Yes, I'm going to turn it in for replacement when I get back to Paradise. Why?

Holmes looked grim. *The attacks may have started.*

What? Oh, do you think the poles are shifting? Are some volcanoes exploding?

*Very possibly. Come, Watson! Come, Baroness! We have little time to waste. On to the **University of Naples Federico II** and our new friend, the volcanologist. The game is…*

"*Afoot!*" they silently chorused.

*****

"Signore Holmes and Dottore Watson! What a pleasure! When I received your wire I was, how you say, besides myself with excitement," Father Mercalli said, welcoming them in his thickly-accented English.

You'd be even more excited if you know I was standing 'besides' you, Padre, giggled the Baroness. *Me and my dog!*

"You mentioned a very serious situation involving volcanoes," he continued. "That, of course, is my **specialità. How can I assist you?"**

"**Father** Mercalli, we have reason to believe that someone intends to trigger a series of volcanic eruptions around the world," said Holmes. "They may even have started already."

Father Mercalli looked mortified. "Oh, Madonna! My fears are coming true."

"What do you mean?" asked Holmes.

"Signore, I am here in Naples because of the relative proximity of Mt. Etna, Vesuvius and Stromboli. There are a number of other Italian volcanoes, but those three are the ones most famous for their destructive history, and for launching intense scientific study. Remember Pompeii, Herculaneum? They are all active. But they are as nothing compared to The Ring of Fire."

Watson looked up. "I found a few references to the Ring of Fire, but really couldn't get a proper picture of it."

"It is what the name suggests. The rim surrounding the Pacific Ocean east, north and west. Look at this map," he said, pointing to a large yellowing paper nearly covering a small table. "Seventy-five percent of Earth's volcanoes—more than 450 — are located along the Ring of Fire on both sides and in the interior of the Ocean. South America, North America, Asia, Islands and Archipelagos. Ninety percent of Earth's earthquakes occur along its path, including the planet's most violent and dramatic seismic events. The Ring of Fire has existed for more than 35 million years. The four largest volcanic eruptions on Earth in the last 12,000 years occurred at volcanoes in the Ring of Fire. More than 350 of the Ring of Fire's volcanoes have been active in recorded time. If you were to select locations for volcanic mischief, the Ring would be it."

"You spoke of fears. What did you mean?" asked Holmes.

"There have been rumors circulating among seismologists and volcanologists for some time of accelerated activity around the Pacific Rim. Some of us believe it may be induced."

"Induced? How?"

"That I do not know, Signore, but there have been a series of irregular spikes that do not seem to match our predictions. Of course, earthquake and eruption forecasts are very inexact processes. There is also the airship report."

"An airship report?" Holmes's eyes bulged. "Explain!"

"Last year, a group of observers taking measurements at Krakatoa in Indonesia spotted a small airship floating about the caldera. It bore no markings and seemed to be making practice runs around the perimeter. Then it disappeared and has not been seen since. Not a trace. Most peculiar."

"That sounds quite curious, indeed. Could it have been sightseers?"

"No. No sane sightseers would have approached the caldera at such close quarters."

Watson thought out loud. "We obviously need to go to the Pacific Rim if we are going to pursue this further. Can you recommend someone we should approach in that vast territory?"

"Several. I would suggest Professor John Wilson. You'll find him at the new University of Indonesia in Batavia. He, like you, Dottore, is a physician but he is a volcanologist par excellence. You may also wish to call upon Madame Greta Stark. She is Director of the Pacific Rim Research Project. Also in Batavia."

Juliet whooped telepathically. *At last, another woman! I was afraid this was going to be a stag affair.*

"Well, it would seem our next stop should be Indonesia - specifically Batavia," agreed Holmes. "Have your Italian volcanoes been behaving themselves?"

"At the moment, but I am concerned. They, too, are possible subjects for trouble."

"If you detect or even suspect any irregularities, will you please contact us immediately?"

"Of course, Signore. Is there any other way I may be of service to you?"

"Perhaps two letters of introduction to Professor Wilson and Madame Stark."

"Uno momento!" He ran to his desk and scrawled a few lines, folded the papers into two envelopes, smiled and shook our hands. "Go with God!"

Juliet chortled. *Little does he know.*

*****

On the way back to the ship leaving that evening for London, Holmes made several decisions. He would contact Mycroft, which did not fill Juliet with great joy, and ask him to use his good offices with the Admiralty. It was they who had responsibility for the development and deployment of airships. He also wanted access to a warship, if any, that was patrolling the Pacific. Finally, he wanted a comprehensive briefing on the relationship of Indonesia and His Majesty's Government.

He then turned to the Baroness. "Milady, are your flight and navigation skills up to an aerial trip to Batavia and its environs? I'd like you to discover whatever you can about this Professor Wilson and Madame Stark. I'd also like you to see what you can find out about this mysterious airship. It is probably somewhere in the Indonesian Archipelago."

"What, and give up singing in the choir? Try and stop me! I'll need a better compass, however, and a few reliable maps. Pookie will be my wing dog. Indonesia sounds huge."

"It is. Listen to this: Father Mercalli gave me this description along with the letters of introduction…

"Indonesia is the largest archipelago in the world. It consists of five major islands and about 30 smaller groups. There are a total number of 17,508 islands of which about 6000 are inhabited. Islands are mountainous with dense rain forests, and some have active volcanoes. Most of the smaller islands belong to larger groups, like the Spice Islands.

"It is on a crossroads between two oceans, the Pacific and the Indian Ocean, and bridges two continents, Asia and Australia. Indonesia has many high mountains, the highest of which are over 12,000 feet with some 400 volcanoes, of which 100 are active.

"There are tropical rainforests and jungles, as well as swampy mangrove areas. Indonesia's most fertile land is on the island of Java. The country stretches 3,200 miles east to west. The largest islands are Sumatra, Java, Kalimantan, Sulawesi, and the Indonesian part of New Guinea."

Lady Juliet threw her hands up in mock frustration: "Oh, good. Just a walk in the park. Well, Heaven is infinite so I shouldn't complain. Back I go."

*****

Giuseppe Cei, recently deceased himself, looked up from his desk in the Heavenly Hangar to see Lady Juliet flitting into the room. "Ciao, Baronessa!" he said, smiling. "One of my favorite students. What's on your hyperactive mind?"

"Giuseppe, I'm going on a long-distance flit on Earth. I could use a little advice and counsel."

"How come you're making all these earthly trips? You got a boyfriend down there? Does Mr. Raymond know?"

"You amorous Italians are all the same. It's Raymond who is sending me." This was a slight stretch of the truth, but still within heavenly veracity limits. "And no, I have friends down there who are 'boys' but no boyfriends. Now, Pookie and I are off to Indonesia."

"Did you know Pookie won our Top Gun Dogfight Award? First female to do it."

"I'm not surprised. She's a tough little bitch." Lady Juliet did a double-take. "Oops! Can I say that?"

Giuseppe shrugged. "Why not? That's what she is, according to the Celestial Kennel Club."

"Thank goodness for that. So, when you were flying and setting records, did you ever have to cross the Pacific?"

He laughed. "No, I flew mostly in France. Paris, actually. With our aeroplanes, we were lucky if we could cross the River Seine, although I did fly around the Eiffel Tower."

"Do you think an airship could cover the Pacific?"

"Now, that's a different story. One of those flying gasbags could make it, although it would take quite a few stops to refuel and make repairs."

"Repairs?" asked Lady Juliet.

"Those engines and the fabric covering the bag would take a beating. Also, they're filled with hydrogen. Dangerous stuff. Blow up in an instant. I wouldn't want to chance it, but some idiot probably would."

"Well, this idiot is going to flit to the Indonesian Archipelago. No aeroplane! No airship! Just me and my dog. By the way, the compass you gave me to go to your native Italy went haywire. I ended up in Milan on my way to Naples."

"That's the third time I've heard of that. There's nothing wrong with those compasses. The magnetic poles on Earth are acting up. It's going to make your over-water trip a bit tricky. But, hey, you're immortal, so you'll just have to live with it. Ha, ha!!"

"Very funny, Giuseppe. Hmmm… I could use a few maps and two celestial flight suits. One for me and one for Pookie. She's coming along."

"Very well, let's see. World, Pacific and Indonesian maps. One high fashion rig for you and a small dog suit for the Top Gun. By the way, you'll probably be flitting by night on Earth. Aren't you glad you took the course?"

"I thought it was useless with Paradise's non-stop sun but now I'm glad I did. Anyway, Heavenly Traffic Control is off my case. No more near misses with those chariot speedsters. Thanks for that!"

"My pleasure, Baronessa! Let's test your night acuity first, and then, off you go. Have a good trip."

*****

On board the RMS *(Royal Mail Ship)* Colossus traversing the Mediterranean from Naples toward England, Holmes and Watson had ample time to consider the bidding, as it were. The Great Detective had wired home to Mycroft's office inquiring about Professor John Wilson at Batavia University and Madame Greta Stark, Director of the Pacific Rim Research Project. Professor Wilson's credentials and bona fides were quite legitimate and his expertise in both medicine and volcanology unquestioned.

Mycroft's message read: "Madame Stark was a different item. A virtual scientific unknown until two years ago, she used her deceased husband's abundant wealth to finance several rather unusual programs of which the Pacific Rim—the 'Ring of Fire'— was the most extensive. Based in Batavia with branches in Iceland and Italy, little, if any, of the results achieved by this group found its way into publicly available information bases. Most of their work is committed to private, some say 'clandestine' enterprises. Little is known about her personally. Living alone in Batavia, she eschews the communal niceties usually enjoyed by ladies of significant financial and social standing. In short, she is a bit of a mystery."

Maintaining telepathic contact with Lady Juliet, Holmes asked her to pay special attention to Madame. The Baroness had not yet begun her global journey but was testing her simulated night flying skills with Giuseppe. Finally, she was good to go. Giuseppe gave her a thumbs-up.

"All right, Pookie," she said to her fluffy friend, "we're off. I must say your flight suit fits you quite well. Mine is a little bit loose but it will do. At least it's the right color, not that anyone will notice. Now, out of the Pearly Gates and turn left. A sharp dive and we'll be over the ocean. When we get to Batavia, we have to find Professor Wilson at the University, as well as finding the Pacific Rim Research Project and Madame Greta Stark. Mr. Holmes and his brother seem to think there's something fishy about her. No, not eating fishy. Pookie, that's all you think about!"

From the ship, Holmes made telegraphic contact with the Admiralty, asking about any incidents involving unidentified airships in or around the Pacific. Airships were still something of a rarity in aviation circles and were carefully watched. Most of them tended to operate in Europe or the United States.

One report came back, a repeat of the Krakatoa sighting by the volcano research team. However, an intelligence request to the War Office asked for verification of a Japanese firm who supposedly was going into the business of making and selling medium size, attack-class dirigibles to the highest bidders. That attracted some attention including that of our heroes.

"Contact the Baroness, Watson. Tell her to keep a sharp lookout for airships and any landing sites they may be using in Indonesia. Probably the proverbial needle in the haystack."

Watson balked: "What makes you think dirigibles are involved in this, Holmes? In fact, what's involved here at all? So far, we have collected a lot of odd facts but no real data. The Ring of Fire has been around for millions of years. What makes it so much more important now? We've been trekking around in pursuit of who knows what. Now we have Lady Juliet in the Far East. Both she and Pookie may just be chasing their tails."

"Valid points, Watson, but the stakes involved in runaway volcanic action are too high to ignore. We may be wasting time and effort, but let's keep going. I'm sure Lady Juliet is having the time of her life."

She was. After landing in Batavia, the amazed Baroness took in the density of the population and the packed homes, roads and byways. She shook her attractive head. "Pookie, this is incredible. This place makes London look like a bucolic village. So many people squeezed into so small a space. What a waterfront! Fantastic. We'll have to find the University. It's new, but it's built around a medical school. What do our maps say?

Aha, let's flit this way. No flirting with the dogs. You don't know where they've been. Professor Wilson, where are you?"

The Professor had just completed a lecture and headed for the University refectory for lunch. He was a tall American, over sixty, with a slight age-induced stoop. A shock of grey hair framed his wrinkled face and his dark brown eyes were overshadowed by heavy black brows. He wore the gown of the academician and carried the inevitable briefcase full of lecture notes and books. He waved at colleagues and students as he passed. The Baroness, sitting on top of an unoccupied table in the dining hall, was favorably impressed, but appearances could be deceiving. Pookie seemed to like him—her tail wagged as he passed by.

He seated himself next to a young associate, turned to the waiter who approached the table and asked. "Arief, what poison is the kitchen dispensing today?"

"Your favorite, Professor—ristaffel."

"Fine, I'll prepare myself for a seared tongue and a burned mouth." He turned to his neighbor and said, "These classes on liver disease always put me in a sour mood toward local food. Nothing I'd like better than a good steak and potatoes. Oh, well. How goes the volcano survey, Bakti?"

Lady Juliet and Pookie both perked up their ears.

The youth responded, "Well enough, Professor. My contract with the Pacific Rim Research Project is allowing me to pay for my ailing mother's medicines. Madame Stark is most generous with her money. She acts as if she doesn't care what she does with it. The survey, as you might expect, is promoting major differences of opinion. There are only a small number of sites we all agree are now or will shortly be active. Of course, there's always Krakatoa. That goes without saying. We have to issue a preliminary report this week. It's keeping me busy. I have to return to the Center right now. I wish you were working on it with us."

"I do too, but this semester's medical lecture schedule has taken up all of my time. Ah, here comes the ristaffel. Call the fire brigade!"

"Well, Pookie, the Professor seems out of the volcano business for the moment. That narrows our search a good deal. I wish I knew what we were searching for. This preliminary report may be exactly what Mr. Holmes and Doctor Watson want. Let's follow Bakti to the Center, wherever that is."

It was only a short walk to the waterfront where a two-story building seemed to be engaged in a battle with the oncoming tides. A medium-sized steamship was tied up at an adjacent wharf and was being loaded with an assortment of containers, tanks and foodstuffs.

The two spirits swooped inside, passed a native receptionist and headed toward an office block. An elaborate frosted glass door bore the sign: DIRECTOR. Inside, a conference was proceeding. Bakti entered and seated himself at the back of the room. The wraiths sat next to him on a cabinet.

A tall pale woman in a white dress was leading the discussion. "What is your confidence level on this material?"

An officious-looking Sumatran cleared his throat and said, "As you know, Madame Director, volcanoes are notoriously unpredictable. However, after performing major surveys and on-site reviews, we feel the first ten on the list are due for some major activity within the next five years. Seven are within the Ring of Fire. The rest are scattered around the world."

"Five years?" The tall woman was not pleased. "Is that as much precision as you can bring to this study? I was hoping for much more."

The gentleman was eager to reassure the speaker: "Remember, please, that these are only preliminary judgements. We still have much data to analyze and correlate."

"Accelerate your activities. Expense is no object. We will meet again in two weeks. Meanwhile, I shall be away on a short business trip." She picked up some papers in front of her. "Meeting adjourned."

Lady Juliet looked at the dog. "Where do you suppose she's going and how is she getting there?"

The second question answered itself within half an hour when the director walked out of the building carrying a small suitcase and headed for the steamship which had just completed loading. The captain assisted her up the gangplank after smartly saluting. "Welcome aboard, Madame Stark. We will be casting off in just a few moments. Our usual destination?"

She nodded. "Thank you, Captain. Yes, and the usual protective measures, please. I shall be in my stateroom and am not to be disturbed."

The Baroness smiled, "We won't disturb her, will we, Pookie? She may disturb us. Let's see what she's up to." They swooped into the room where the director had laid out on a table the written estimates developed by the research team and was studying them.

She shook her head in frustration, then started talking to herself. "Not precise enough. He will not be pleased, but a summons is a summons. He is obviously anxious to set his mad scheme in motion."

"Whoa, Pookie!" Lady Juliet wondered, *Who is 'he' and what is his mad scheme?*

Suddenly, the ship's engines stopped. The skyline of Batavia had sunk below the horizon and only the waters of the Pacific were visible. A small crew was actively deploying camouflage netting and disguising the vessel as an oversized fishing boat. They were quite agile and quick and the ship was soon underway again.

The Baroness had flitted outside to watch this exercise and was becoming increasingly intrigued by the entire situation. She would wait until they reached their destination before telepathically contacting Mr. Holmes and Doctor Watson. But they needed to converse! She wondered if they had reached London yet. She had gotten one message from Doctor Watson asking her to keep an eye out for airships. Not in Batavia, certainly. Maybe at their destination.

One of the over 11,000 Indonesian islands designated as uninhabited and unnamed actually played host to a rather elaborate but well-hidden facility. A splendid manor; a large barracks; a sizeable blockhouse and a huge hangar-like structure were all tucked beneath a major growth of tropical foliage. An open area in front of the hangar was all that distinguished this atoll from its thousands of fellows. That and a seaside mooring and roadway that led to the complex.

Good Heavens, Holmes

A substantial steam vessel heavily camouflaged as a native fishing boat was tied up at the anchorage. A group of sailors and uniformed men were busy rolling heavy tanks, large containers and two small vehicles off the ship and up the roadway to a storage area in the blockhouse. One other item distinguished this picture from all others in the archipelago. Three medium-sized airships filled the hangar with their significant girth.

A woman in a flowing white dress carrying a briefcase sauntered up the roadway from the ship and turned toward the manor house, where she was greeted by a butler dressed in full formal livery, in spite of the oppressive heat. The oceanic breezes did little to cool the area during the day – a fact that inhibited the lift characteristics of the airships. The evening was different. Then a major flurry of activity surrounded the unmarked behemoths as they were towed into the clearing and prepared for takeoff. Right now, with the exception of the supply ship's unloading process, things were relatively quiet.

"Madame Stark, welcome back to the island," said the butler. "The Adjudicator is awaiting you."

"Thank you, Hasan. I am here as he requested." He turned to escort her, but she stopped him. "Don't bother. I know the way."

"Hello, Hasan," said Lady Juliet to the butler as she floated by. "We don't know the way but we'll just follow her, if you don't mind. C'mon Pookie!"

Tall and slim, in her forties, with streaks of grey in her simple coiffure, Madam Stark strode down an elaborate hall to an open-air breezeway where she found her host, ensconced in a substantial ornate rattan chair. Ceiling fans rotated slowly but

228

seemed to make little difference. The man was dressed in a linen suit and his short grey beard was finely trimmed. He still had a full head of hair, carefully combed. A sardonic expression wreathed his face.

Her sharp blue eyes took him in and she allowed a little smile to nudge her otherwise expressionless mouth.

He smiled in return. "Greta, welcome. Thank you for coming."

"Did I have a choice, Bernhard? Or should I call you Mr. Adjudicator?"

"Adjudicator?" asked Lady Juliet, unheard by the couple. "Now there's a formidable title. Who is this fellow?"

"Formality is necessary only in the presence of others," Bernhard said. "I have heard little from your Pacific Rim Research Project lately. I wish an update. Am I getting my money's worth? But first, before you begin, a cooling beverage." He pulled a silk cord dangling nearby from the ceiling. The butler appeared. "Hasan, bring refreshments." The butler nodded and left.

"Please Greta," the Adjudicator said, "be seated. It gets beastly hot during the days here, but as you know, the evenings are quite pleasant. In more ways than one. I delight in watching my formidable Air Force leap into the sky at twilight. I have ridden with them. Not often! There is some danger involved, of course, but it will be worth it. Oh, it will be well worth it, provided we get guidance from your scientists."

Greta sat down, her eyes fixed on the man before her. "My 'scientists' have amassed an immense amount of data about active volcanoes in the Ring of Fire," she said. "They believe we are on a protective mission to reduce the impact of eruptions and earthquakes."

The Adjudicator laughed. "A protective mission! Little do they know. They are selecting my targets for me. Do you have the names and locations for us? Our flight tests have been highly successful and we are ready to initiate our assault. The Rim, the Ocean and the mainlands! None are safe. All subjected to explosive bursts, poisonous gasses, burning ash, enveloped skies, floods, tremors, tsunamis, and fire, fire, fire. Spreading worldwide across land, sea and sky. The Ring of Fire. My Ring of Ire! Europe, Asia, North and South America, all eventually destroyed. The end of so-called civilization. We will then emerge from our safe havens and claim this shattered Earth for our own."

Greta remained unmoved: "What will be left to claim?"

"Enough to begin a new world under my direction. I have carefully planned our recovery but first the Earth must endure a cleansing purge."

"Where are these havens of safety?"

"Northern Australia, a place called... Palmerston. Actually, they just changed the name to Darwin. Ironic! It has no active volcanoes or much seismic activity. Externally induced phenomena will reach it, however, so we must live in hiding for a while. We even have a refuge in Antarctica that I hope never to use. I'm sorry, dear Greta, but you must wait to be called to join the refugee group."

"I still don't understand how you plan to bring this off!"

"Delayed incendiaries, my dear. Incendiary bombs with dozens of thin, Thermite-filled canisters set off by magnesium fuses, dropped into active calderas from my airships. The explosions are timed to allow the ships to exit and flee to our havens."

"How will you control the success of the bombardment? Some will be duds."

"It doesn't matter. It will only take a small number of successes to set off the cataclysm. Some initial eruptions will cause further eruptions provided they are strategically placed. That is why your work is so critical."

She reached into her bag and pulled out an elaborate chart portraying the Rim as well as isolated targets in the Mediterranean, North Atlantic and the east coast of Africa. "I don't know how far your airships can reach, but our scientists included all these locations because they thought they were a potential natural danger."

Another laugh. "Indeed, they are. And we, Madame Stark, will be the unnatural causes to bring those dangers to a fiery conclusion. Thank you! I shall study these charts carefully. Farewell, Greta. Have a good journey back to Batavia. I shall call you when it is appropriate to seek shelter."

She wondered. Would he call her, or would he betray her? She shook her head, turned on her heel and returned to the steamer, ready to make its return trip to Batavia and her Center.

While this conversation was going on, a horrified Juliet who had been listening in after following the woman scientist, turned to her dog and said, "These two are insane, and the world is nearing total destruction! We need to flit, Pookie! First to Batavia and then to London. Mr. Holmes and Doctor Watson should be there by now. We have to stop this. I hope there's enough time. We could use some divine intervention."

Perhaps at Godly inspiration, nature did intervene. Much to the Adjudicator's frustration a series of monsoons and a tropical cyclone descended on the atoll and surrounding islands immediately and lasted for several weeks. The complex was battened down and the airships could not take off. Not so, the celestial pair who flitted across the globe and landed at 221B Baker Street.

"Mr. Holmes, Doctor Watson! It's much worse than we imagined," Lady Juliet cried, flitting into their front room. She then proceeded to relate what she had learned. "I would have destroyed them then and there if I could. Being incorporeal is so frustrating! It's up to you two, now."

*****

"You will just have to trust me on this, Mycroft. I cannot tell you my source, but it's most reliable. We are faced with a disaster of cosmic dimensions unless we act rapidly and completely."

Holmes's voice rattled around the walls of the Stranger's Room in the Diogenes Club. Mycroft waved at his brother to keep his voice down, while Watson looked on. The Stranger's Room tolerated discussion, but only at a discreet volume.

"It is not me who needs to be convinced, Sherlock," said Mycroft. "You are asking the Admiralty and the American Navy to essentially invade an island that is nominally governed by the Dutch East Indies Company. This Bernhard de Groot owns the atoll and is entitled to his government's protection. He may indeed have airships housed on his property but they do not violate any international laws. In fact, there are *no* international agreements at all governing the ownership or operation of airships. What you are asking could trigger a major global incident."

The Baroness gritted her ethereal teeth and resisted taking a useless swat at the elder Holmes brother. *You are a pompous bureaucrat, Mycroft Holmes,* she silently spat. *The end of the world is upon us and you're citing the absence of regulations governing airships! We need your help, not your fusty platitudes. Ooh, you make me so mad! Hit him, Mr. Holmes! Doctor Watson, do something!*

He answered telepathically, *Calm yourself, Baroness. We need to plot out an alternate solution.*

Like holding him for ransom until the Admiralty agrees to send gun boats to occupy that Island of Doom. Maybe the Americans would be more reasonable, Mr. Holmes. Or, Heaven help us, the French. Forget the Russians. I'm still smarting over Volkov.

While she was ranting, Tobias, Mycroft's assistant, knocked and entered the room. "Forgive the intrusion, gentlemen, but His Majesty's government has received a message and the Prime Minister wants Mr. Holmes to urgently deal with it. Mr. Holmes Senior, that is. It is a global telegraphic missive from an apparent madman but the PM wants it verified as a crank letter as rapidly as possible."

The Baroness turned her attention to Mycroft and watched as he took the flimsy sheet in his hands.

He read it and turning pale, shook his head and passed it on to his younger brother, "As you always say, Sherlock. See what you can make of this. No doubt, an elaborate hoax."

Watson rose from his seat and read over Sherlock's shoulder. The other shoulder was ethereally occupied by the Baroness. Pookie growled and wagged her tail furiously. The dog sensed something amiss. She was right.

Holmes read the letter aloud:

"To the incompetent, pernicious fools who pretend to rule the countries of the world. Attention!"

"You have been tested in the crucible of light and justice and been found irretrievably wanting. A single solution presents itself. Total annihilation of you and your sinful populations. I have been commissioned by a higher spirit to carry out this noble work and I have prepared a catastrophic ending for the so-called civilizations of the Earth. There is no way you can avoid the fiery end prepared for you. Flee, if you can. Resist, if you dare. It will be to no avail."

"This is my first message to you. I want to entertain myself and watch you flail hopelessly against the fate that inexorably awaits you. My next missive will go to the general populations of the world, aided and abetted by the deplorable press that infests the minds and hearts of all those weak-minded degenerates. I await the delicious panic, rebellion and destruction that my words will create. And then, Armageddon!"

(signed) Most sincerely, The Adjudicator.

Lady Juliet shouted and Pookie barked. *It's him! Bernhard de Groot is the Adjudicator. I heard Madame Greta Stark call him that. Mr. Holmes, he's going to do it. His airships, bombs and active volcanoes are just waiting. She set up the targets and he built the apparatus. Capture her. He won't take her to their safe havens. Not yet! The arrogant fool. Pressure her! Faced with a horrible fiery choking death she herself brought on, she'll give him away. Speaking of arrogant fools, convince your brother.*

Sherlock turned away from Lady Juliet's tirade, concentrating on Mycroft. "This is no hoax. Bernhard de Groot is the Adjudicator. My highly reliable source has established that. You have trusted me in the past. Do it now. Convince the Prime Minister. So we risk an incident with the Dutch East India Company. Who cares, for God's sake?"

Yes, Mr. Holmes, said the Baroness, *for God's sake.*

Holmes continued: "Which would you prefer, Mycroft? A diplomatic spat, or watching the world collapse around itself? We shall go to Batavia immediately and face down this Madame Stark and her Pacific Rim Research Project. Can you arrange a swift destroyer to take us there?"

Lady Juliet flew between Holmes and his brother, addressing Holmes directly: *Pookie and I will come, too. We know where to find her. But we'll flit, won't we, girl? I'm getting rather fond of this global travel. First a stop back at the Pearly Gates to give a progress report to Raymond, make an adjustment to my flight suit, get a new compass... and a new pack of Heavenly Chewies for Pookie. She deserves it. Then we'll see you in Batavia. I hope we're not too late.*

*****

Two weeks later, aboard HMS Acheron, China Sea destroyer, the ship's captain was conferring with his two special passengers, Sherlock Holmes and Doctor Watson. "We are approaching Batavia, gentlemen. It is time for the Acheron to develop 'engine trouble' and put in a call asking to dock and make repairs. We will get you ashore by whatever means are feasible, restore our 'sick' power plant and stand ready to move on to our next port-of-call, an uncharted atoll as I understand it. You will have the coordinates, if your mission is successful?"

Holmes smiled, "Thank you, Captain. Yes, we will. Once again, thank the Admiralty. I understand there is an American gunboat in the vicinity as well."

"Yes, the USS Yorktown has been shadowing us and will follow us when we resume our voyage. Between us, we have sufficient firepower to offset anything this Adjudicator maniac can develop."

"Have you had any experience with airships?"

"Not as such, although we do use static balloons for target practice. Airships, of course, are powered and have an active crew so our gunners will have something of a challenge, if it comes to that. The Captain of the Yorktown is concerned that we will be bombed."

"The Adjudicator wants to reserve his incendiary bombs for volcanic targets. I suspect we will be harassed by gunfire."

"You may be right, Mr. Holmes. Of course, the airships have one very serious vulnerability -hydrogen. Volatile material. They are a floating bag of the stuff. One well-placed shot and Poof!"

The first mate came up and saluted. "We have received permission to dock in Batavia, Sir. We will limp in under reduced power and tie up in the Dutch East India Navy Yard. We'll get our passengers ashore without even wetting their feet. I assume you gentlemen will know where you're going once you're on land?"

"Not yet, but shortly. We have an associate to meet."

"Sorry we can't accompany you, even in disguise. It would be an international incident if the Royal Navy was discovered, or its officers arrested."

"Understood! We are renegade civilians." Watson pulled out his Webley service revolver and Holmes waved his swordstick.

As the Acheron pulled up to the dock, a little white dog let loose with a series of unearthly barks. The Baroness, in her scarlet flight suit, recently adjusted, was standing by expectantly. *My goodness, ships are even slower than London cabs,* she telepathically told her friends. *We've been waiting for you for ages, measured in Earth time, of course. Well, hurry up! We have to cross the waterfront. Madame Stark is in her offices. We checked. Pookie doesn't like her much. The skipper of her supply ship is also on board his vessel. If she won't tell you what you want to know, he probably will. I assume you're armed? By the way, I know where this atoll is. Why do you need Madame Stark?*

We want her as a hostage, Holmes told her. *I'm stealing a cab. The Batavia police will no doubt be on our tails.*

Do you honestly believe that fanatic will care if the two of you capture her? The Adjudicator has no regard for her personally. All he wants is her money and her project's information.

We know. We want her to betray him.

Hardly likely, Mr. Holmes. She's in love with him.

Indeed, but Hell hath no fury like a woman scorned.

237

I wouldn't know. I've never been scorned. Shot, yes but scorned? No! Doctor Watson, are your wounds up to all this exercise?

Watson nodded. *Yes, Milady, my injuries seem to go quiet when there's action to be had.*

I hope so.

The trio approached a small building. *That's her headquarters up ahead,* said Lady Juliet. *There's only a receptionist. He may be armed. Her ship is at the wharf. I'm sure they have weapons. You can park the cab on the dock. I'll set up a distraction.*

How? Watson asked. *You're disembodied.*

A little brain to brain communication. Watch! Get ready to invade!

Lady Juliet floated over to the man sitting behind the desk and placed her ghostly fingers around his head. She concentrated. Suddenly, the receptionist jumped from his seat, flailed at his uniform and slapped at the surface of his desk to ward off the swarm of imaginary mosquitoes who were surrounding him. Holmes and Watson slipped past, entered the Director's office and, waving their weapons, signaled her to be silent and come with them. She made an attempt at resistance, but facing the pistol, changed her mind.

They rushed past the guard again, unnoticed. He was still intent on warding off the invisible swarm. Lady Juliet rejoined her companions as they raced back to the HMS Acheron, where their captive was hustled up the gangplank and into the hold. The idling engines miraculously redeveloped full power. The captain saluted the dockmaster, thanked him and the Dutch East Indies Company for their assistance and retired to the bridge.

All was not quiet and serene in the stateroom where Greta Stark was unceremoniously deposited. "Kidnappers! Abductors! Snatchers! How dare you take me hostage! Who are you? What do you want? You'll answer to the Adjudicator for this."

Holmes stood by the door. "Exactly what we want, Madame Stark. I am Sherlock Holmes and this gentleman is Doctor John Watson. We are here at the behest of His Majesty's Britannic government to ensure the Adjudicator does not succeed in his wild plot to destroy the Earth. You are both outlaws. His aerial attack armada, operating on information from your Pacific Rim Research Project, is designed to create volcanic havoc worldwide. Very few will survive."

"That is exactly what <u>we</u> want, Mr. Holmes. Oh yes, I have heard of you, Mr. Genius Detective. Do you honestly believe you can stop us? Bernhard has planned every step of the program very carefully, and I have supplied the target information after in-depth investigation. Until now we have studiously concealed our means and purposes. How did you find out? Of course, his threatening message to the leaders of your world has triggered reactions, but it's too late. Armageddon is upon us."

A telepathic conference ensued, while Watson kept Madame Stark covered with his pistol.

Holmes, this woman is worse than de Groot, said Lady Juliet, disgusted. *Throw her overboard!*

To what end, Baroness? She has completed her mission. Our true adversary is on that atoll. I am hoping that he will alter his plans in order to save his co-conspirator from hanging.

Can Sherlock Holmes be so naïve? She's served her purpose. He won't care a fig. Take my word for it. She turned to Watson. *What do you think, Doctor?*

I agree with Lady Juliet, Holmes. He'll abandon her without a single regret. Not only is he mad, he's also a swine.

Madame Greta looked at the pondering pair in wonderment. They were clearly in some sort of communication, but how? What were they doing?

The Baroness noticed her staring. *Oh, Greta, my dear, we are discussing your fate. Little do you know about Pookie and me. Let's keep it that way.*

They were interrupted by a knocking on the door. Holmes undid the lock and the first mate popped his head in. "Mr. Holmes, we are approaching the atoll. The Yorktown is right behind us. Both ships are on full battle alert. We will commence firing once we are within range. The dirigibles are our primary targets. Then the blockhouse, the barracks and the manor. "

Madame Stark was wide-eyed. "Oh, you fools. Don't you see? Those airships will bomb you to cinders with their incendiaries. You don't stand a chance."

"No, Madame, your friend the Adjudicator needs those airships and bombs to set off his volcanic explosions. He will *not* attack. He will use the airships to escape."

However, it was a hot afternoon and the aircraft were having difficulty developing sufficient lift. A well-placed shot from the Yorktown turned a dirigible struggling to take off into a flaming inferno. The hydrogen that filled the gasbag combined with the Thermite incendiaries to create a roaring firestorm.

In the manor house, a rattled de Groot abandoned his office and ran to the hangar. He dragged several of the crew members from the gondola of a ship that was as yet unscathed by the flames of its sister craft and threw the engines into maximum speed. Lightened by the reduced crew, the dirigible moved forward and rose into the sky. The gunners aboard the Acheron and Yorktown fired at the moving target but failed to score a hit as it moved on its aerial trajectory. They then concentrated their fire on the remaining airship and turned it into a flaming hulk which exploded catastrophically. Finally, they lobbed rounds into the hangar, blockhouse, barracks and manor house, for good measure.

A landing party from both ships came ashore, and amid small arms fire, mopped up the remaining resistance. They hauled all of the Adjudicator's small 'army' into longboats and brought them on board. They would be taken to Batavia where, since most of them were Indonesian, they would stand trial.

The Captain of the Acheron stepped away from the bridge, shook the hands of Holmes and Watson and said, "Mission accomplished, gentlemen."

"Thank you, captain, but I'm afraid congratulations are premature. Our adversary has escaped and may yet bring about a world catastrophe. Meanwhile, please take Madame Stark to your brig."

*****

Six weeks later, back in London, a major conference was about to begin. Hastily called by His Majesty's government, delegates from the major powers who had received the heart-stopping threats from the Adjudicator filed into a large meeting room. There had been some of the usual competitive grousing about which country should host the event and Britain, with its absence of volcanoes, was questioned as the appropriate host. The Dutch, especially, were chagrined that the climactic episode took place in their colony, but they were unwilling to lead the discussions.

Thus, since no one else emerged in a leadership position besides the Americans, who were deemed to be too geographically inconvenient for most delegates, the task fell to the British. Mycroft Holmes, with the assistance of his brother and Doctor Watson, took the extraordinary step of physically bestirring himself to chair the session—a near miracle in itself.

Helped substantially by the Baroness, who was, of course, present but not visible, Sherlock Holmes related the events and described the conditions leading up to Bernhard de Groot's fantastic plot. The Italian representative, relieved that Stromboli, Etna and Vesuvius would be left to their natural caprices, suggested a vote of thanks for Holmes, Watson and the captains and crews of HMS Acheron and the USS Yorktown for disposing of the threat and proposed they permanently adjourn and disband the committee.

"I'm afraid you have missed a most important point, sir." Mycroft rumbled. "The Adjudicator, de Groot, survived the shelling of his enclave, and has escaped to parts unknown with a small group of supporters, an operating airship, an arsenal of

Thermite incendiary devices and as far as we know, a strong determination to still carry out a reduced version of his pernicious plot. We have some reason to believe he is in Australia but that country, as we know, has broad expanses of unexplored landscapes. We have yet to find him."

Lady Juliet shouted, unheard, *But Mycroft dear, we will! You can bet on it!*

Proposals were made to fund an expedition to Australia to hunt down the Adjudicator, his minions and his Satanic devices. In typical bureaucratic fashion, discussion outweighed purpose and international jealousies rose, but were finally assuaged. A request to lead the group was presented to Sherlock Holmes by no less than the Australian representative who was torn between "having a bunch of foreign jackaroos tromping around in the outback" and "having the world breathing down our bleeding necks" if the Australians took on the assignment by themselves.

Holmes, who was getting on a bit in years, was reluctant to "tromp about in the outback" and said as much. He felt that he and Watson (and of course, the Baroness and Pookie) had made major contributions to, thus far, prevent the end of the world. Someone younger and more energetic should take up the palm. Unfortunately, a likely colleague, Sexton Blake, had been injured as a result of a criminal ambush and was hors de combat in this particular instance.

Finally, after a lengthy discussion with Watson and the Baroness, Holmes hesitantly agreed to lead an excursion to dispose of the Adjudicator and the threat he still represented. "Let's find Madame Stark. She is a British citizen and is incarcerated somewhere here awaiting trial. The Captain of the

Acheron had turned her over to the Foreign Office. Mycroft will know where she is."

Juliet scrunched up her attractive face. "Do you think she knows where the Adjudicator is; and if she does, will she tell us?"

Holmes replied, "He abandoned her to save his own skin. As I said, 'Hell hath no fury…'"

"Yes, I know, 'like a woman scorned.' Well, I have to get back to the Pearly Gates. I've been gone too long already."

Holmes frowned, "Giving up on the cause?"

She grinned, "I have to talk Raymond into letting me go off to Australia. He should. Our assignment from the Almighty isn't finished yet. I'm going to trade in this flight suit for a scarlet safari dress, get some different maps from Joe, and get another sack of heavenly chewies for Pookie. See you at 221B. Don't leave without me. Actually, we'll probably flit without you… if I knew where I was going! Australia is huge."

Mycroft located Greta Stark at HM Prison Holloway and Holmes and Watson went to interrogate the former research director. With uncombed hair, she sat at a rough table in a formless grey dress. A sharp contrast to her fashionable appearance at her Center in Batavia.

"Ah, my kidnappers! Well gentlemen, you got your wish. As you can see, I am installed in durance vile for what may be a very long time. The British are a vengeful people. Did you come to gloat?"

"No, we came to negotiate. We want information only you can give us. We believe de Groot is in Australia but we don't know where. You can tell us."

"Why should I? As they say, what's in it for me?"

"We cannot get you released, but we can get you set up with house arrest and access to your considerable fortune. You would still be restrained but in relative comfort. Yours is a heinous crime and even house arrest will be met with significant public protest."

"Rightly so," agreed Watson.

"However," Holmes continued, "we are assured it can be arranged if you cooperate."

"You want me to help capture the Adjudicator?"

"Yes, before he tries again."

"The bastard fled leaving me to the wolves... you!"

"It would seem so."

"Do I have your assurances of house arrest? I want to hear it from someone in authority."

"The Holloway Prison Governor has been instructed to carry out the order. We will summon him for you."

A round of discussion and negotiation followed. Madame Stark seemed to arrogantly disregard the seriousness of her situation and insisted on having petty concessions made before she finally agreed. Watson thought, *It's a shame the Baroness isn't here. She'd love to rant at Madame Stark.*

At the moment, Juliet was in her mansion, stocking up on Heavenly Chewies for her canine companion in preparation of her journey Down Under. Ominous name, if you lived in Heaven.

Back to the here and now. Holmes, barely controlling his temper, asked once again. "Where is he, Madame?"

"Hiding in plain sight. The city that's at the so-called Top of Australia's Northern Territory used to be called Palmerston. Now they call it Darwin. On the Ocean. He's there. He has a complex similar to the one he had on the Indonesian atoll – an opulent home; a barracks; a large blockhouse and a huge hangar housing at least two airships. One rescued from the atoll, I suppose, and a bigger one constructed there. He calls it the Royal Australian Airship Development Center. I was there in the early days. The locals are thrilled. He employs a number of them. Little do the poor fools know what they're really doing. The territorial government welcomes him. He calls himself Gert Blumfeld. Oh, he has another small facility in Antarctica. He doesn't want to use it. He hates the cold. But if he needs to, he will."

Watson shook his head. "So he still intends to carry out his demonic plans."

"Of course! I'm positive he is unshaken in his determination. I'm sure your attacks have just increased his resolve. You'd better hurry with your attempts to save the world. Those volcanoes won't wait. Neither will he."

"You do realize that even here in London, you will not be safe, if he succeeds? He's a maniac!"

"He's the Adjudicator."

*****

Sea travel distance and time between London and Darwin via the Suez Canal is approximately 10,000 nautical miles - over 14 days at 25 knots. Flit distance from Heaven to Darwin is infinite with 0 time required. Once again HMS Acheron had been called up by the Royal Navy to support the Adjudicator Expedition. The newly formed Royal Australian Navy committed HMAS Yarra, one of its few destroyers, to join the assault in its waters as necessary. Holmes and Watson with a small detachment of Royal Marines were billeted on the Acheron. It also carried one of the first Avro D Floatplanes on its deck.

Behind the Pearly Gates, Baroness Crestwell was engaged in improving her swoop proficiency and becoming a well-known personality with HTC (Heavenly Traffic Control). She proudly demonstrated her emergency recovery abilities and received a DFC (Distinguished Flitting Citation) for her troubles. Pookie was not idle and earned a Renowned Flying Dog insignia which she sported on her red neckerchief. Were they ready for Australia? You bet!

"Pookie, my dear," said Lady Juliet, giving her companion a scratch on the head, "I wonder how the Trans Pacific expedition is faring. Perhaps we should join the ship and assist our mortal companions? No point in sitting about and plucking our harps if we can be of some use. I'll pass the idea on to Raymond."

Pookie barked and looked at Lady Juliet, expectantly.

"Yes, Pookie, I've restocked your supply of Heavenly Chewies. Never fear! Let's go!"

The senior Director required little persuasion and authorized the long (long for Earth-time, that is) flit to the HMS Acheron to be followed by joining the Expeditionary Force. Looking quite heavenly (but actually devilish) in her scarlet safari outfit, Lady Juliet went to check in with flying ace Giuseppe Cei in the Heavenly Hangar. She waved to him as he came jogging over.

"Ciao, Baronessa. Look at you! Off on another flit?"

"Greetings, Joe. Yes, another flit. This time it's to Australia. I need the usual navigation paraphernalia. I have to find a ship in the middle of the Pacific and then swoop on to Darwin, wherever that is."

He smiled. "Well, that certainly sounds interesting. If I wasn't running this flight school, I might ask to join you. This local flitting with students can get boring. Hold on! I'll get your stuff."

Giuseppe returned in a few minutes with a large package. He handed it to Lady Juliet. "How's Pookie doing? She's quite a little zoomer."

The dog barked and executed a series of backflips.

Lady Juliet laughed. "Showoff! Come on, we have to track down a ship! Thanks, Joe!"

"Fly safely, Baronessa. Watch out for the chariots."

*****

Lady Juliet flitted over the sea, with Pookie in tow, searching for the *Acheron*. "Water, water, everywhere! To say nothing of fish, fishing boats and floating fisheries."

She pointed at a boat in the distance. "Look at that clipper ship, Pookie. Don't see many of them anymore. The Pacific is gigantic. That's what they should call it. The Atlantic and the Gigantic. Now where is HMS Acheron?"

The dog whined. "I'm sorry," said Lady Juliet, "I'm too busy to get you a Chewie. Oh, wait! There's the ship. You've spotted it, you wonderful mutt. I owe you an apology. Look, there's an aeroplane on the deck. That should be fascinating. Joe would love it. Crazy Italian. OK, Pookie, down we go. Mr. Holmes, Doctor Watson! Here we come."

Good Heavens, Holmes

Down on the destroyer's deck where they were watching the Royal Marines go through their paces, Watson looked up and saw a scarlet-clad apparition and a ghostly white dog standing on a gun turret across the way. The woman waved and the dog wagged its tail furiously. Watson turned to Holmes who said, "I see them, Watson. Well, our journey has just become more interesting." Telepathically he called, *Lady Juliet, welcome aboard. Your navigation and flight skills are extraordinary.*

Lady Juliet and Pookie swooped down onto the deck. *Yes, Mr. Holmes, I'm getting quite proficient. Won an award, in fact. So did the dog. Ooh, look at all those handsome Marines. I'm glad I came. Alright, Pookie. One Heavenly Chewy coming up! So, gentlemen, what's afoot?*

Holmes and Watson both chuckled. This woman was truly unique, dead or alive. *We are nearing Darwin,* said Holmes. *One more day at sea. We have been cleared to enter the harbor where we will be joined by the Royal Australian Navy destroyer Yarra. The plan calls for us to enter the Elizabeth River and sail inland for a short distance before deploying the floatplane in search of de Groot's Royal Australian Airship Development Center. We suspect it is nearby since he's using local labor. Once again, the airships and the bombs are our primary targets. We don't know how many there are or how well these people are armed. If de Groot learned anything from our last encounter, it's how vulnerable those craft are. I'm sure he's increased their protection, but he still has to depend on hydrogen – a major weakness."*

Lady Juliet considered this. *Do you have any idea whether he still intends to attack the volcanoes?*

He hasn't fled with his airship just to set up an Australian Development Center, thought Watson.

No, thought Holmes, *we're sure he's fanatically resolute. I'm betting Krakatoa will be his first target, followed by Mts. Pinatubo and Mayon, as well as several other coastal pyrotechnic piles. Those explosions will be enough to poison the global atmosphere and set off a series of earthquakes and tsunamis. The entire Ring of Fire will go unstable. Over time, no one will be safe anywhere on Earth, He must be stopped.*

*****

The staff at the Royal Australian Airship Development Center was divided into two units. Those who were aware of Blumfeld's true identity and intentions and those who weren't. The former group was exceedingly small, consisting of airship pilots and crew, and on-the-ground armorers. Hasan was still with de Groot, assisting in managing logistics, routes and reports on the activity levels of the target volcanoes. A small but effective number of armed guards patrolled the area, especially the hangars.

The ground crew and mechanics were under the impression that the Center was exactly what it claimed to be – a research facility for lighter-than-air flight. Two airships were fitted out and on standby - the medium-sized Japanese version that had migrated from Indonesia to Darwin; and a larger, longer range vehicle that had been designed, developed, and constructed at the Darwin facility.

A third ship, the twin to the long-range version, was under construction and occupied the activities of most of the local workers. There was little management expectation that it would ever be completed and fly. It was a ruse designed to head off any suspicions raised by the locals or their government. Reviews by the Royal Australian Aviation authorities were few and far between and generally favorable. It helped that the examiners were aeroplane specialists who knew very little about the design, care and feeding of dirigibles. Circumstances seemed to favor de Groot and his ambitions.

Under the supervision of trusted guards and technicians, a stockpile of Thermite incendiary bombs rested inside the blockhouse. They were carefully maintained and made ready for transfer to the two active dirigibles. Equal care was being taken for the copious number of tanks of hydrogen needed to keep the gas bags aloft. Strict discipline was required and de Groot, aided by Hasan, saw to it.

But, while a lookout noticed a military floatplane flying in the vicinity and reported it, no one could see the invisible wraith in her scarlet safari suit as she stealthily wandered through the facility. Nor could they hear her telepathically reporting back to her contacts on the HMS Acheron that was maintaining steam in the Elizabeth River.

Two of the airships look ready to go. Their gas bags have been loaded with hydrogen. The bigger of the two looks, to my unlettered eye, to be designed for much longer range travel than its smaller counterpart. Remember, the small one made it here from Batavia, so we can expect the big one to cover substantially greater territory. The gondola is quite a bit larger. There are guns on both of them. The third ship is in pieces and unlikely to be ready for anything for quite a while. The bombs are still in storage, but I think they can be loaded very swiftly.

The Captain of the Yarra signaled to the Acheron to please stand by. A longboat broke away from the Australian destroyer and headed across the river to the British craft. A young lieutenant swung up the Acheron's boarding rigging and reported to the captain. "Commander Darby's compliments, sir. He did not want to signal this discussion. You should be aware that this is the monsoon season here in the North, and heavy rain and cyclones are quite likely. In fact, we have been told to expect a very heavy storm in the next six hours. You may wish to haul in the floatplane and secure it fast to the deck. It will also be near impossible for our friend to launch his airships in this kind of weather. You may want to consider a gunnery exercise on his facility during the storm. It won't be as effective as a clear weather strike but unless he has something that is a match for naval guns, it will be quite one-sided."

The Baroness cried aloud, "Holmes, NO! There are innocent local workmen there who will be killed along with de Groot's villains. You can't!"

The Great Detective had listened to the conversation between the naval officers, and as head of the expedition, he intervened. "Gentlemen, I must admit it would be tempting to blast his operation into kingdom come, but please remember that he is employing a number of citizens of Darwin who believe they are gainfully employed in advancing the state of the airship art. We cannot allow them to perish indiscriminately. We must devise a way of destroying his lethal capabilities without wanton slaughter. He and his airships are our targets."

Good Heavens, Holmes

Watson said, "Let's look at the process. The airships are the delivery vehicle but they are worthless to him without the Thermite incendiaries. We need to destroy his bombs."

He then mentally added, *Lady Juliet. You said they are carefully guarded by de Groot's thugs within the blockhouse?*

Yes, they are. There's an immense stockpile of them.

Holmes looked at Watson and laughed, "I bow to your wisdom, Doctor."

The Baroness agreed but then said, *Wait, those airships are incendiaries too, with their hydrogen filled bags. He could still get Krakatoa and Pinatubo erupting by plunging the dirigibles suicidally into the calderas. We need to destroy the bombs and the ships.*

Holmes was listening and said telepathically, *I am surrounded by expert tacticians. Excellent thinking, Milady.*

The captain and lieutenant looked confused. "What do you want us to do, Mr. Holmes?" asked the captain. "That storm is approaching rapidly. We need to protect our own ships."

"We invade! Let's use the cover of the storm to attack the blockhouse, captain. First, the Royal Marines can herd all the workers into the shelter of the barracks. We can sort the guilty out from the innocent after this is over. You may have some experience with that, Baroness. Goats and sheep from the Pearly Gates."

The captain asked, "Who is the Baroness?"

"Forgive me, Captain, a literary allusion."

Lady Juliet chuckled, *A weak recovery, Holmes, but it will have to do.*

He continued, "Then we can surround the blockhouse and ignite the Thermite bombs on a delay fuse so no one is injured. The fire will be terrific. We will then destroy the dirigibles. If de Groot behaves according to his usual pattern, he will attempt to take one of the airships and head for the volcanoes on a suicide mission. We will have to shoot him out of the air. Is the floatplane armed?"

"Yes, but it is battened down and hardly set up for combat."

"It may have to play the part if the ship's guns can't bring him down. Meanwhile, get the Marines ready to invade. No killing! Now, let's wait for the weather to change and hope de Groot knows about the storms and will delay his mad excursion."

*****

The Adjudicator was not happy. "Hasan, what is happening?"

"Our enemies have assembled on the Elizabeth River, Adjudicator. They seem to be waiting to descend on us."

"Well, prepare the airships for attack. I shall not tolerate another attempt to forestall my noble mission. Earth must suffer fully and terribly. Now!"

"Sir, we must wait. There is a dangerous storm there on the horizon. The airships cannot go aloft. They will not survive the buffeting and rain. It is the monsoon season and the winds are treacherous. Lightning could destroy all our work. If I may, sir, hold off until the rain passes. Only then can you wreak your vengeance on those heathen vessels. Right now, the severe weather is against us. But, it will not last."

"Nature must know I plan to destroy the world. Ha! It is no matter. I shall not be deterred."

Hasan replied, "Your enemies can do nothing. They, too, are subject to Mother Nature's whims. They will be caught in the storms."

*****

"Let's get going before the winds get too stiff." This from the sergeant-major leading the Marine contingent. A longboat was lowered into the river and the armed men clambered down the ropes and into the seats. "Protect your weapons. Remember, shoot only in self-defense. We are here to prevent bloodshed, not cause it. Alright bosun, shove off!"

The rowers propelled the boat with great effort over the rising river waves. Lady Juliet stood at the prow like a medieval figurehead with Pookie at her side. Holmes and Watson were seated aft. They reached the causeway and the invaders scrambled out and ran toward the buildings and the hangar. The guards fired a few half-hearted shots at the oncoming assault, then turned and ran. The workers looked on in panic and then they too ran, looking for shelter from the now soaking rain, wind and lightning. A small Marine contingent forced them into the barracks, blocking the doors after them.

The sergeant-major and several explosives experts broke off and ran to the blockhouse, smashed the locks and descended on the stacks of Thermite bombs. "Careful, you men. This stuff is treacherous. We have to ignite the fuses and get out smartly. This whole place will be an inferno in a few minutes. The airships are next. We can't let them fly, although the weather may see to that."

In spite of their ages and wounds, Holmes and Watson had joined the attackers and had headed for the huge hangar and its hydrogen-filled inhabitants. The Baroness flitted along. Pookie growled and charged ahead. The guards, mechanics and ground crew had all joined the fleeing mob, leaving the dirigibles untended except for two pilots and a flight crew member. Suddenly, a wildly gesticulating figure ran onto the apron rolling a Maxim machine gun in front of him. It was de Groot! Followed by Hasan! The Adjudicator fired a burst from the Maxim at the invaders but hit nothing. "You there, pilot, get in the gondola. Start the engines." He jumped into the car of the large ship waving a pistol. "Hasan, release the restraining cables."

The pilot protested, "Sir, we can't go out in this storm. This is a cyclone. Winds over 75 miles an hour. The ship will be torn apart." The Adjudicator steadied the pistol and shot the man. He turned to the second pilot and shouted, "He was a coward! Are you courageous enough go on this sacred mission?" Hasan was petrified. The British party watched, amazed and immovable. The pilot trembled and took up the tiller. "Sir, we have no bombs."

"It doesn't matter, idiot! This ship is the bomb. We will make the ultimate sacrifice."

Juliet screamed telepathically: *Holmes, stop him! He's going to plunge that damned dirigible into one of the volcanoes and set it off!*

I know, Baroness! He's going to try, but he won't make it!

By now, the nose of the dirigible had emerged from the hangar's cover and was being battered by the fierce wind and rain.

The engines strained to achieve some forward progress. The pilot struggled to retain some form of control. Hasan had unleashed the shackles and cowered against the wall of the cabin. He would not dare to escape and save what little life he had left. The Adjudicator was standing on the open portion of the deck where the Thermite bombs would have been positioned, shouting into the howling winds. "Onward, upward! I will conquer you yet, Mother Earth! This world deserves to perish! I am its nemesis! When I die, all will die!"

The frames of the hangar began to creak and rock back and forth in the screaming winds. The sergeant-major signaled to the task group to move out and head for the sturdier barracks. Suddenly, there was a fearful blast. The Thermite bombs were beginning to explode in the blockhouse. It was only a matter of time before the entire structure would collapse and burn to the ground. The windows of the manor house had been blown in and a portion of the roof torn off. No safety there. The barracks was still intact and the only secure place left. The team rushed for it.

As they struggled to run through the windswept rain, their path was suddenly illuminated by a blinding light, followed by a crackling burst. A lightning bolt had struck the hangar. Another hit the structure and set the smaller airship ablaze. Its hydrogen exploded, sending shrapnel into the air and causing the hangar to collapse on the larger, semi-emerged dirigible that was still fighting its way against the forces of Nature.

The battle ended. Flames crept along the smooth lines of the ship's gas bag and small explosions broke out along the ribs finally concluding in one titanic burst. Hasan and the pilot had jumped from the slowly moving gondola but de Groot had stood firmly in his place, arms stretched upward, fists shaking mightily. Then like the ship itself, he disappeared in a surge of fire.

A day passed before the storm began to blow itself out. Both the Acheron and Yarra, pummeled as they were in the river, sustained minor damage but were still capable of getting underway back to the harbor at Darwin. Hasan was wounded trying to escape and the surviving pilot, crew and guards were taken into custody by the Royal Marines. Once they had identified themselves, the locals were allowed to leave, but unfortunately they no longer had jobs to return to. The wreckage of the Center was just about total with only the barracks remaining reasonably intact. No one could be found to claim ownership. What remained of the airships were burnt out hulks, not even fit for salvage.

It was over.

Holmes and Watson managed to secure berths on a fast passenger liner headed back to London where they would be tasked by His Majesty's Government to put together a credible story to release to the international press and the hordes of "interested" parties trying to take advantage of the situation. Lady Juliet delayed her return to Paradise in order to see closure brought to the incident. Raymond would just have to wait.

Mycroft reassembled the international committee and another round of bureaucratic squabbling began. He announced to the crowd of delegates, "One thing de Groot had proven. Volcanoes, earthquakes, storms, tsunamis, fires and floods all have much wider impacts than we originally believed, if we thought about it at all. National and international boundaries count for nil during a cyclone, typhoon or hurricane. If the magnetic poles shift, we are all affected."

In the midst of small-minded bickering, some enlightenment manifested itself. Certain members committed their countries to devising cooperative protection techniques, warning systems and education. It was something, but not enough.

Lady Juliet, for the moment, abandoned her whimsy and wondered (telepathically, of course) what would befall the world if we stayed on our current course. Holmes and Watson were without answers.

*****

In a Kensington flat, Madame Greta Stark, under house arrest, whiled away the hours with alternating bouts of self-pity and self-hatred. She had allowed herself to be duped by the charlatan de Groot. She actually loved him. Obviously, her affection was not reciprocated.

The Home office was keeping her on a tight leash. So too was Indonesia. Her Pacific Rim Research Project had been disbanded although the results of their scientific inquiries were preserved and turned over to several international bodies, geographic organizations and individual practitioners. Father Giuseppe Mercalli and Professor John Wilson were two of the beneficiaries who received comprehensive materials along with a stipend.

She was somewhat surprised when she received a wire from Sherlock Holmes, suggesting he and Doctor Watson drop by for a chat. She had little choice in the matter. They were coming today at two o'clock. *No doubt to lord his victory over her! Oh well,* she thought, *it beats being caged up in Holloway Prison.*

As the hour struck, she heard a knock on her door. She had no servants. Only a charwoman who 'did' for her several times a week. She rose and went to the door, ignorant of the ethereal dog and scarlet clad phantom flowing into her foyer. Standing in the corridor were two men, impossible to mistake either one of them. Sherlock Holmes and Doctor John H. Watson. "Hello, gentlemen. Come in! I don't get many visitors nowadays. Scotland Yard has to approve of anyone who wishes to grace my doorstep. I assume you have their clearance?"

"Madame Stark," said Holmes. "Thank you for seeing us. This is not really a social call."

"I suspected as much, Mr. Holmes. Have you come to gloat? You can assure me of one thing immediately. Bernhard is really dead? I have never been officially informed."

"Yes, Doctor Watson and I were witnesses to his demise. A rather grotesque event. And no, gloating is hardly appropriate."

Juliet telepathically piped in. *He certainly didn't make it to the Pearly Gates, girlie.*

"I am not surprised that his death was unusual… de Groot was… an unusual man. How did it happen?"

"He was incinerated on board one of his airships. It blew up in a typhoon."

"Those damned airships. He lived by them, and now you tell me he died by them."

"Sadly, yes! But now, to the purpose of our call. It involves de Groot."

"I didn't think I would be the object of your interest. What do you want?"

"Information! We know his money came, ironically, from volcanic diamonds and his dirigibles came from a firm in Japan. What we don't know is where the thermite bombs came from. It is illegal for private citizens to have such incendiary weapons. Exceptions are sometimes made for construction companies and similar organizations who have use for explosives. They will operate under a restrictive license. This is not dynamite. These are firebombs of extraordinary destructive power."

"Oh! Mr. Holmes, such naiveté! Where else would one procure such weapons than from a weapons manufacturer?"

The Baroness snorted. *I really don't like this chit. Neither does Pookie.* The dog growled and snapped at Greta.

Holmes nodded. "The thought occurred to me that a highjacked military shipment might have been involved."

"You may wish to have your vaunted Military Intelligence investigate. I cannot help you."

"There is a strong suspicion that your fortune financed the acquisition of the bombs, Madame."

"That suspicion would be misplaced. The Adjudicator had no need for my money."

"So you are unwilling to assist us in discovering where the bombs came from?"

"Willingness has nothing to do with it. I am unable. Sorry, Mr. Detective. Another case for you to investigate. I am confident you will find a solution."

"I share your confidence and I am certain our investigations will lead back to you."

"I am already subject to His Majesty's penal system. What further damage can you do?"

"A return to Holloway?" suggested Doctor Watson.

She turned pale.

Back in Baker Street, the four musketeers joined for one last session before going their separate ways. Holmes was going to his new retirement cottage in Sussex Downs to tend his bees. They were currently in the care of a local farm boy. Also, Holmes had finally convinced Mrs. Hudson to sell up her Baker Street property and join him at the Downs.

Watson was trying to compose an apologetic approach to his long-suffering wife. He once again had stayed away too long and now had to make up for his absence. A splendid dinner, jewelry and flowers might go a long way toward making amends. A splendid dinner would go a long way, regardless.

The Baroness smiled. "Gentlemen, this has all been great fun, especially flying. But we have to get back to Paradise. Pookie and I are competing in an aerobatic contest. We have come up with a daring and dramatic series of maneuvers. My shaggy dog and I don our red flight suits and zoom up into the heavens. Then, we flit, float and fly in loops and figure eights. Next, we soar, sweep and swoop in plunging circles. Finally, we slip, slide and glide to a spectacular touchdown. We call it - A Stunt in Scarlet."

About the Author

Harry DeMaio is a ***nom de plume*** of Harry B. DeMaio, successful author of several books on Information Security and Business Networks as well as the seventeen-volume ***Casebooks of Octavius Bear*** adventure series.

He is also a published author of Sherlock Holmes and Solar Pons stories for Belanger Books and the MX Sherlock Holmes series. A retired business executive, former consultant, information security specialist, elected official, private pilot, disk jockey and graduate school adjunct professor, he whiles away his time traveling and writing preposterous books, articles and stories.

He has appeared on many radio and TV shows and is an accomplished, frequent public speaker.

Former New York City natives, he and his extremely patient and helpful wife, Virginia, live in Cincinnati (and several other parallel universes). They have two sons, one living in Scottsdale, Arizona and the other in Cortlandt Manor, New York; both of whom are quite successful and quite normal, thus putting the lie to the theory that insanity is hereditary.

His e-mail is hdemaio@zoomtown.com

You can also find him on Facebook.

His website is www.octaviusbearslair.com

His books are available on Amazon, Barnes and Noble, directly from Belanger Books and MX Publishing and at other fine bookstores.

Belanger Books

Lightning Source UK Ltd.
Milton Keynes UK
UKHW021607130123
415295UK00016B/1241